Beneath these Stars
(Lucy Mitchell Book 2)

By Hannah Ellis

This is a work of fiction. Names, characters, places, and incidents either are the products of the author's imagination or are used fictitiously. Any resemblance to actual persons, living or dead, businesses, companies, events, or locales is entirely coincidental.

Text copyright © 2017 Hannah Ellis
All Rights Reserved

Cover design by Aimee Coveney

To Mario

with love

Acknowledgements

This book wouldn't have happened without a lot of help and support.

As always my parents top the list! Thanks so much for everything you do.

A big thank you to the amazing people who helped me by reading and giving feedback at the various stages: Dua Roberts, Fay Sallaba, Sarah-Jane Fraser, Kathy Robinson, Anthea Kirk, Sarah Walker, Natalie Sellers, Sue Oxley and Meghan Driscoll. Your input is invaluable.

Many thanks to Jane Hammett for another great editing job. Your suggestions are so helpful and the book is better because of you.

Aimee Coveney, I am absolutely in love with these book covers! Thank you so much.

To my friend, Pete Anglesea, at Flat White Kitchen, Durham. My inspiration for *The White Kitchen* came from you. I always love hearing about your success and I promise to visit one of these days!

I really appreciate the people who answered my random questions to help make the book as factual as possible: Jenny Addrison and Dan Forrester, thanks for the info on Manchester; Michaela Smith and Fiona Parkinson, thanks for answering my questions about teaching (even if you did just Google it, Fi!); Mark Ellis, thanks for ruining my day with your input about police procedures! Any facts that are not quite right are down to my interpretation and not their lack of knowledge.

Mario, thanks for everything. I love you.

Prologue

It was a perfect summer's day. Everything about it was perfect. We'd spent the whole day outside in the sunshine. The flowerbeds were bursting with colour, and I watched a butterfly hover over the pale pink peonies before fluttering away. The sky was a crisp bright blue and I'd spent the day surrounded by family. Thinking about it made me smile. Because they weren't actually my family. Not yet anyway.

"What are you grinning at?" Adam asked, flopping down next to me on the picnic blanket in his parents' garden.

"Nothing," I said, running a hand through his sandy-brown hair and gazing into his sparkling blue eyes. "I'm just happy. It's been a nice day. I really like your family."

"You're drunk, aren't you?" he asked, eyeing the glass in my hand. "Is my sister making cocktails?"

"Yeah. It's nice." I took another sip of the mojito and gave him my flirty eyes over the glass.

"Am I going to have to carry you home?"

"I'm just happy," I said, giving him a shove. "Leave me alone."

Becky appeared at the back door and shouted up to me. "Ready for another one?"

"No, I'm okay, thanks."

"Why are you trying to get my girlfriend drunk?"

Adam asked, grinning.

"So I can interrogate her without it being weird," she said, a smile playing on her lips.

It was the first time I'd met Adam's sister and her family. She and her husband, Will, lived in France with their two little girls and were in the UK visiting for a week. It had been fun, spending the whole day with them, and I enjoyed Becky's company. She had a positive energy that seemed to infect those around her.

"Uncle Adam!" three-year-old Emily shouted. "Swing me 'gain!"

"I'm still dizzy!" he told her, making silly faces when he jumped up and chased her around the garden. She squealed when he caught her and swung her up in the air, turning around and around with her over his head.

"She just ate," Becky shouted. "If she pukes everywhere, you're cleaning it up."

Adam's mum, Ruth, appeared beside Becky, a tea towel in her hand. "Stop throwing the poor child around."

"That's what uncles are for," he said, sticking his tongue out as soon as Ruth disappeared back into the kitchen. "Is it my turn on the scooter yet, Hailey?" he asked, looking towards the garage while he lowered Emily to the ground. Hailey rode round in circles on the patch of flagstones between the garage and the house.

"It's pink," she told him in her obnoxious eight-year-old way; with a look that said he was an idiot.

"Just my colour," he said. "Stop hogging it."

Little Emily looked up at him with a big grin on her

face. "You're too big!"

"I am not!" he said, moving towards Hailey.

"Go away!" she shouted. A giggle escaped her as she manoeuvred the scooter away from him and down the driveway.

"Come on," he said. "One turn!"

"If you break a limb falling off a child's scooter, I'm not coming to the hospital with you," I told him.

He disappeared around the front of the house after Hailey, with Emily following close behind him.

"So you two are getting pretty serious?" Becky asked, sitting beside me on the blanket.

"Are you really going to interrogate me?"

Her nose wrinkled when she grinned. "Yeah, 'fraid so!"

"Okay," I said, a smile spreading across my face. "Yes it's serious."

Adam and I had been together just over a year. We'd met on a reality TV show. It was out of character for me, agreeing to take part in the show, but I'd just lost my job and they offered to whisk me away to Spain for a week in the sun. Adam was a cameraman on the show and he'd spent the week filming my every move. Even then, when he was working, it was easy to see what a kind and compassionate person he was.

Once the show was over and I got to know him properly, I fell for him completely. He was easy-going and so much fun to be around. It hadn't taken me long to realise he was the one I wanted to share the rest of my life with.

"That's good," Becky said. "Because my dad is totally smitten and I don't want you breaking his heart!"

"I'm a big fan of your dad," I told her. Tom was a gentleman; kind and gentle, always with a twinkle in his eye. He'd made me feel like family from the first time I met him, and I always enjoyed his company.

"Well, you obviously make Adam happy," she said, drinking her cocktail through the straw. "How are you finding village life?"

"So far, so good." I'd only moved into Adam's cosy house in Havendon a month before, but I was enjoying my summer in the quaint little village. Ruth had been trying to teach me about gardening, and I spent many lunchtimes in the local pub with Tom. Whenever Ruth was at one of her many committee meetings he'd appear and treat me to lunch. The summer was slipping away too fast and before I knew it I'd be starting a new job as a teaching assistant and my lunches with Tom would come to an end.

"Do you think you'll ever move back here?" I asked Becky.

She shook her head. "No, we're happy where we are. I love France and we have a good life. I always enjoy coming back for a visit, but I can't imagine living here. You two should come out and visit us sometime."

"I'd like that. I just need to talk Adam into taking some time off."

"Good luck. I've been bugging him for years to come out and see us, but he's always busy with work. Although I'm amazed he's quit the TV studios. He's really going to set up on his own?"

"His contract at the studio is up in a month and then he's all set to go it alone," I said. "I'm excited for him."

Adam had finally made the decision to leave his job as a camera operator with Realnet Direct TV (RDT) and follow his dream of still-photography. It was a risk; he was a valued member of the team at RDT and they'd been a good employer, but his passion had always been photography and he would finally be doing what he loved.

Becky looked at me seriously. "You must be good for him. We've been telling him to sell his photos for years but he hasn't listened to us. Come on…" She stood up. "Let's have a nosey at his collection while he's out of the way."

I followed her to the garage and she retrieved a key from under a plant pot to open the side door.

"I love it in here," I said as we walked into the musty-smelling room and gazed at Adam's photographs. They were all different sizes, framed, and stacked against every wall.

"Me too," she replied, as Hailey appeared and nestled under her arm. "Even when I was a kid and the garage was just full of junk and bikes, I loved hiding away in here. It was my favourite place. Now it's full of Adam's photos I could sit in here for hours."

"What are you doing in my garage?" Adam called from the doorway. Emily wriggled and giggled while he held her like a rag doll under his arm.

"Checking out my talented brother's collection before he sells everything and becomes rich and famous!" Becky said.

"You always did live in your own little dream world," he said, setting Emily down. "I'm glad some things don't change."

"Where are Will and Dad?" Becky asked.

"I think they slipped off to the pub," Adam said. "I'm not sure why I didn't get an invite."

"Someone's got to entertain the kids," she said.

We moved back outside and I sat at the patio table, sipping cocktails with Becky while Adam played with the girls. Ruth came out with a tray of snacks and coaxed Emily inside to give her a bath and put her to bed. When Will and Tom returned from the pub they were in high spirits and we sat outside while the light faded and the sky filled with stars.

Adam and I finally stumbled home late in the evening, tipsy and laughing. We had no idea that our relaxed day in the sun would be the last time we were all together as a family.

Part 1

Chapter 1

Exhaustion had come and gone. I was way beyond it. I existed in a zombie-like state, unsure what had happened to my life and how it had become so unrecognisable.

"Lucy?"

I'd cleaned the kitchen before finally collapsing on the couch when a little voice interrupted me. I looked into the big tearful eyes of the five-year-old who regarded me from the living room doorway.

"I wet the bed."

"It's fine," I said, on autopilot. "It's doesn't matter." I walked over and put a hand on her silky blonde hair. "Let's get you cleaned up and back into bed."

She followed my lead. We had this routine well practised, though thankfully it happened less and less. I stripped her bed and put fresh sheets on it while she undressed in the bathroom, then I showered her off and helped her into clean pyjamas. "Back to bed now. I'll tuck you in."

"Lucy," she whispered at the top of the stairs. "Can I say goodnight to Mum?"

"Of course you can."

Swallowing my emotions, I picked up the soiled sheets for the wash, balling them to carry under one arm, leaving a hand free for Emily. We walked down the stairs together. I dumped the sheets in front of the washing machine then opened the back door. Cold air hit us and I unhooked my thick cardigan from the back of the door, wrapping it around Emily before I picked her up and stepped outside.

"Which one is she?" Emily whispered, under the star-studded sky. I breathed a sigh of relief that it wasn't cloudy.

"See the three stars in a row?" I pointed. "She's the one in the middle." The middle star on Orion's belt. Because that was the only constellation I knew.

"Will she come back to see us soon?"

"No, sweetheart. She can't. Remember? But she watches you and she loves you so much."

The star thing had started when I'd let Emily watch *The Lion King* – without vetting it first. She'd decided her mummy was a star, just like Simba's daddy. After that she stopped asking me where Mummy was, so it felt like a good thing to me. The stars seemed to help her. At least, late at night, when she was tired and confused, it was a comfort.

"Is Daddy there too?"

"Right next to Mummy," I said. She raised a hand to wave and rested her head on my shoulder. I hugged her to me, shivering. She'd be asleep before I got her up the stairs.

Adam came in the front door as I walked through the kitchen. He ran a hand over his niece's hair and the scar on the back of his hand reminded me of our old life. Before everything fell apart.

"She okay?" he asked.

"She wet the bed again," I said. "I'll take her back up now."

Adam was asleep on the couch when I returned downstairs, an almost full bottle of beer dripping condensation onto the table in front of him. I watched him for a moment before pushing my feet into a pair of tattered trainers, grabbing a jacket and slipping out of the front door into the night. I should probably get to bed but I knew I wouldn't be able to switch my brain off. My steps were quick and even as I walked down to the village and then up the gentle hill beyond the community centre. I was starting to feel that I knew the village of Havendon better than I knew my own face.

The village was deserted but I kept my head down anyway. It was easier if no one knew about my visits to Tom. I'd feel better for talking to him. I always did. Adam's dad was the one I always turned to. I was only twenty-eight, and my life had changed so dramatically over the past year and a bit that I struggled to make sense of it.

Maybe I shouldn't be talking to Tom, but I couldn't seem to stay away. I felt better as I approached, knowing he would listen without judgement, and quietly comfort me. Tom was the only one who I could talk to properly. And If I didn't talk to someone, I might just explode.

Hannah Ellis

Chapter 2

"Don't bother making me sandwiches," Hailey said when she joined her sister at the kitchen table the next morning. "I won't eat them."

I'd stopped hearing her comments about the lunch I packed for her a long time ago, and continued putting the sandwiches in her lunch bag.

"I want coco pops too!" Emily demanded, watching Hailey help herself.

"They're just for the weekend," I said, snatching the packet from Hailey and returning them to the cupboard.

"But Hailey's eating them," Emily whined.

"Just eat your muesli, please, Emily. I put extra raisins in for you."

She pushed her bowl away. "No!"

Hailey crunched loudly on the coco pops and laughed at me. Not out loud, of course, but the corners of her mouth twitched to let me know she was thoroughly amused.

"Muesli's really good for you," I told Emily while I put their lunch bags in the hallway with their schoolbags.

"I want coco pops!"

"What's wrong?" Adam asked, walking down the stairs and registering the look on my face.

"Hailey's having coco pops," Emily said loudly. "I want some too."

"Okay." He moved to the cupboard and pulled out the packet.

"Adam, I've just told her she can't have them! Hailey's not supposed to be eating them either."

"Morning!" Ruth sang, letting herself in the front door.

"Gran," Emily called. "Lucy says I can't have coco pops."

"Of course you can," Ruth said, taking the packet from Adam and pouring her a bowl.

I sighed in defeat. "I'm going to get ready for work."

"Did you make lunches for the girls?" Ruth asked.

"With the schoolbags," I replied through gritted teeth. She insisted on asking me every morning, as though I might have forgotten. Like I was the most incompetent person in the world.

"What's up?" Adam asked, following me into our bedroom. I sat on the end of the bed, exhausted. It wasn't even 8am and I was already wishing the day were over.

"Nothing."

"Does it really matter if they have coco pops for breakfast?"

"Probably not," I conceded. "I wish your mum would let me take Emily to school instead of coming to take her every morning. I drive right past the school."

"She likes to be involved, that's all. It's good for her."

"She *is* involved!" I said irritably. "She's here all

the time, undermining me and telling the girls they can have coco pops for breakfast when I've already said they can't."

"What is the big deal with the coco pops?" His eyes flashed with anger as he moved to the dresser and picked up his wallet.

"They're full of sugar, and I want the girls to have a healthy breakfast. Why does that make me the bad guy? And it's not the bloody coco pops! It's the fact they are allowed to ignore anything I say to them."

"They've been through a lot. Who cares if they have coco pops for breakfast? If that's what makes them happy, let them."

"It's been over a year," I reminded him. Sixteen excruciating months had passed. In that time we'd moved into his parents' house while Ruth took over our lovely little house. Life had been dominated by loss and grief and trying to figure out how to look after Adam's nieces. It had been a time of falling apart, muddling through and just barely getting by, taking one day at a time. "And I know exactly what they've been through," I snapped. "But I don't think being made to adhere to a few rules is going to damage them. They're kids; they need rules."

"Adam!" Ruth's voice drifted up. "You need to get going or you'll be late."

I sighed as Adam replied that he was coming. I hated her intruding in our lives. It was relentless: she was round every day, checking up on us and pointing out every mistake I made and everything she would do differently.

"Lucy!" Ruth's voice came again. "Can you pick Hailey up today and take her to her appointment?"

"Yes!" I shouted before turning to Adam. "I take her every Friday! Why does she always have to ask me as though I'm going to forget?"

Every Friday I pick Hailey up from school to sit outside an ugly grey government building for an hour while she has grief counselling.

"Why do you let her get to you so much?" Adam asked. I wasn't sure whether he was referring to his mother or Hailey, but it didn't really matter, I didn't have an answer for either. I stood up to get ready, and when Adam moved to kiss me, I reflexively withdrew.

"Hey!" His eyes softened and he snaked his arms around my waist. "I know it's hard, but we'll get through it. I love you."

I buried my head in his neck, savouring his scent. "I love you too."

I only wished I could turn back time to when it was just the two of us and the future seemed bright and happy.

Back downstairs, Emily hugged me and I kissed the top of her head, feeling slightly better for the huge grin she gave me before she skipped out of the door, her grandmother close behind.

The twenty-five-minute drive to work was my favourite part of the day. St Jude's Primary School in Kingstown had become my refuge. Kingstown was a small town halfway between our little village of Havendon and my old place in Manchester.

When I met him, Adam already lived in Havendon, and we'd been talking about me moving there with him, so when the teaching assistant job came up I'd jumped at the chance to leave the bustle of the city.

Moving in together had seemed so natural.

I was supposed to spend a year at St Jude's as a teaching assistant and then do my teacher training there the following year.

Things didn't quite go to plan. Everything was great at first. We had four months of living together as a couple, and when I looked back it seemed we didn't have a care in the world. We were so blissfully happy. Then came that awful day, the unforgettable week. Everything changed overnight and, before I knew it, work had become a place where I could switch off from my problems for a while.

I'd put off the teacher training and arranged to work fewer hours so I could be home for the kids in the afternoon. Adam took Hailey to school in the morning and I picked her up on my way home. It was the worst part of my day, those twenty minutes in the car with Hailey, who seemed to hate me unconditionally.

My working day flew by too fast, as always. I pulled up outside Hailey's school and saw her chatting to another girl, which was something of a miracle in itself. She'd not settled well and didn't have any close friends. The teachers said it would probably take her some time to settle in. She kept herself to herself, but they weren't concerned. They seemed to think that was just her personality.

It was Ruth who had decided that private school would be a better fit for Hailey, since it could offer intensive language tutoring for Hailey to keep up with her French. It was a big school, catering for children from three to eighteen years, and even I found the place daunting. In Havendon the schools were divided into Infants, Juniors and Secondary. Nice cosy schools where everyone knew each other. It was a shame, I thought, that Ruth had set her sights on Cromwell School for Hailey, but she had been adamant it was for the best.

"Hi," I said, trying to sound cheerful when Hailey climbed into the back seat of the car. I turned to drive back the way I'd come. "How was school?"

"Fine," she mumbled. This was a good day; a lot of the time she refused to say a word to me.

"What did you do?"

I was honoured with a glance in the rear-view mirror, an eyebrow raised. "School stuff," she muttered, turning away to gaze out of the window, dismissing me.

"A kid threw up in my class today," I said. "Right before lunch. The smell was so bad, it put me off eating. If someone threw up every day, I'd be skinny in no time!" I looked back, but she was staring out of the window, ignoring me.

"I'll wait here," I said needlessly when I pulled up at her counselling session. The vibrations shook through the car when the door slammed.

I listened to the radio for a while, turning it off when I couldn't take the noise any more. When I started to feel claustrophobic sitting in the car, I walked up and down the road. Hailey climbed back into the car precisely an hour later.

"How long do I have to do that for?" she asked.

"I don't know," I told her honestly. "We can ask Adam."

"She's an idiot," Hailey stated. She'd never had anything good to say about Mrs Miller. "And it's a load of crap. How come Emily doesn't have to go any more?"

Emily had seen the grief counsellor for a while, until it was decided she was coping with everything well and it was no longer necessary. Hailey was a different matter.

"I'm not really sure. We can talk to Adam about it later."

This was my usual tactic when I didn't know how to reply or lacked the energy for discussion: defer to Adam or Ruth or some vague time in the future. Settling back into silence, I drove the familiar roads home almost on autopilot.

"I've done a casserole for dinner," Ruth said when I walked into the kitchen of what was supposed to be my house, but still felt like hers. It had seemed logical for Adam and me to move into his parents' house with the kids. For a start, it was bigger than Adam's house, and the girls were familiar with their grandparents' house, having stayed there many times. It was the house their mother and Adam had grown up in. It should've been comforting for them to be somewhere they knew.

However, even a year later, I felt as though I was intruding in someone else's house.

"Great, thanks," I replied. "It smells delicious." Again, I had the feeling Ruth thought me utterly incompetent; as though none of us would eat if it weren't for her. I kissed Emily on the top of her head while she coloured happily at the kitchen table.

"I spoke to Adam," Ruth told me from her place at the stove. "I said I'd babysit tonight so you two can go out for a drink."

"That'll be nice." I took a seat opposite Emily,

smiling when she held up her picture, showing me the row of flowers she'd drawn. It was hard to always come home and find Ruth there, to have my nights out planned and dictated by her. I would've preferred to stay at home and watch a film, but it was easier to do what I was told. Adam should have rung and told me about the evening plan. It was irritating to hear it from Ruth.

"It's the quiz tonight," Ruth said. "You could win a meal in the pub!"

"I doubt it; we've never been very good at the pub quiz."

Emily looked up at me and I poked my tongue out at her, making her laugh.

"You should be good at it," Ruth continued. "You've got more brains than most in this little village."

"We always struggle with sport and celebrity gossip," I said. Ruth turned and smiled at me just as Hailey walked into the room.

"I thought you *were* a celebrity?" Hailey said.

"Once upon a time," I said, ignoring her mocking tone. "And only for about five minutes."

Thankfully, the attention created by my appearance on a reality TV show had been short-lived. It was almost three years ago and had been a strange part of my life, but something I looked back on fondly. I'd remained friends with the others on the show, and even though the media attention had been overwhelming at the time, on the whole the experience had been positive.

"What's for dinner?" Hailey asked, moving to look over Ruth's shoulder at the pot on the stove.

"Chicken casserole," Ruth said. "How was your day?"

"Fine."

I was happy that Ruth got the same curt reply as I had.

"How was your appointment?" Ruth asked quietly, unable to refer to it as anything other than an appointment, as though Hailey might just have been at the dentist and not at counselling to help her deal with the loss of her parents.

"Fine."

Hailey shot me a look and I smiled discreetly. There were occasional moments when we were united in our thoughts about Ruth.

"Mrs Miller is still telling me it's okay to be sad that both my parents are dead. I think I've got it. I hope you're not paying her a lot."

Ruth's ability to skirt subjects often brought out the blunt crassness in Hailey. The awkward silences that fell after Hailey's shock statements usually made me want to laugh inappropriately.

Emily looked up with wide eyes, waiting for someone to react.

"We'll wait for your Uncle Adam to get home before we eat," Ruth said. "Unless you're really hungry?" She looked around at us and I shook my head, suppressing a laugh and avoiding looking at Hailey who would no doubt be thoroughly amused by how uncomfortable she'd made her grandmother.

Hannah Ellis

Chapter 3

I walked hand in hand with Adam into the village that evening. The sun had long since set and the air was crisp, my breath fogging in front of my face. I focused on the feel of Adam's hand in mine, trying not to dwell on the fact that the past year had turned physical contact into something rare, something to treasure. I missed our intimacy, which had got lost somewhere along the way.

"I hope Hailey behaves for Mum," Adam said. "She seemed determined to wind her up over dinner."

"She's been like that since we arrived home." I was secretly happy it wasn't me bearing the brunt of Hailey's moods for once.

Adam's hand tightened around mine as we approached our old place. I should've known better than to look. I usually kept my head down and didn't allow the memories to surface. The blue curtains were like a ghost of the past, drawing me back to that awful winter day.

It was a Sunday. We'd been enjoying a late breakfast after spending the morning tangled together in bed. The smell of bacon permeated the air as we chatted and laughed. We were so caught up in ourselves that we'd ignored the phone when it rang, which I felt guilty about with hindsight.

There was snow on the ground but, the way I remember it, the sun was shining in the window so brightly that everything glowed. I don't know how true the memory is but we were smiling and laughing, glowing right up until Adam opened the door. The knocking was so insistent that it couldn't be ignored, and I wondered later when we had realised something was wrong. Certainly by the time we saw the look on Ruth's face as she stood in the doorway, but in my memories the awful knocking sound was an indicator too. Grey clouds hung behind Ruth, proving my memories weren't entirely accurate. A crisp sunny day had turned grey and overcast in a moment.

Adam asked her what was wrong. His brow furrowed, knowing something had happened. I could see him age in front of my eyes, even before Ruth spoke. I immediately thought of his dad, Tom, who'd already had one heart attack.

"It's your sister," Ruth managed. "It's Becky." The words were forced. Her voice, an echo of a whisper, didn't belong to her. "There was a car accident."

"Is … is she …?"

The sentence went unfinished. What was he going to say? Okay? Alive? Dead?

Ruth shook her head, her eyes wild with horror and disbelief. "We need to get to France. The girls are all alone." Her ragged voice cracked and she turned, stumbling back down the path.

"Go with her," I prompted Adam, rooted to the spot. "I'll find your passport and pack your things."

"I think those curtains are the only thing she hasn't changed," Adam commented, pulling me back to the present.

"It's annoying," I said without thinking. "She changed everything about our home to make it hers, but she won't let me touch anything in her house. Everything has to stay the same. It's still *her* house." Her ornaments and pictures were still scattered around and it annoyed me daily. I couldn't bring myself to ask her to move them.

He flicked his head to look at me, and I knew I'd said the wrong thing. "You *can* change things. You've never seemed interested in changing anything. It's our home; we can do what we want with it."

"It doesn't really feel that way." It wasn't just the house that didn't feel my own, but my life too. I decided to keep that to myself.

"You don't think of it as home?" The mixture of surprise and concern in his voice unnerved me. I should be more careful what I say.

"I don't know." I paused, not wanting to talk about it. All I wanted was a nice quiet evening. "I think of *you* as home."

He draped an arm around my shoulder, drawing me to him and kissing the side of my head. My heart raced and I realised the romantic words I'd surprised myself with were probably a lie. They had been true once – but now I wasn't sure at all.

Adam greeted Mike in the bar and I said a quick hello while avoiding eye contact, letting my gaze roam around the pub. Mike chatted to Adam, only addressing me to ask what I wanted to drink. I wondered if anyone else felt the awkwardness between us, or if it was just me. For a while I'd tried to avoid him completely, but it wasn't easy given the size of the village and the fact he was the landlord of the only pub in a six-mile radius. I'd settled for politely ignoring him and was thankful he paid me the same courtesy.

He'd never mentioned the incident, apparently as happy as I was to pretend it had never happened. The village was a minefield of memories for me.

I went to grab a table while Adam waited for Mike to pour the drinks.

"Do you want to do the quiz?" Adam asked, placing a glass of white wine in front of me.

"Not really," I said. I had a flashback to the first time I'd visited the pub, on my first date with Adam. It was so clear in my mind – a happy memory that made me so sad. "Go on then, let's do the quiz," I said quickly, changing my mind. I needed something to focus on, to stop my mind wandering and to make sure we didn't spend the evening drinking in an awkward silence.

As expected, we didn't do very well in the quiz and, as usual, Mike dropped in two extra questions for our benefit: 'Name a participant on the reality TV show, *A Trip to Remember*', to which everyone would write my name. Then 'Name a cameraman on the same show'. It always caused much amusement around the pub, and I found the attention embarrassing.

Although we knew most of the people in the pub, we didn't speak to anyone.

"I wish you'd sell your photos," I told Adam wistfully, glancing at one of his pictures which graced the wall over our table. The pub had his pictures hanging all around and we had a garage full of his framed photos – masterpieces which, in my opinion, shouldn't be hidden away.

"I'm tired. Let's go," he said, finishing his pint. Before the girls came to live with us, I would nag him all the time about giving up his work at the TV studios to pursue his dream of still photography. I'd finally managed to convince him, and he'd been in the middle of setting up a website and had found a restaurant keen to display his work. Then his sister died and his plans were put on hold. He didn't take photos any more; he'd packed his beloved Nikon at the back of a cupboard, along with so many more of our dreams.

I finished my wine and we walked home in silence. I checked on the girls before I climbed into bed, leaving Adam on the couch, flicking through the TV channels, a beer in his hand.

Hannah Ellis

Chapter 4

The best thing about Saturdays was the absence of Ruth in the morning. I woke with Emily's arm across my chest and no sign of Adam in our bed. Carefully, I peeled Emily off me and crept downstairs. Adam slept quietly on the couch. I picked up three empty beer bottles from the table beside him. His arm dangled limply off the couch and I bit my lip too hard before leaving him and heading to the kitchen. The back door was unlocked when I went to put the bottles out in the recycling bin.

I glanced at the garage. The key was in the door. Adam kept it locked and the kids weren't supposed to go in there, but Hailey sneaked in sometimes when she thought no one was looking. Adam hadn't noticed and I kept quiet about it. I didn't blame her; it was a nice place to hide away, surrounded by stacks of Adam's photos.

I made coffee and when I looked again, Hailey was sitting on the swing at the top of the garden, staring in my direction. She looked away when I forced a smile.

"Uncle Adam's sleeping on the couch," Emily told me, padding into the kitchen in her pyjamas.

"He stayed up too late watching telly," I said.

"Can I wake him?"

"Leave him a while. You hungry?" I grabbed the

chocolate cereal from the cupboard and shook it into a bowl while she grinned her approval. "What do you want to do today?" I asked, sitting opposite her to drink my coffee.

"Can we go swimming?"

"I guess so."

"You always want to go swimming," Hailey commented, strolling in through the back door.

"I like swimming," Emily said.

"I'm not going," Hailey said. I ignored her, certain she was just trying to get a rise out of me.

"Good," Emily said, munching her cereal. "I can just go with Lucy."

Adam stretched his neck and arms as he came in, looking sleep-deprived and crumpled. "Where you going?"

"Swimming," Emily told him. "But Hailey doesn't want to go."

"She can stay with me, then." Adam got himself a coffee and came to sit with us.

"Do you want some breakfast?" I asked him.

"These look good." He smiled at Emily and picked up the packet of chocolate cereal.

"You want some, Hailey?" I asked.

"I'll have muesli," she replied, getting the box from the cupboard while I directed my amusement into my coffee.

"I'll take Emily swimming this morning and nip to the toy shop for a present for the twins," I said. "You've not forgotten we're going over for cake tomorrow, have you?"

My half-brothers were turning eight and I'd opted out of going to their party in favour of a quiet family get-together the following day. I didn't think Hailey would appreciate a bowling party with rowdy boys two years younger than her.

"Do I have to go too?" Hailey asked.

"Yes, we're all going," I told her.

"Oh, *great*," she said, oozing sarcasm, pushing her muesli aside and leaving the table.

"Can you put your bowl in the dishwasher?" I raised my voice but she hurried up the stairs and ignored me.

"Pick your battles," Adam said, standing to clear the table.

"Let's get dressed and get our swimming things," I said to Emily, taking her hand when she got up from the table.

"See you later," I called when we left the house ten minutes later. Adam shouted 'bye' from the living room and Hailey was no doubt waiting for me to leave before she came out of her room. She'd enjoy the time with Adam: she doted on him and was always vying for his attention.

"I don't think Hailey likes me," Emily said as we pulled out of the driveway.

"You and me both," I muttered under my breath.

"What?"

"Of course she likes you. But she's your big sister and sometimes big sisters can be mean. She loves you really."

"I don't like her," she stated.

"Yes, you do."

"No, I don't. She's always mean."

I decided a change of subject was in order. "Are

you going to jump in at the deep end today?"

"Yes!" She grinned at me and I caught her eye in the rear-view mirror. She'd been scared of jumping into the water until recently. We'd spent a lot of time practising, moving from the shallow end, and gradually getting deeper until she was more confident.

"I bet you'll be the best in your swimming class soon."

She went swimming once a fortnight with school and she'd hated it at first but seemed fairly relaxed about it now.

"Billy's the best," she told me. "But I might be as good as him soon."

The public swimming pool was in Brinkwell, a small town a fifteen-minute drive from our village. We spent an hour in the water, which wasn't nearly warm enough for my liking, and then I coaxed Emily away with a promise of chips for lunch. We had a walk around Brinkwell and spent too long in the toy shop choosing presents for Max and Jacob. Emily begged me for everything she saw. I finally relented and bought her a cheap plastic jewellery set consisting of a sparkly silver tiara with matching necklace and ring. She insisted on wearing it all immediately and I walked to the café with my little princess swinging on my arm.

I called Adam and told him we were eating lunch out and he should find something for himself and Hailey. He said they were watching TV and Hailey was making him watch some show about high-school girls who were secretly mermaids. I knew it well.

"I'm a real princess now," Emily said when I ended the call. I looked over to see her adjusting her tiara across the table from me.

"Yes, you are!"

"What do princesses eat for lunch?"

"Whatever they want," I said.

"Sausages and chips?"

"Definitely," I assured her.

"I thought so!"

Emily chatted incessantly on the drive home and made me turn the volume up when a song she liked came on the radio. I glanced at her in the mirror and smiled when she tried to sing along to the music, though she clearly didn't know all the words.

Pulling up in the driveway, I took a deep breath before following Emily inside the house.

"We're home!" I called, peering into the living room to be met with a glare from Hailey. Adam was asleep on the couch beside her.

"What's on?" I asked.

Hailey fixed her focus on the TV. "*Mermaid High*."

Still? No wonder Adam was asleep.

"I don't like it," Emily said.

"Don't watch it then," Hailey snapped at her.

Emily looked up at me. "Can I watch *Frozen*?"

"No!" Hailey answered.

"Later," I told Emily who burst into tears.

"Hello!" Ruth's voice rang out behind me as she let herself in. I shushed Emily. It would be nice if, for once, Ruth could walk in to a scene of happy families rather than crying and bickering.

"What's wrong?" Ruth asked, dropping a shopping bag on the hall floor and moving into the living room.

"I want to watch *Frozen*," Emily said tearfully.

"Watch what you want." Hailey passed her the

remote. "I'm starving. What's for lunch?"

"You've not had lunch?" Ruth asked as Hailey walked past us. "It's the middle of the afternoon."

"Emily and I ate in Brinkwell," I said, defensively. "We've been swimming."

"Can you make pancakes, Gran?" Hailey's voice drifted in from the kitchen.

"The poor girl will waste away," Ruth said huffily and left the room.

I nudged Adam awake. "How can you sleep through that?"

"What?"

"Everything! Why didn't you get Hailey any lunch?"

"She wasn't hungry." He sat up, looking dazed and confused. "We had milkshakes."

"That's great. Thanks a lot."

"What's the problem now?"

"Nothing," I snapped. "Your mum's in the kitchen making pancakes."

"So what's the problem?"

I sank into the armchair. Emily moved from where she'd been standing by the window to climb onto my lap. Sometimes I forgot she was there. She seemed to be able to make herself invisible: she'd stand quietly, watching and listening, taking everything in. A little sponge. "Why don't you go and have some pancakes?" I said to Adam calmly.

"Can I watch *Frozen*?" Emily asked when Adam wandered out.

"How about we go down to the playground for a bit?"

She turned her nose up.

"I'll buy you some sweets on the way…"

"Okay. But can I watch *Frozen* later?"

"Yes. Promise."

"We're just nipping down to the playground," I called when we were already out the front door. "Won't be long." We left before anyone had a chance to comment.

I bought Emily sweets as promised and parked myself on a bench by the playground to watch her play. The playground was in the corner of a field at the edge of the village. It was picturesque and I was happy we had it to ourselves so I didn't have to make small talk with other parents.

I picked at my fingernails, smiling at Emily occasionally when she shouted for me to watch her.

"Hi." A voice interrupted my thoughts and I looked up to find Angela standing beside me. I managed a smile but my heart raced. I felt like I never had a moment to myself and I couldn't escape people's judgement.

"Hi," I said and she joined me on the bench.

"I saw you from the road and I thought I'd come and say hello. I've not seen you for a while."

"The boys at home?" I asked, ignoring her dig. She'd tried to befriend me when the girls came to live with us. Apart from being the school nurse and seeming to know everyone in the area, she'd also been best friends with Adam's sister, Becky, when they were growing up. It always felt like she was checking up on me – keeping an eye on her friend's kids to make sure they were being properly looked after. I'd taken to ignoring her calls and declining her invitations until she'd finally taken the hint and left me alone.

"Yes, I've just been up to the pub to talk to Mike about ordering drinks for the Easter picnic. How I get roped into these things I'm not sure." She rolled her eyes and I managed a smile. "I thought I'd get some peace and a bit of fresh air so I left the kids with Ben and walked over. They're no doubt glued to the TV and eating junk."

"I left Hailey with Adam this morning and they did the same," I told her. "Ruth's up there now making sure they eat."

"So you thought you'd escape for a while?"

"I can't do anything right," I said, suddenly unable to keep my thoughts to myself. "Ruth always arrives at a bad time. She comes in and finds the kids bickering and Hailey complaining that no one feeds her. And of course Adam's fast asleep on the couch so it's all my fault."

"Sounds like our house! You're doing a great job, you know." She patted my arm and my eyes filled with tears. "What's wrong?"

"Everything," I whispered, wiping my eyes. I watched Emily fly higher and higher on the swing. "Nothing. I'm fine. I'm just tired."

"Kids will do that to you. Mothers-in-law too." She smiled. "And husbands."

"I don't have a husband," I corrected her as fresh tears sprang to my eyes. "Somehow I ended up with the kids and mother-in-law without getting myself a husband."

"Sorry."

I shrugged. "That's life." *Mine, apparently, anyway.*

"Are you guys okay?" she asked, her voice full of concern.

"Yeah, we'll survive."

Angela turned to look at Emily and I watched the look pass across her face. I saw it often when people looked at the girls. Sympathy and sadness for the poor little things.

"They're lucky to have you," she told me. "I don't know how Adam and Ruth would have coped without you around. The girls too, of course."

"I'm sure they'd manage."

She looked at me for too long, making me uncomfortable.

"I'll give you a push," I shouted to Emily, getting up and heading towards the swings. "It was nice to see you," I said, looking briefly back at Angela.

Emily and I spent an hour there, playing tag and chasing each other around. We swung side by side on the swings and spun on the roundabout until we were dizzy.

"Uncle Adam!" Emily shouted, running into his arms when he approached us. He lifted her off the ground to spin her around and make her giggle. "Watch how high I can push myself on the swing," she said, running away from him.

Adam put an arm around me, kissing the top of my head before whispering "sorry" into my ear. I looped my arm around his back and rested my head on his chest.

"Don't be angry with me," he said. I wanted to tell him I wasn't, but I couldn't bring myself to lie. "I love you."

"I love you too," I replied automatically.

Hannah Ellis

Chapter 5

Ruth left shortly after we arrived home. Emily sat happily in front of the TV, finally getting to watch her film, and I went to work in the kitchen, cooking a nutritious dinner rather than reaching for frozen pizzas – which was what I really felt like.

"Can I do anything?" Adam offered, handing me a glass of wine.

"Peel the carrots," I said.

Hailey walked into the kitchen and took a seat at the table. "Gran said I can stay with her tomorrow. So I don't need to go with you for the twins' birthday."

"It's not up to your gran," I told her, looking at Adam for moral support.

"I was thinking I might not go either," he said. "They won't mind, will they?"

"I already told Kerry we'd all be there." Kerry is my stepmum, and one of my favourite people in the world, although I didn't see enough of her any more.

"I just really wanted a relaxing weekend without having to drive into the city," Adam said. "I have to drive in and out all week."

I shook my head, breaking off from washing the broccoli to glare at him. "I'll drive. You just have to sit in the car…"

"I spend half my time in a car."

"But it's the boys' birthday."

"Okay," he said with a sigh.

"I just thought it would be nice if we all went," I said.

"Okay."

"I don't even like Max and Jacob," Hailey complained. "Why can't I stay with Gran?"

"We're all going," Adam said.

Hailey huffed and stood up, then stomped all the way to her room, where she stayed until I called her down to dinner. We ate in front of the TV in an attempt to minimise conversation. There was less chance of bickering that way.

By the time the girls were in bed, I was emotionally drained. I sat down on the couch with Adam, glass of wine in hand, unable to concentrate on the crime thriller he'd put on. I stared at the screen for a while, but when I saw Adam was asleep beside me, I got up and headed quietly out of the front door. I was halfway up the hill, intent on visiting Tom, when I glanced at my watch. Surprised by the time, I realised it was probably too late to visit him.

There was something liberating about wandering the streets so late at night. I continued up the hill and circled back through the village.

"Evening." Mike made me jump when he walked out of the pub, collecting ashtrays and glasses from the lone table out the front – the smokers' table.

"Hi." I swallowed hard, frozen to the spot.

"Coming for a drink?"

"I was just out for some fresh air before bed," I told him.

He hovered in the doorway, his hands full. "Up to you. The place is empty." He left me on the street, wondering whether I should risk being alone with him. Would he try and talk to me, dredge up the past, or let me drink in peace? A drink would be nice and I wasn't in a hurry to get home.

"Wine?" he asked, pulling a bottle of white from the fridge and unscrewing the top while I perched on a stool at the bar and nodded my reply.

"Thanks." I watched him return the bottle to the fridge and turn to load glasses from the bar into the dishwasher. I'd always liked Mike. He was in his early forties, attractive, and easy to chat to. He was a nice guy. I sipped my wine and watched him work.

"Don't mind if I clean up around you, do you?"

I shook my head and he moved around the room wiping down tables and straightening tables and chairs. After hoping he wouldn't talk to me, I soon switched to wishing he would.

"I'd better get out of your way," I said once he'd finished cleaning and took the empty wine glass from the bar in front of me. "How much do I owe you?"

"Nothing."

I thanked him and slipped off the stool.

"Lucy," he called softly when my hand connected with the door handle. "Are you okay?" His words were so loaded that my eyes filled with tears.

"Yeah." I turned, nodding while I tried my best to convince him – and myself. "Just a bad day."

He walked around the bar towards me. "I'm going to have a drink before I turn in if you want to join me?"

I hesitated. "I'd better not."

He smiled kindly. "If you ever need to talk, you know where I am. Or if you just need a drink after a bad day…"

I thanked him again and slipped back outside. I walked quickly home, aware of how long I'd been gone.

It was quiet when I returned and crept like a burglar into my own home. Adam stirred on the couch as I slipped out of my shoes and jacket. I stopped and lingered in the shadows, waiting until I was sure he was sleeping before continuing up the stairs and into our bed.

Chapter 6

My bad temper flared the next morning when I looked at Adam lying on the couch, watching TV. "Maybe you should just stay here," I said gruffly.

"I said I'd come," he replied. "What have I done now?"

"I'm trying to get the girls organised to go to Dad and Kerry's and you're just lying around doing nothing."

"It's Sunday. I had a long week."

"Right, so I do nothing all week?"

"I'm coming," he said, standing up. "What do you want me to do?"

I glared at him. "Stay here – it's fine."

"I said I'm coming. Why are you in such a bad mood?"

"I'm not," I said, taking a breath and adopting a falsely calm tone. "I honestly don't mind if you don't come. Stay here with Hailey."

Hailey appeared in the doorway. "I don't have to go?"

"We're all going," Adam told her.

"Hello!" Ruth's voice – and the sound of the front door opening and closing – reached us just before she did. "Hailey said she might spend the day with me. What are the rest of you doing?"

"I'm taking Emily to my dad's," I said. "Adam and Hailey were going to stay here, but if you want to spend some time with Hailey then that's great." I realised it would take more than a day out together to turn us into a happy family, and I just didn't have the energy.

"Lovely." Ruth beamed at Hailey. "You can come to church with me."

I did a mental happy dance and had to stop myself from high-fiving Ruth. I watched with amusement as Hailey's face fell.

"Oh, I've decided to go with Lucy," she said. "It's the twins' birthday. I was just about to get dressed."

"Adam, have you got time to do a few jobs for me?" Ruth asked.

"Maybe later," he said. "We were all going out, actually."

"Stay and help your mum," I said. "We won't be long. I just need to put in an appearance and drop off the gifts."

Adam eyed me wearily and I almost felt bad. He clearly didn't want to come though, and if I'd known how much it would put him out I would never have suggested we all go. At that moment I really wished I could go alone.

"Great, that's settled then," Ruth said. "I just need you to put some curtains up. I finally found some to replace those tatty blue ones in the front room."

"Hurry up and get dressed, Hailey," I said. "I want to leave in a few minutes." She scarpered up the stairs and I shouted for Emily to come and put her shoes on. "Tell Hailey we're waiting in the car," I called over my shoulder once I'd rushed Emily into her shoes and jacket.

"Lucy," Adam called, following me outside. I helped Emily with her seatbelt before I closed the car door and turned to Adam.

"What?"

"I'm sorry," he said. "I feel like I can't do anything right. We should all go to your dad's."

"Yes, we should, but I shouldn't have to strong-arm everyone into going. You clearly don't want to come, so don't. Go and help your mum get rid of our tatty curtains!"

"Can I sit in the front?" Hailey asked, coming out of the house.

"Yes." I couldn't face another argument. The path of least resistance was the way I was going for the rest of the day. "I'll see you later," I said to Adam.

"What do you want me to do? Tell her not to take the curtains down?"

"Of course not. I'm sorry I said anything. I'm just tired – ignore me." I gave him a quick kiss and left him standing on the driveway as I drove away with the girls.

Hailey begrudgingly agreed to play I spy with Emily, and the drive was painless. Shy, the girls stayed by my side when we went into my dad's house – a sign that we didn't visit often enough. I hugged Dad and Kerry, and the boys hovered around me until I handed over their gifts. When we followed them into the living room I was surprised to find my mum there too.

"Hi." I hugged her. "I didn't know you'd be here."

She and Kerry had always had a slightly unconventional relationship. I'm not sure I'd call them friends – I certainly don't think Kerry would describe their relationship that way – but they'd always been on good terms.

I was a result of a fling when my mum was working in Dad's office. All very cliché. I grew up mainly with my mum, but Dad was always involved and when Kerry came on the scene, when I was four, she became my third parent. My favourite parent, if I'm honest. She was the most dependable of them and always had time for me. She was the one I went to for advice or to talk my problems through.

"I thought I'd call in," Mum said. "Kerry said you were coming over, and I haven't seen you for so long."

"Sorry," I said. "Life's hectic, you know."

"Oh, I know. I wasn't criticising; I just wanted to see you and I had to drop the boys' presents off anyway." I looked over at Max and Jacob, who had opened their Lego constructor kits and were assembling them on the coffee table.

"Good choice," Kerry said to me. "Who wants a drink?" We put in our drink orders and she looked at Dad, who dutifully went to the kitchen.

"I've got a little something for you girls too," Kerry said, retrieving two gift bags from behind the couch. They thanked her politely. Emily opened hers excitedly, and produced a jewellery-making kit complete with hundreds of tiny beads. Hailey's smaller bag held a box with a silver necklace and dolphin pendant. She thanked Kerry again and I helped her put it on. I wasn't sure whether to be happy that she was an angel child while we were out with my family or annoyed that they didn't see what I had to put up with every day. Mostly, I think it just irritated me that she couldn't be like that all the time.

"Did Adam have to work?" Mum asked.

"No. Ruth needed him to help her with a few things, but he sends his love."

"That's a shame," Kerry said. "We haven't seen him for ages."

"Can I make something now?" Emily asked me quietly, looking eagerly at her box of treasures.

"Let's save it until we're home. You don't want to lose the little bits."

"I can get her a tray," Kerry said. "She can sit at the table with it."

Dad came back in, carrying hot drinks for us. I took my coffee and watched Emily sit at the table with Kerry, looking seriously at her box of beads.

"You can help me if you want," Max said, looking up at Hailey. She moved on to the floor and leaned over the pieces of Lego spread on the coffee table. "Help me find the next pieces," he said, pointing to the instruction booklet.

"So it's kind of like a jigsaw puzzle?" she asked.

"Exactly," Max replied.

"I used to be good at puzzles," she said, plucking a tiny blue Lego brick out of the pile and handing it to Max.

"That's not fair," Jacob said. "Of course you'll win if you've got help."

"It's a competition?" I asked.

"Everything is a competition," Kerry said, shaking her head.

The Lego kept the boys and Hailey busy for a good half hour, and then Kerry brought out a cake and we sang 'happy birthday'. It was all very pleasant and relaxed. I wished our house were as calm.

Hailey went into the garden to play football with the boys and I watched them through the window while Mum helped Dad carry the plates and cups into the kitchen.

"They look like they're having fun," Kerry commented from beside me.

"I should come over more often," I said. "A happy imposter seems to have taken the place of my miserable child."

I felt her looking at me, trying to read me. "They're good kids," she said quietly, glancing at Emily who was enthralled with her beads.

"When we're here anyway," I said.

"You doing okay?" she asked.

"Yeah, we're okay." I moved back to the couch. Dad sat next to me, and Emily climbed onto his lap.

"I made you a necklace," she told him, draping a chain of pink and purple beads around his neck.

"Thanks," he said. "It's beautiful."

"I can make one for everyone," she announced proudly.

"I'm not sure we'll have time today," I told her. "But you can make them at home and bring them another day."

When Mum left, I shouted to Hailey that we'd have to go soon too. She was racing around with the boys and when a look of annoyance flashed across her face, I decided I'd have another coffee. We ended up staying for sandwiches and more cake and left late in the afternoon, promising to visit more often.

I was surprised at what a pleasant day I'd had with

the girls, and wished Adam had joined us. At home there always seemed to be so much tension – and it reappeared the moment we walked through the door. Hailey's dark mood returned and she snapped at Emily for no reason before stalking up to her room.

"I'll have to nip over to Brinkwell," I told Adam while I peered into the fridge. "There's nothing for the kids' lunches tomorrow."

"Sorry," he said, immediately defensive. "I didn't know, or I would've gone this afternoon. I can go shopping."

"It's fine. I'll go."

"Honestly, I don't mind. I can go."

I felt suddenly sorry for him. He walked on eggshells around me, wondering what I was going to snap at him for next. I walked over and circled my arms around his neck.

"I'm not angry at you," I said. "Play with Emily for a bit and then get them into bed."

He raised his eyebrows. "As long as I'm not in your bad books."

"You're not. I won't be long." He smiled and kissed my nose.

I returned to a quiet house an hour later. Adam grinned lazily at me as he lay sprawled on the couch. I perched beside him.

"You've not commented on my decorating," he said.

"Sorry." I fingered the row of plastic yellow beads around his neck. "They suit you."

"Not those," he said. "I decorated in here while you were out today."

"Okay," I said slowly, moving my eyes around the

room until I reached the window. "Wow!" I laughed.

"I figured if Mum didn't want the tatty old curtains we could have them back."

I leaned to kiss him. "I really love them."

"Even though they don't actually fit, and Mum's going to go crazy?"

I beamed at him. "*Because* they don't fit and it will drive your mother crazy!"

Chapter 7

"Morning." I greeted Jean Stoke cheerfully as I passed her in the hallway on the way to my classroom. She was the head teacher at St Jude's – a caring and reasonable boss, but not my biggest fan, due to the number of absences I'd had, and me cutting back my hours. When I'd started at St Jude's, I'd done so with the intention of becoming a full-time qualified teacher. But then the girls had arrived in our life and after a couple of months of Adam and Ruth trying to juggle the girls' after-school care, I'd suggested that I cut my hours for a while so I could pick up Hailey from school and be home with the girls in the afternoons.

It had been a temporary arrangement, but it showed no sign of changing. There'd been a few occasions – or perhaps more – when the girls or Ruth had been ill and I'd needed to take time off. Jean had been understanding about the situation, but I had the feeling she might be losing patience with me.

I slipped into the classroom and began setting up for the day. Sarah Willis, the class teacher, arrived not long after me. She was part of the reason I enjoyed the job so much. It was my second year at the school, and I'd been in her class the whole time. She'd requested me for another year despite my absences and issues.

We had grown close, and confided in each other about our lives.

Sarah was a mum of three and had always been supportive of my unusual family life. It was nice to be able to offload everything to her from time to time.

"I had the craziest weekend," she told me. "All three kids are up on eBay but there're no takers so far."

"Maybe you over-priced them?"

"At this point, I'd pay someone to take them away! Seriously, I don't know what was going on this weekend; I don't think they stopped bickering for a second. Jack was even shouting at Henry in his sleep! What did I do to deserve three boys? You're lucky you've got girls."

"Yeah, right!" I said. "My weekend wasn't much fun either."

"What are we going to do at Easter? Two weeks of being home with them. I swear I'll end up in an asylum."

"Which could be a nice break!"

"Exactly. Only a mother could dread having two weeks off work."

"Well, at least…" I paused.

"You can't think of anything, can you?"

"No. I don't think there are any positives." We smiled at each other and moved in sync around the classroom, preparing for the day's lessons.

The bell rang and the kids began to file in. I smiled as the children greeted me. "Hi, Jess!" I beamed. "I love your hair today. Did Mummy do it? It's beautiful. Hi, Freddie, what a great hat! Can you put it with your coat for play time? We don't wear hats in class, remember?"

They settled down quickly and we fell into our daily routine. I loved my job. Working with Sarah was great, and I loved the kids. My working day always went too fast and at 2.30pm, when I left to pick Hailey up, it was generally with a sinking feeling.

The week went by at its usual variable pace, with time seeming to slip into fast forward when I left the house in the morning. My working day whizzed by in a blink and then, the moment Hailey stepped into the car, time would slow almost to a halt and the hours often felt like they lasted for days.

I always had to force myself to chat to Hailey on the drive home, and Thursday was no different. "How was school?" I asked, trying my best to sound chirpy.

"Crap."

Without replying, I put the car into gear and pulled away, turning up the radio and wondering why I bothered. At home, I emptied out her lunch bag and found her lunch untouched. We'd been through this before, but I thought we'd moved on.

"You didn't eat your lunch," I said, walking into the living room.

"I didn't like it," she told me. "I hate your lunches."

"What would you like in your lunchbox?" I asked calmly.

"I don't care."

"Well, if you don't like what I make for you, you need to tell me what you *do* want."

"I *said* I don't care. Leave me alone."

I went into the hall and shoved the lunchbox back

into her schoolbag. I'd empty it later, when Ruth wasn't around to comment.

"How was your day?" Ruth asked when I joined her and Emily in the kitchen. Emily was standing on a chair at the sink, helping Ruth with the washing up.

"Good, thanks." I held back from adding that it had gone downhill as soon as I left work. "How was school, Emily?"

"Good," she said. "I made an Easter card for you but it's a surprise."

"Lovely!"

"Yep. And I get to stay home and play with you for the holidays."

"That's right," I said with a sinking feeling at the thought of the Easter holidays the following week. "We'll have lots of fun."

"You've got holiday club too," Ruth reminded her. She'd signed both the girls up for the programme at the community centre – it was just in the mornings and only the first week of the holiday but I was glad I'd get a bit of peace.

"Will my friends be there?" Emily asked.

"Yes," Ruth said. "Rosie will be there and Emma, and lots of other kids from school."

"Okay, I'll go then," Emily said, as though she had a say in the matter.

Chapter 8

The weekend went by in a haze of bickering and sniping that was held at a modest level by Emily's presence in the house. If it weren't for her sparkle of innocence forcing a measure of cheerfulness from us, I dread to think how we'd get through the days together. Really, I should have been happy that it was the Easter holidays and I had two weeks off work. Needless to say, it was not something I could get excited about.

"You're really making me go to this *kids'* club?" Hailey asked over breakfast on Monday morning. I'd put toast in front of her and she hadn't commented, clearly saving herself for bigger battles.

"You *are* a kid," I reminded her.

"You're a kid until you're twenty-one," Emily announced while she munched noisily on her toast. "Uncle Adam told me."

I smiled at her and sat down, clutching my coffee.

"I don't want to go," Hailey said. "And I don't think it's fair. Why can't I stay home with you?"

She really must hate the thought of it if staying with me seemed preferable.

"All the local kids go. You might make friends," I said.

"That's stupid. I'm not allowed to go to the local

school but I have to go to the local kids' club in the holidays?"

"I didn't think you minded not going to the local school."

"Of course I mind. I have to go to a school that's far away with a load of rich, stuck-up brats when I could walk down the road and go to school here like a normal kid."

"You are normal," I told her. "Your gran just thought Cromwell School would be better for you."

"I don't see why. It's a crap school."

"Hailey," I hissed, glancing at Emily.

"Sorry, but I think it's a bad school. Why do I have to have extra French lessons in my break-time? That's not fair."

I didn't know what to say, because I agreed with her on that point. Ruth had been adamant that Hailey should keep up with her French, and had decided Cromwell School was the best place for her. I didn't disagree about the French, but my suggestion had been for her to go to the local school and have lessons with a French tutor outside school. My opinion had been overlooked once again.

"I told Gran I want to go to Havendon Juniors," Hailey said when I didn't reply. "But she says I'm not allowed."

I was surprised. Hailey had never been keen on school, but I thought it was school in general she hated, not her specific one. "Talk to Adam," I suggested.

"Can you talk to him?"

"I guess so."

"Please," she said quietly, her big eyes boring into

me. "The kids at Cromwell are mean."

"I'll talk to Adam," I promised her, hating how vulnerable she looked.

She tensed and looked away from me. "He'll just do what Gran says, though," she said gruffly, challenging me. I kept quiet, feeling uncomfortable. She was probably right.

"Good morning!" Ruth's voice reached us. Hailey rolled her eyes theatrically.

"Can't *you* at least take us?" she asked, quietly. "It won't be as embarrassing as turning up with my gran."

"She wants to take you," I murmured back. Ruth appeared in the doorway.

Hailey looked at Emily and whispered, "I'll give you a pound if you cry and say you want Lucy to take us."

"Can you lend me a pound?" Hailey grinned at me when we walked down the drive together. We'd left Ruth getting on with some cleaning after Emily's award-winning performance. Emily swung happily on my arm as we walked in the sunshine down to the community centre. Hailey went quiet when we got there.

"You're really making me do this?" she asked.

"You might enjoy it," I told her.

"Morning!"

I turned to see who had spoken. It was Angela, arriving with her boys, Zac and Harry.

"You coming too?" Zac asked Hailey, who nodded in response. "Come with me if you want." He didn't wait for a reply, but turned and beckoned her with a flick of the head. She gave me a weak smile and followed him, shaking Emily off when she tried to hold her hand.

"See you later," I called, but neither of them looked back.

"They'll be fine," Angela said. "You got time for a cuppa?"

"Yeah," I agreed, thinking I would do anything to avoid going back to Ruth. "I'd invite you to our place, but Ruth's there."

"Come to mine," she offered. "I've got cake."

"Sold!"

I followed her to her car.

Ruth called me to find out where I was before I'd finished my coffee at Angela's. I politely told her where I was, feeling like a teenager who'd stayed out past her curfew. She offered to cook for us, but I said I would fix something when I got home.

"She might actually drive me crazy one of these days," I told Angela when I hung up. Reaching for my fork, I tucked into the carrot cake she'd put in front of me.

"I'm sure she means well," Angela said. "But I don't envy you. She does like to have her nose into everything."

"She just seems to make everything more difficult. She thinks she's doing me a favour by cooking and cleaning, but it just makes me feel like it's not really my house. I took the girls to McDonald's the other week and then got in trouble because she'd made lasagne."

"I'm always thankful that my mother-in-law is a safe distance away and she doesn't make any unexpected visits."

"You're lucky," I said. "Hailey told me today she wants to change schools. I think I'm supposed to convince Adam and Ruth."

"Do you think Adam would go for it?"

"Probably not. He tends to go along with what Ruth says. She really thinks the private school is best for Hailey, but I'm not convinced. She doesn't seem to have made any friends."

"I was surprised Ruth didn't want her in the local school. It must be so hard on her, though. I bet keeping busy with the girls is the only thing that keeps her going."

"I know. I have to remind myself daily to be patient with her."

"I don't know how you do it," she said. "Everything – not just putting up with Ruth. It can't be easy."

"We manage."

"Do you want another cuppa?"

"Go on, then. If I'm not in your way."

"Not at all. You're keeping me from a mountain of washing which I'm quite happy to avoid."

We ended up chatting all morning and suddenly it was time to pick the kids up again. I apologised for outstaying my welcome, but Angela insisted I hadn't and she was glad of the company.

We walked into the community centre together. Emily came running up to me with a mask she'd made out of a paper plate which vaguely resembled a lion. I asked where Hailey was, and Emily pointed to the back door which led out into a field. Through the window I could see Hailey chatting to another girl while Angela's son, Zac, kicked a ball around them. Hailey suddenly darted forward and kicked the ball away from Zac, laughing as she did so.

"Looks like they're having fun," Angela said. I nodded, unable to speak. I couldn't remember seeing Hailey laugh so freely.

"That's Imogen Webster with Hailey," Angela told me. "She lives next door to us. She and Zac are fairly inseparable."

"Hi!" Hailey said when they came running inside.

"Hi. Did you have fun?"

"Yeah, it was good."

I waved to Angela while I herded the girls out of the door and back up the road to home. They chatted about their morning, one on each side of me, oblivious to the fact that I couldn't process two conversations at once. I nodded along, catching the odd sentence from each of them. Apparently the holiday club wasn't so bad after all.

Ruth was gone when we got back, and the kitchen was as clean as I'd ever known it.

"Where are my colouring books?" Emily asked, sitting at the kitchen table. This was the trouble with Ruth cleaning up for us. We inevitably spent a long time searching for missing items. I'd often asked Ruth if she'd moved something and she'd swear blind she'd not touched it, then I'd find it in a completely random place. Hailey got especially annoyed when Ruth put her clothes away in Emily's room or vice versa.

"Gran must have tidied them up," I said. "Let's have a colouring book hunt!" I made a game of it and we finally found the missing books in Emily's bedroom, which was annoying since Emily loved to sit and colour at the kitchen table when I cooked – and Ruth knew that.

I decided not to get annoyed by it and instead enjoyed the rare tranquillity in the house. We had lunch and the three of us watched a movie before I suggested Emily and I do some baking. Hailey surprised me by helping too. After we'd made a disgustingly rich chocolate cake, we made spaghetti Bolognese for dinner.

Adam looked pleased when he came in and found the three of us laughing in the kitchen. We had the radio on and were singing and dancing and being a bit silly.

"Hi!" He picked up Emily and danced her around before moving over to give me a kiss. "What's going on here?"

"We cooked dinner," Emily told him.

"And chocolate cake," Hailey said, running her finger along the sticky icing on the side of the cake and licking it.

"Hey!" I cracked a tea towel in her direction and she jumped out of the way, laughing.

We had the nicest dinner that I ever remember us having together. Sitting around the kitchen table, the girls told Adam all about the holiday club. Adam even chatted about the TV show he was working on, which made me realise we didn't talk much any more. It was rare for me to hear anything about his work.

After dinner, the girls disappeared into the living room, leaving Adam and me to tidy the kitchen.

"Do you want a glass of wine?" he asked, taking a bottle of beer from the fridge.

"No, I'll wait until the girls are in bed and then I

can relax properly."

"Shall I read to Emily?"

"No, it's fine," I said. "I'll do it."

He grabbed my hand when I finished loading the dishwasher, pulling me to him and kissing me.

"Dinner was great," he said.

"It was, wasn't it?"

"That's a bit modest," he said teasingly, nuzzling my neck.

"You know what I mean! Now get off me – I need to get Emily bathed and into bed."

"Good plan." He flashed me a boyish smile. I gave him another quick kiss, looking forward to the girls being in bed so we could spend some time together.

I'd been lulled into a false sense of security by the nice day I'd had with the girls, and had let myself be optimistic about bedtime. I called to Hailey to get ready for bed while I helped Emily out of the bath. I wrapped her in a towel and ushered her into her bedroom, where she put on her pyjamas before I read her a quick story and kissed her goodnight. When I tiptoed across the room, her eyes looked so heavy I was sure she'd be asleep within moments.

I was wrong.

"Lucy," she said when I reached the door.

"Yes, hon?"

"Does Mummy know I'm going to holiday club and not school?"

"Yes, she knows," I whispered, hoping that would be enough.

"Does she still love me?"

I moved back to sit on the edge of the bed. "Of

course. She'll always love you. I told you that."

"I forgot."

"Don't forget. Never ever forget!" I said in a sing-song voice and tickled her, hoping I could distract her. I wanted her to giggle and fall into a peaceful sleep.

"Can we go outside and say goodnight?" she asked.

I pulled back the curtain slightly, revealing a hazy sky. "The clouds are hiding the stars," I said.

"Can we wait until the clouds go away and then go outside?"

"Okay. Let's wait. I'll lie with you and we'll wait." I snuggled beside her, watching the sky through the window, certain she'd fall asleep any moment.

I was wrong again.

"What are you doing?" Adam asked when I carried Emily downstairs an hour and a half later. I'd just nodded off when Emily nudged me and told me she could see stars.

"She wants to look at the stars for a minute," I told Adam.

"It's time for bed, Emily," he said, stroking her hair. "You should've been asleep ages ago."

"I want to say goodnight to Mummy."

Adam gave me a look. The look said he disapproved but didn't want to cause a fuss. He didn't like Emily's fixation with stars. He'd told me as much once; he thought it was confusing for her, and unhealthy. He'd never made an issue of it, though, just let me get on with it. The look he gave me was yet another thing that made me feel I had no clue what I was doing. It was true, of course. I had no idea.

We were only outside for two minutes before Emily fell asleep on my shoulder. She opened her eyes when

I tucked her back into bed, and asked me to stay with her. I lay down, pulled the duvet over both of us, and didn't stir until morning.

Chapter 9

"I'll walk the girls down, if you don't mind," I said to Ruth the next morning. "I think it's good for me to meet some of the other parents. I never get to know anyone since it's always you dropping Emily off and picking her up."

She looked surprised. It had taken me a while to come up with this excuse. Hailey was adamant she didn't want to be dropped off by her grandmother, though, and I didn't want Ruth to be offended.

"That makes sense, I suppose. Did you have a nice time with Angela yesterday?"

"Yeah, I did."

"Oh good, you've put some washing on," she said when the machine started its noisy spin cycle. "I can stay and hang that out for you, and then stick another load in. You don't want it getting on top of you, and it's a lovely breezy day – it'll dry in no time."

I focused on my coffee, taking deep breaths and worrying that one day I might just bite my tongue right off.

Hailey made a beeline for Zac and Imogen as soon as we reached the community centre. Emily spotted her school friends and was off without a second glance at me. I waved at the two women in charge and then hung around to say hello to Angela, who was talking to another mother near the doorway.

"Morning!" She smiled warmly when she saw me and finished her conversation with the other mum. "How are you this morning?"

"Fine," I said. "Apparently I'm in mortal danger of the washing getting on top of me, but apart from that everything is good!"

"Oh dear." She chuckled. "Was Ruth over again this morning?"

"Every morning," I said. "I must have been an awful person in a previous life!"

"Come for a jog with me," she said. "Channel the anger!"

We headed out of the community centre. I glanced around at the girls but they were engrossed with their friends. "I don't know when I last did any exercise," I told Angela. "There's a good chance it could kill me."

"Come on – I don't go far or fast. It'll be good for you."

"Okay. If you promise not to laugh at me."

"Cross my heart!"

We walked up the hill together to our house. I left Angela chatting to Ruth in the kitchen while I rummaged around for something sporty to wear. I finally found a suitable outfit and hurried down to rescue Angela.

I managed to jog for half an hour and then couldn't ignore my screaming lungs any longer. I stood, bent over, my hands on my knees, while I tried to catch my breath.

"You said you wouldn't laugh," I reminded Angela. She held her hands up and made a zipping action across her lips.

"You did better than I expected," she said.

We spent the next hour wandering the hills around the village, chatting about whatever came to mind, mainly complaining good-naturedly about our families. We were walking back through the village when Mike appeared at the door of the pub.

"Looking energetic, ladies!"

"I don't feel it," I told him.

"Is your coffee pot up and running?" Angela asked.

"It certainly is," he said, standing aside and holding the door for us.

"Perfect," Angela said. "I assume you'll put it on a tab? We've no cash."

"No problem," he told us.

I took a seat at the nearest table and laid my head down on the table, groaning. "What have you done to me?"

"I told you. It's good for you!" Angela said.

"Anyone want some gossip to go with the coffee?" Mike asked, setting two steaming mugs down in front of us.

I sat up quickly. "Definitely!"

He pulled up a stool and leaned towards us conspiratorially. "Last night Ron Bishop came in for a few drinks…"

I looked at Angela.

"The old guy with the golden retriever," she told me. "His wife died a few years back."

I nodded and looked back at Mike.

"So last night old Ron got a bit tipsy and ended up sitting with Sheila…"

"Sheila from the shop?" I asked.

Mike nodded. "Shop Sheila. So they got chatting

and stayed until closing. When they were leaving, Sheila tripped on the doorstep." Mike raised his eyebrows. "And old Ron had to see her home safely."

"And?" I asked.

"She tripped," Mike said again. "Ron had to lend her an arm to make sure she got home okay!"

"That's the gossip?" I looked at Angela, who was smiling as she sipped her coffee.

"I thought it was quite exciting," Mike said. "She tripped!"

"She didn't fall on her face, though?" I asked.

"Of course not," Mike said. "That would be a serious incident, not idle gossip!"

"This isn't really gossip, though," I said.

"You city folks," he said. "This is as good as it gets, I'm afraid. What were you expecting? Some big scandal? Dream on!"

I gave him a playful nudge.

"So just to make sure I've got this right for when I tell Adam … Sheila tripped?"

"She did indeed," Mike said. "I wouldn't lie to you!"

Chapter 10

I enjoyed chatting to Angela and Mike, and stayed too long. When we left the pub I only had time to go home for a quick shower and change before I had to pick the kids up.

Hailey ended up going home with Angela, desperate to play with Zac and Imogen. Emily and I had a quiet lunch of sandwiches and crisps and then nodded off in front of the TV. When I called Angela, she told me that the kids were all playing on the field opposite their house, and invited me to bring Emily over to play with the younger kids on the playground.

Hailey waved when we arrived. She was running around on the hill and seemed to be having a great time. Emily spotted a friend on the playground and I followed when she ran in that direction.

I took a seat on a bench next to another mum and said a quick hello to her.

"I'm Karen," she said. "Imogen's mum. I've seen you around but we've not met properly."

"I'm Lucy."

"I know," she said lightly.

I turned and smiled at the amusement on her face. "I'm still famous around here, then?" I asked.

"For so many reasons."

I appreciated her honesty.

"The kids have been having a great time," she told me, glancing back at the hill.

"I'm glad," I said. "Hailey was dreading the holiday club, but she's having a fantastic time. To be honest, I wasn't looking forward to the holidays either, but so far, so good! Have you got a little one too?"

"Yeah, Ella's the little blondie." She pointed to the girl on the slide. "She's three and a half."

I turned to see Hailey, Zac and Imogen running into the house next to Angela's.

"That's our place," Karen said. "They'll no doubt be out again in a minute."

She was right: they reappeared a few minutes later, carrying kites, and ran to the top of the hill to fly them.

It was late afternoon when I finally loaded the girls into the car and headed home for dinner. Adam was late and the girls were watching TV in their pyjamas when he arrived home. He gave me a quick kiss and collapsed into an armchair.

"Did you have a good day?" he asked as Emily crawled into his lap.

"Lucy's going to take us shopping for kites tomorrow," Emily told him. "Then we can go up on the hill to fly them."

"We were over at Angela's place and the other kids all had kites," I explained to Adam.

"We've got kites in the attic," he said. "Do you remember, Hailey? I bought them one summer when you were little."

"When Emily was just a baby?" Hailey mused, looking up from the TV. "You and Dad took me out to fly kites but wouldn't let me have a turn…"

"Yeah." He smiled. "I thought you might have forgotten that part. I'll go up in the attic later and find them."

Of course, he didn't get up to the attic that evening, and when I sat at the kitchen table with the girls the following morning all thoughts of kites had vanished.

"Lucy," Ruth huffed. "You didn't hang the washing out. I told you I was putting another load in the machine."

"I forgot all about it," I said, refusing to let her get to me.

"You'll have to put it on to wash again now."

"It's fine. I'll do it later."

"What on earth were you doing all day that you couldn't manage to hang out one load of washing? You didn't even fold the other load." She glanced at the washing basket, which was full of crumpled but clean clothes. I thought I'd done well remembering to take it off the washing line before I went to bed.

"I was busy having fun with the girls," I said. "We're on holiday."

"You're going to have no clean clothes to wear soon," Ruth said irritably. "Shall I walk the girls down this morning so you can get on with some jobs?"

"Yeah, okay."

Hailey shot me a disapproving look, which I ignored, getting up to put the washing machine on. I spent the morning ironing and cleaning and then had half an hour to relax with a cup of tea before I went to pick the girls up. Again, they were chatty and full of excitement when they gave me a rundown of their morning over lunch.

"Did Uncle Adam get the kites out?" Hailey asked as I loaded plates into the dishwasher.

"No, I think he forgot.".

"Can you get them?" she asked.

"I guess so," I told her. "Let me put a movie on for Emily and then I can go up and have a look."

Luckily, I managed to avoid knocking myself out with the attic ladder when I pulled it down through the trapdoor. That had been my main worry. I groped in the dark until I found the light switch. Blinking, I took in the mess of boxes and random objects in the attic. Unsure where to start, I randomly pulled up the lids of boxes to look for the kites. The creak of the ladder alerted me to Hailey's presence a short while later.

"Wow, what a mess!"

"I know," I said. "We should've left it to Adam."

"They must be around here somewhere." She copied me and checked some more boxes.

"Bingo!" I said eventually, opening a huge cardboard box and discovering an array of outdoor toys. "There's all sorts of things in here."

I looked at Hailey, who was crouching over a smaller box.

"Is this my mum?" She held a photo up to show me and I moved to take it from her.

"Yeah," I said, taking in the image of Becky and Adam sitting on their bikes, grinning into the camera.

"How old do you think she is there?" she asked, biting her lip and fighting off tears.

I flicked the photo over. A date was written on the back, in Ruth's handwriting. "About your age," I told her after a quick calculation. "Maybe a bit younger."

She sniffed and nodded, taking the photo back and

replacing it in the box. "It's full of photos," she told me, delving into the box and pulling out an album. "They're all of Mum and Uncle Adam. Where's this?" she asked, pointing to a photo of Becky on a beach as a teenager.

"I don't know. Why don't you take them down? You can ask Adam about them later."

"Thanks," she said, flashing me a shy smile. "Did you find the kites?"

"Yeah. You go down the ladder and I'll pass things down to you."

We managed to cart the boxes downstairs and then played in the garden for a while with our newfound treasures: bats and balls, stilts and roller-skates, and skipping ropes. I was surprised Ruth hadn't suggested getting them out before.

We drove over to Angela's place with the kites late in the afternoon. We flew them on the hill with Zac and Imogen before heading into Angela's house to eat and warm up.

Hailey was laughing when we finally arrived home, but stopped abruptly when she walked into the hallway. She turned to look at me, panic in her eyes. I glanced into the living room. Adam sat on the floor, his childhood photos spread out around him, tears streaming down his face. Quickly, I directed Emily into the kitchen and ushered Hailey in after her.

"Why don't you make milkshakes?" I said to her. She stared at me and swallowed hard. "It's fine," I said, rubbing her arm. "Just watch Emily for a few minutes, okay?" She nodded. I pulled the living room door shut behind me and knelt beside Adam, hugging him. There was a time when it felt like whenever I entered a room, I would find someone crying. I don't know when that had stopped, but Adam's tears took me by surprise.

"I still can't believe she's gone," he said when he finally managed to speak.

"I know," I said, stroking his hair and kissing his damp cheek. "I'm so sorry."

When I looked up, Hailey was in front of me, tears in her eyes. "I'm sorry," she said. "I should've left them up in the attic."

"Come here." I took her hand and pulled her in for a hug. "It's fine."

Adam straightened up and took a deep breath, attempting a smile for Hailey. "I just miss her, that's all."

She wiped her tears with a sleeve. "Me too."

"See this one…" Adam picked up a photo from the floor. "That's my T-shirt. She was always stealing my T-shirts. I used to get so annoyed at her. It's not like I could wear her clothes."

Hailey picked up another photo. "This is the tennis set we found in the attic today, isn't it?"

Adam took it from her. It was a photo of himself when he was about Hailey's age, holding a tennis racket and grinning into the camera. "Your gran never throws anything out."

I left them reminiscing over the photos and got Emily ready for bed. After reading her several stories I went back downstairs. Hailey and Adam were laughing and I decided to leave them alone. I made myself a cup of tea and went upstairs to read in bed.

Chapter 11

The next day, I was disappointed to wake and find Adam had already left. I hated his long hours and wished he was home more. I was happy about the long weekend: he'd be home for four days and – for once – I was looking forward to us all being together. Hailey had been like a different person the past week. She was actually fun to be around. I'd stopped having to watch what I said around her, and she was kinder to Emily too. It made the house a much happier place.

The kids were so eager to get to holiday club on the final day that they were ready to go when Ruth arrived. I felt a bit sorry for her. We didn't need her in the school holidays and she could surely see that – although she clearly thought I was terrible at housework and took every opportunity to point out the mess I made of it! I was probably doing her a favour by letting the house get into a state. It gave her something to do – and something to complain about.

"You going jogging again?" Ruth asked, taking in my outfit.

"Yeah. Angela invited me along with her."

"That's nice," she said. "Do you need anything doing around here?"

"I'm not sure." There was obviously plenty she could do, but I wished she would just leave me to do things as and when I wanted to.

"I could cook you a nice lunch if you want?"

"That would be good," I said.

Hailey glared at me when we walked out of the front door. "I hope it's not fish pie. I hate her fish pie."

I secretly agreed.

"I can't believe you've got me doing this again," I told Angela outside the community centre. Exercise had never been high on my list of things to do, but I was glad Angela had talked me into jogging. I enjoyed the fresh air, and being able to jog for half an hour on my first attempt had left me with a small sense of achievement.

The kids wandered off, chatting away to each other in their little groups, and Angela and I set off at a slow pace down the road.

"What will we do next week when there's no kids' club?" I asked once we were out of the village, jogging along a footpath that ran along the fields in the valley.

"Zac and Imogen are signed up for sports club over in Brinkwell. They did it last year and loved it. Why don't you see if you can sign Hailey up?"

"Sounds great," I said, my breathing ragged. "I'm sure she'll be keen if Zac and Imogen are going. She'll get bored if she's stuck at home all week."

"Yep, they're at an awkward age. I try and sign them up to as many clubs as possible over the school holidays. It works out better for everyone."

"I've still got a lot to learn," I said. "It's good to get some tips."

"You're amazing with them, though," she said

kindly. "And they adore you."

"It's only recently that things seem to be getting easier. I feel like Hailey and I are finally managing to get along. She was awful before."

"That's understandable, isn't it?"

"Of course. Just tough to live with sometimes."

"I still can't believe it," she said. "Life is so unfair sometimes."

I nodded, my lungs burning.

My second attempt at jogging actually felt worse than the first. Every part of me screamed at me to stop. I had a stitch, then cramp. My muscles hated me, my lungs were refusing to do their job, and I collapsed on a bench near the playground after half an hour.

"I'm sorry," I panted. "I'm pathetic!"

"You're not," Angela assured me. "It gets easier."

"I might just decide that jogging isn't my thing."

"You can't ditch me now! I like having a running partner. It makes it much easier."

"I'm done for today," I told her. "I might need to call a taxi to get me home."

"I've got to go shopping anyway. I need stuff for the Easter picnic tomorrow and it's easier to do it without the kids."

"Ruth's doing the food for us. She insisted. She's also making us lunch today. She likes to keep busy, I guess."

"She always did – and now more than ever, I suppose."

We walked together back to Angela's car and then I walked slowly up the hill, shouting hello to Ruth when I walked in the house. I headed straight upstairs for a shower. The place smelled delicious – and, thankfully, there was no whiff of fish.

"I did a sausage casserole," she said when I came back down. "I know the girls always enjoy that."

"Me too. And I've earned it today!"

"I think you could eat what you want anyway. You're so skinny these days. You should eat more."

She was always trying to feed people. She thought everyone was too thin.

"I was thinking of signing Hailey up for the sports club next week in Brinkwell," I told her. "Imogen and Zac are going and she's had a great time with them this week."

"That's probably a good idea," she agreed.

Hailey asked me if she could go to sport camp as soon as I picked her up. She was delighted when I told her I'd already called and signed her up. We had lunch with Ruth, and then the girls showed her the box of toys we'd found in the attic. Ruth sat outside to watch the girls play. Later that afternoon, she took them to the playground, leaving me at home.

I was sitting on the couch with a cup of tea, enjoying the peace, when the phone rang. It was Adam.

"Hi, babe." He sounded distracted and busy.

"Hi – everything okay?" I asked.

"Yeah. It's all crazy down here, though. I'm going to have to work tomorrow and probably Saturday."

My heart plummeted.

"We're not going to get finished until late tonight, so Carl said I could stay at his place. Do you mind?" He worked with Carl and they'd been friends for years. I'd also met Carl when I was on the reality TV show. I liked him and his wife a lot, though I hadn't seen them for a while. Before we lived together, Adam used to stay in the city with Carl a lot.

"I suppose not."

"Sorry. I think I'll be too tired to drive."

"Yeah, okay." What else could I say? "What about the family picnic tomorrow?"

"Sorry."

"It's a public holiday," I complained.

"I know but TV doesn't really stop, does it? I'll get double pay."

"Okay." I sighed, irritably. "Just call me tomorrow and let me know if you'll make it home tomorrow night."

"Lu—"

I hung up, furious with him. Why couldn't he see that we needed him at home more? He used money as an excuse to work long hours, but I had the feeling he preferred to be at work than at home with us. It hurt.

Hannah Ellis

Chapter 12

The weather had been unseasonably mild and thankfully it stayed that way for the Good Friday picnic, which took place in the field at the back of the community centre, with the community centre as the backup location in case of bad weather. I was happy about being outside.

I'd been asked about Adam's whereabouts roughly seven thousand times in the space of half an hour. Or so it felt. I'd smiled politely, saying he had to work. It was a shame, yes, but unavoidable. People asked me about the girls with a sympathetic tilt of the head. They were doing great, I'd reply. Yes, kids are resilient. Yes, it was an awful tragedy. I think their hushed tones annoyed me more than the questions themselves.

We'd come last year too, at Ruth's insistence, but hadn't stayed long. I'd had Adam by my side the whole time and the girls clung to us. They hadn't made local friends then, and were still in a state of shock. I remember thinking the picnic had been awful last year, but it seemed worse this year, as I was by myself and the girls were off playing with their friends, not needing me at all. Ruth was busy circulating, and I felt awkward and alone. I waved a greeting at Angela, who was chatting to an old couple, and tried to catch the eye of Imogen's mum, Karen, but she seemed to be bickering with her husband.

I smiled at an old woman who walked past, and quickly buried my head into our picnic hamper in the hope she wouldn't stop to chat.

"If you find Narnia through that hamper, you'll let me come with you, won't you?" I turned to find Mike crouching beside me. "It looked like you were trying to get in there."

"I wish! How can I escape this?"

"It's awful, isn't it?" He handed me a plastic cup of what appeared to be Coke. "This stuff helps."

I took a sip and coughed, not expecting it to contain vodka. "Alcohol is frowned upon at the picnic," he told me. "Since it's a family day. It's ironic, because it's the only day I really feel the need to drink."

I took another sip. "Is there more where this came from?"

"Yes," he said, smiling.

I offered the cup back.

"Keep it. Just don't drink it too quickly. We don't want to get into trouble with Ruth."

"Aren't you going to ask where Adam is? It seems to be the question on everyone's lips today."

He sat on the picnic blanket next to me. "I don't need to ask. I know everything about everyone around here."

I raised my eyebrows at him.

"I overheard Ruth telling her knitting crew that Adam is working himself to death. A martyr to his family, apparently."

"Is it only me who thinks he's got it easy today?"

"That would definitely be my opinion." He took the

vodka-laced Coke from me and took a swig. "But I guess we're the minority."

"Do you ever think about living somewhere else?" I asked.

He scanned the field, looking thoughtful "No. It's my home. I wouldn't want to go back to city life. Would you?"

"You lived in the city?"

"Yes." He grinned. "I grew up in Manchester. I'm like you; I only ended up here by accident."

"Adam said you took over the pub from your uncle…"

"Yeah, I did."

I poked him in the ribs when he didn't elaborate, and he laughed at me. "Fine. It was eight, nearly nine, years ago. I may have been slightly heartbroken and my uncle asked me to come out here for a while and help him with the pub."

"Oh God, he died and left you the pub, didn't he? Is this village cursed or what?"

"No," he said, chuckling. "Worse than that! He moved to the coast, bought some ramshackle old cottage to do up, and he goes surfing every day. I'm not even kidding – he's sixty-five years old and he surfs every day while I slave away in his pub for a pittance. He's promised the pub will be mine when he pops his clogs, but I'm fairly sure he'll outlive me."

"Well, I'm glad he's not dead."

We looked up at the sound of someone calling for Mike. "We're out of orange juice," the man shouted. "Can you run and grab some more?"

Mike waved and stood up.

"I never bring enough drinks over," he told me,

quietly. "Gives me an excuse to keep going back to the pub for more."

"You're a pro! Don't suppose you need any help?"

"That would be a brave move. Don't people gossip about you enough?"

"People gossip about me?" I asked with a grin. "What on earth would they have to say about my boring life?"

"I'll find you later," he said. "I need your advice on something."

He left me alone – and intrigued. I finished the drink in one long gulp and looked around for the girls. They were playing happily, so I dragged myself up and walked purposefully over to Angela and her husband.

"You have to let me sit with you," I said. "I'm so bored!"

They shuffled around to make room for me.

"I was going to come and save you earlier, but Mike beat me to it," Angela said.

"I can't believe Adam isn't here," I complained.

"I know," Angela's husband Ben said. "It doesn't seem fair, working on a public holiday. He'll be on double pay, though. I'd work for free if it got me out of this!"

"Ben," Angela hissed, slapping his arm. "It's a nice family day together!"

"We could have a nice family day in front of the TV," Ben said. "I could have a beer then as well. I don't understand why we're not allowed a drink. Can't we get Mike to spike the punch again?"

"No!" Angela laughed. "He got into trouble over that. And he didn't spike it; he just didn't know that alcohol wasn't allowed."

"I got a vodka and Coke from him," I confessed.

Ben shook his head. "I hate you!"

The rest of the afternoon was bearable. I stayed close to Angela and Ben for most of the time, rounding up the kids with Ruth to eat a late lunch together. A barbecue was fired up, manned by a couple of locals, offering hot dogs and burgers to go with the drinks, which were included in the ticket price. Ruth had brought salad to go with it, and crisps and biscuits which the girls feasted on before running off to find their friends again.

An announcement was being made about a game of cricket when Mike sidled up to me. "Unfortunately, I didn't bring enough lemonade so I'm going to go and fetch some more." He gave me a serious look. "I'd advise you to make yourself scarce while they pick teams. Do not get involved in the cricket game, whatever you do."

"I was thinking it might be fun."

"It's not," he told me. "It's the exact opposite of fun. They say it's a friendly game but it's not. People get competitive. Save yourself!"

"I might just nip to the toilet…"

"Good plan. I'm just fetching some lemonade," Mike shouted to the man who was organising the cricket.

As I headed into the community centre, I pretended not to hear Ruth calling for me to come and join in. The game was in full swing when I went back outside. I sat on our picnic blanket to watch from a safe distance. Emily was sitting with a couple of girls from her class, diligently making daisy chains. Hailey was perched on the wall by the road with Zac and Imogen.

A friend of Ruth's strode towards me and I fought to remember her name. Then it came to me: Mary. I stood and smiled politely when she got near. She drew me in for a hug and asked how I was.

"I saw you visiting Tom a while back," she said quietly. I'd wondered what her agenda was when she'd marched over to me so purposefully. Thank goodness Adam wasn't around. I'd never told him about my visits to Tom. It was difficult for me to bring up. Sadly, no one seemed to want to mention Tom, and I worried it would just cause upset if they knew I'd been talking to him.

Mary tilted her head, waiting for me to respond.

I smiled benignly, staying quiet. I didn't owe her any explanation.

"Life can be so cruel, can't it?" she said after a moment. "How's Ruth doing?"

"Up and down," I said vaguely. "It's hard for her. But she puts on a brave face."

"Whenever I try to talk to her, she clams up and says she's fine." She tutted. "Of course she's not fine. How could she be? I can't even begin to imagine how she feels. I couldn't cope if I were her."

"She focuses on the kids," I said, uncomfortable with the conversation. Thankfully Mike sauntered over, and Mary excused herself to re-join her husband.

"You saved me!" I told Mike, settling myself on the blanket again.

"You're welcome! I brought you another drink," he said, sitting beside me and handing me my second alcoholic beverage of the day. "But in return I need your advice on something."

"Okay. What?"

"Well, don't laugh … but what do you think of this?" He tapped on his smartphone and then passed it to me. "Remember, you're not allowed to laugh."

"Oh," I said, scanning the page. "Internet dating?"

"Yes. I know it's ridiculous, but apparently that's what people do these days. What do you think of my profile?"

"It looks fine."

"Fine?"

"Good. I meant good. Did you match with anyone yet? Or whatever you do?"

"I found a few possibilities," he told me, tapping the phone to bring up a woman's profile. "But I've not actually messaged them yet. Do you think she's got funny hair?"

"You can't judge her on her hair!"

"So you do think she has funny hair!" he said, grinning.

"How would you like it if she judged you on your looks?" I clicked back to Mike's profile to scrutinise it properly.

"What's wrong with my looks?"

"You've picked a good photo, actually," I said. "Do you think that's a good idea? They might be disappointed when they see you in the flesh…"

"Okay, give me the phone." He went to take it from me and I held it out of his reach. "I thought you were older than that," I said, reading through his personal details.

"What?" He snatched the phone back. "Are you serious? How old did you think I was?"

"I don't know. Older than thirty-eight!"

He stuck his bottom lip out.

"Sorry! Don't look at me like that. I thought you were … er, thirty-nine, that's all."

"Liar!" He smiled. "Remind me not to ask you for advice again."

"I'm sorry. I was only joking around. I think it's a good profile."

"You've made me self-conscious about it now!"

"Don't say that." I looked at him, feeling bad for not taking it seriously. "I honestly think it's good. I'd date you." An awkward silence fell as soon as the words had left my mouth. Mike shifted his gaze to the cricket game.

"I told you they get competitive," he said after someone yelled at the batsman when he missed the ball.

Then a shadow fell on me, and I looked up – at Adam. "How did you two manage to get out of the big match?" he asked.

"Hi!" I grinned at him and he kissed me before shaking Mike's hand.

"I meant to warn you not to get involved in the cricket," Adam said, draping an arm around my shoulder and pulling me to him. "Any idea who's winning?"

"I've not got a clue," Mike said. "No broken noses yet, though, so it's going well."

Adam smiled and I threw him a questioning look.

"Jim took a ball to the nose one year," he told me. "It was a blood bath." I looked around, trying to remember which one Jim was.

"It livened things up," Mike said, standing. "I'd

better go and check on the drink situation. I'll catch you later."

"I'm hoping we can sneak off soon," Adam said.

"It's all right for some," Mike replied. "Arrive late and leave early. You've got the right idea!"

I moved closer to Adam when Mike had left us, happy he was there.

"Sorry I had to work," he whispered.

"It's fine. Angela and Ben looked after me. And Mike."

"That's good. I thought you'd be going crazy by now."

"I'm glad you made it," I told him.

"Me too."

Then Emily spotted him and ran straight at him. "Uncle Adam!" she called, flinging herself at him. He did a fake fall onto his back and threw her up in the air, zooming her around above him until she squealed for him to put her down.

"Can we get Hailey and go home?" Adam looked at me. "I just want to be with my girls."

"Yes! Just say hello to your mum first so we don't get into trouble."

"Okay. You get Hailey."

I said a few quick goodbyes and negotiated with Hailey that she could stay a little longer. Adam had Emily on his shoulders as we walked home. I turned and caught Mike's eye across the field, giving him a quick wave before we set off up the hill.

Hannah Ellis

Chapter 13

I was usually up early – dragged out of sleep by an alarm or a five-year-old – and it felt strange to wake up of my own accord. The smell of bacon lured me downstairs, yawning. Adam kissed me and handed me a bacon sandwich.

"This is nice," I said, joining Hailey and Emily at the table. "I thought you'd be at work by now."

"I rang in sick," he confessed, taking a seat opposite me.

"That's naughty," I said, smiling at him.

"Are you sick?" Emily asked.

"No, he's faking it," Hailey told her.

"I'd just rather stay home with you today," Adam explained to Emily.

"Did you tell a lie?" Emily asked, her eyes wide.

Adam looked at me and I took a bite of my sandwich, unable to hide my amusement.

"Sometimes it's okay to lie," Hailey said.

"Well, not really," Adam said, looking lost. "Er … what shall we do today?"

"Gran's coming over to teach me how to knit," Emily announced.

I gave Adam a look and caught Hailey rolling her eyes.

"Oh." Adam stared at me. "But weren't we going to

go out? I thought we were going to go for a little day trip."

"Where to?" Emily asked.

"The beach!" Adam told her.

She eyed him suspiciously. "What about Gran?"

"I'll ring her and tell her we're going out. Maybe she can knit with you tomorrow?"

"Okay," Emily agreed.

"Run upstairs and get dressed then if you've finished your breakfast," Adam said to her.

We watched her skip out of the kitchen.

"So how long have *we* been planning to go to the beach for?" I asked.

Adam raised an eyebrow. "I've been thinking about it."

"You're such a liar!" Hailey grinned at him.

"Do you want to spend the day knitting and getting into trouble about the state of the house?" he shot back at her.

"I'll go and get dressed," she said, smiling. "And find my raincoat!"

"So, we're going to the beach?" I glanced outside and saw the fine mist of drizzly rain.

"In the rain, apparently," Adam said. "And quick, before Mum arrives!"

"Poor Ruth." I sighed, but couldn't hide my smile as I picked up the plates and took them to the sink.

"Poor Ruth?" Adam laughed. "You've changed your tune. You're always complaining about how much she's here!"

"I guess we did see her yesterday," I said. "And we'll see her tomorrow!"

"Exactly. I don't feel like listening to her nagging

all day."

"Welcome to my world!" I said. "And *you* can't complain; you can do no wrong in her eyes. It must be nice to be so wonderful!"

He grinned at me. "Just shut up and get ready, will you?"

I think we packed as much for a day trip as I'd normally pack for a week away. It was a little under an hour's drive to the coast – and, surprisingly, the only bickering was between Adam and me while we debated whether or not to believe the sat-nav. I was convinced it was taking us on its own little mystery tour. Finally we crossed into Wales and hit the coastline.

"We used to go to the beach in France," Hailey said when we pulled into a deserted car park in Rhyl. "But it was always hot and sunny."

"I like a blustery day at the beach," Adam said.

"There's no one else here," Emily commented when we exited the car and looked up and down the long stretch of sandy beach.

"No one else is as crazy as we are!" Hailey said, shivering as the wind whipped around us. At least the rain had stopped.

"It's a perfect kite day," Adam said cheerfully. I made sure the girls were wrapped up warmly, and then put on everything I'd brought, which had looked a lot when I was getting in the car but seemed distinctly insufficient now. The gusts coming off the sea brought the temperature right down, and it was hard to believe that yesterday we'd managed to spend the entire afternoon outside in comfortably mild weather.

I spread out a blanket on the sand and watched Adam help the girls to get their kites airborne. The sound of seagulls squawking hit me intermittently, caught on the breeze as the birds flew low over the water. It was bleak, but there was something exhilarating about the deserted beach and the brisk sea air.

"I'll give it about half an hour before they're complaining they're freezing and want to go home," I told Adam when he sat down beside me.

"They're loving it," he said. "It's you who's got no sense of adventure!"

"Maybe just bad circulation," I told him, rubbing my hands together. He took my hands in his, blowing on them before rubbing them between his hands. I leaned into him and he put an arm around my shoulder.

We watched the kites soar overhead until Emily's dive-bombed and she burst into tears. Adam jogged over to help her while Hailey shouted sisterly words of encouragement. Her voice was distorted by the wind, but I'm fairly sure she was saying something about Emily being a cry-baby.

Then two girls and a guy arrived in wetsuits and nodded at me as they passed me, heading for the water, surfboards under their arms. It was hypnotic watching them ride the waves so expertly. Emily soon came and cuddled up to me, equally enthralled by them.

After a while, I shuffled Emily off my lap and took her for a walk along the beach, looking for shells and shards of sea glass to fill her bucket with. The temperature was more bearable if I kept moving.

When we returned, Adam had retrieved the picnic from the boot of the car. We wolfed down sandwiches and crisps before giving in to the cold and piling back in to the car, turning up the heating.

After ten minutes, I glanced into the back seat: Emily was fast asleep and Hailey looked content as she gazed out of the window. My lips twitched into a smile and I felt myself relax. It hit me: we'd turned the corner I'd been waiting for. It felt like I'd been telling myself for an eternity that things would get better, and for the first time I felt we were doing okay. Better than that, we were happy. Things really would be okay.

How little I knew.

Hannah Ellis

Chapter 14

"They're still glued to the TV," Angela told me when I arrived to pick Hailey up late on Friday afternoon. The older kids had loved the sports club and Angela, Karen and I had shared the driving. After the club, the kids had lunch together and played at one of our houses in the afternoon.

That day they'd all gone back to Angela's place and I'd had a phone call from Angela after lunch to ask if it was okay for Hailey to watch *Star Wars*. The question had caught me off guard and made me feel, once again, that I had no idea what I was doing. I wouldn't even have questioned it had Angela not asked, and then I was left wondering why it wouldn't be okay. I told Angela if it was okay for the other kids then it was okay for Hailey.

"Tea or coffee?" Angela asked when I followed her into the kitchen.

"Tea, please."

"Is Emily with Ruth?"

"Yeah, they were busy baking. I can't believe the holidays are over already." I took a seat at the table and looked out over the fields. "And I can't believe how painless it's been. I was dreading two weeks at home with the kids."

"I'm the same," she said. "It's usually nice to get

back to work for a break. The nice weather has helped, though. It's always easier when I can throw them outside to play."

"I spoke to Adam about Hailey changing schools," I told her.

"And?"

"He thinks it's a good idea. He's going to talk to Ruth, but I think we'll try and get her into the local school in September."

We'd had a good chat the evening after we'd been to the beach, and Adam had agreed it might be good for Hailey to go to school in Havendon and meet more of the local children.

"You won't have a problem getting a place for her. It's Ruth who'll be your obstacle."

"It's not her decision. At the end of the day, it's up to Adam."

"Yeah, but you know Ruth. She likes to have her say." Angela put a cup of tea in front of me and took a seat opposite me.

"I think she'll be okay with it. Especially seeing how much better Hailey's doing now."

"Fingers crossed. I was thinking the other day I'd like to get more family photos taken. Do you think Adam would take some more of us?"

"I doubt it. Unfortunately."

She searched my face, obviously wondering if I was joking. "He won't make time for an old friend?"

"It's not time that's the issue, really – though he doesn't have much of that. He's just stopped taking photos. His camera hasn't seen the light of day for a long time."

"That's a shame. Could you ask him for me?"

"I can try."

Hailey walked in and dropped into the chair next to me. "We watched *Star Wars*!" she told me. "It's so cool! Can we stay a bit longer?"

"No. We need to get home," I said. "Your gran was cooking, and Adam should be home soon. Go and say bye to Zac and Imogen."

She ambled back out of the kitchen and I thanked Angela for having her over.

Hailey talked non-stop on the way home – and all through dinner. I decided I didn't need to watch *Star Wars,* since she'd given me a full, detailed rundown of the plot. We ate with Ruth; Adam ended up coming home late as usual. Ruth had already left when he got home, and Hailey immediately filled him in on her afternoon.

"You watched *Star Wars*?" He looked at me and then back at Hailey, who nodded enthusiastically.

"It's so cool," she told him.

"Who said she could watch *Star Wars*?"

"I thought it would be okay," I said. "The other kids were watching it."

"I can't believe it." He looked sternly at Hailey. "You make me watch bloody mermaids, and then you watch *Star Wars* without me?"

Hailey laughed and leaned into him, her arms around his waist. "You could download it. I'll watch it again."

"Good idea," he said and then looked at me with a cheeky grin. "Are we allowed to stay up late?"

"I was just about to send them up to bed."

"Please," Hailey and Adam said in unison.

"Fine, but wait until I've got Emily upstairs and out

of the way."

They high-fived, then Adam went to heat up his dinner while I went to persuade Emily up to bed.

*****

It was Sunday night before I knew it. I had a sinking feeling about work the next day, which was unusual. I thought I'd be raring to get back. "I like the school holidays," I told Adam, sitting beside him on the couch when the girls were tucked up in bed.

"I thought the girls would have driven you mad. Or my mum."

"It's been surprisingly easy," I said. "Though there've been a few moments when I've wanted to throttle Ruth. But Hailey's been so much better. I think it's been good for her, making friends with Zac and Imogen."

"Really? I thought she was pretty miserable all weekend."

"Probably because you let her stay up so late on Friday. She always gets grumpy when she has a late night. And I think she's upset that the school holidays are over too. She got very annoyed when Ruth asked if her school uniform was washed and ironed."

"She wasn't the only one!"

"Well, she could at least try to be tactful about it! Maybe she could pretend she's come to see how we are, and discreetly ask if we need any help getting things ready for school. Of course I get frustrated when she comes over just to ask if we've remembered to iron their uniforms and buy food for their lunches. How incompetent does she think we are?"

"Very, I guess."

I slapped him lightly on the arm and then snuggled into him. "Did you talk to her about Hailey moving schools yet?"

"No, I haven't found the right time."

"Adam!"

He laughed. "It's going to end in an argument, isn't it?"

"Yes, probably," I agreed. "But I really think it's for the best. Don't you think it's strange that Hailey hasn't made any friends at school?"

"Maybe. I don't know. She's been through a lot. And the teachers aren't concerned."

"Well, maybe they should be," I argued.

"I'll talk to Mum," he told me seriously. "There's no rush, though, is there?"

"I guess not." I hesitated before casually changing the subject. "Angela asked me today if you'd take some more family photos for them…"

"I could do," he said after a pause. "But I don't know when I'll have time." He moved his arm from around me and stood up. "Do you want a drink?"

I declined. When he came back from the kitchen a few moments later he was holding a beer bottle.

"I just thought it would be nice. Angela's been so great with Hailey over the holidays – it'd be a nice thank-you. Plus she still raves about how well the last photos came out. I think she's scared to get someone else to do it in case they're not as good."

"I really don't know when you think I'm going to have time."

"You could do it at the weekend."

"I'd rather not, to be honest. The weekends are

busy enough as it is."

"It'd be fun. Remember when you did the last ones?" That had been when we first met. He'd brought me along for the photo session, when I'd been trying to hide from a lot of unwanted media attention. It was the first time I'd met Angela, and of course I'd had no idea then that we'd end up being friends. It seemed like a million years ago. A different lifetime, almost.

I looked at Adam. He frowned as he remembered too. Maybe that was the problem; he didn't like to remember.

"It's a lot of work," he said. "Just tell her I don't have time."

"Okay," I said, sighing irritably. "Sorry I asked."

"I don't have a problem with you asking, I have a problem with you trying to guilt-trip me into it when I don't want to."

"I wasn't trying to guilt-trip you. To be honest, I'd just like to see you taking photos again. The only recent photos I have of the girls are ones I've taken with my phone."

He groaned and pushed his head back into the couch. "Fine, I'll take some photos of the girls if it will make you happy, but can you please shut up about it?"

I suddenly felt close to tears. "Don't put yourself out," I said angrily. "I'll just shut up." I stood and walked out of the room.

"Lucy!" He followed me into the kitchen. "Lucy! I'm sorry. Why is this such a big issue?"

I sat at the kitchen table and couldn't stop the tears. "Because photography used to be such a big part of who you were. I miss that. You were always so happy when you were taking photos."

"I'm happy now," he said gently, crouching in front of me.

"Are you?" Tears blurred my eyes and I had to blink to focus.

"Of course I am. I've got you and the girls…"

"But why did you give up on the photography?"

"I just put it aside for a while, that's all." He looked away. "We need a guaranteed income."

"But you could set up your photography business like you planned. Sell your photos, make your own schedule, do private photo shoots. You'd be home more. It'd be great."

"I can't," he said impatiently, moving away from me. "I have to think about the girls. I can't afford to take risks any more."

"You could give it a try. If it doesn't work, you could go back to your old job. It would work, though – I know it."

"I don't want to," he snapped, his tone taking me by surprise. "Why do you have to keep going on about it?"

"Because I don't understand. You loved photography and you had plans. How can you just walk away from it?"

"Because it's not fun any more. And you constantly picking fights isn't much fun either."

"I'm not picking a fight!" I yelled, my voice getting louder as Adam stormed out of the kitchen. "I just wanted to talk about it. Like we used to talk about things. I want to understand what's going on in your head."

My heart pounded as silence fell around me. A few minutes later the hum of the TV drifted through to me. It annoyed me that he could just go back to watching mindless programmes while my mind raced. *How could he just give up on his dreams? All that talent just going to waste. And why can't we talk any more? We used to talk about everything. We had all these grand plans for our life. Now we were just coasting.*

When I eventually dragged myself up to bed, I was adamant I wouldn't bring up Adam's photography again. Arguing took too much energy and it was all pointless if he wouldn't even discuss it with me. If he didn't want to try, that was up to him.

Chapter 15

The next day, fighting off sleep, I made sandwiches for Hailey and Emily's packed lunches. We were back into the morning school routine.

"Do you want ham or cheese?" I asked Hailey, when she drifted into the kitchen.

"I don't want to go to school."

"You have to go to school," I told her, making cheese sandwiches for Emily.

"I hate it. You said you'd talk to Adam about me changing schools."

"I did, but it takes a while. You can move in September if you want."

"I want to move now."

"It doesn't work like that," I told her. "What do you want in your sandwiches?"

She looked at me, her cold hard stare boring into me. "I don't need sandwiches. I'm not going to school."

"What's wrong?" Adam asked as he came into the kitchen, Emily by his side. We'd been waking later in the holidays, and being woken by the alarm again was a shock for us all.

"I'm ill," Hailey declared, reaching for the cereal. "I can't go to school."

"You look fine," he said.

"So did you, when we went to the beach, but you still rang in sick." She glared at him, determined that the morning wouldn't go smoothly.

"That was different," he said. "Just eat your breakfast and get dressed, please."

"Why do I have to go to that stupid school?"

"Because it's a good school," Adam replied. "Hurry up. I can't be late today."

"Fine," Hailey snapped, pushing her bowl away and stamping up the stairs.

"I like school," Emily told us cheerfully, tucking into her cereal.

Adam smiled at her. "Good girl."

"Do you want something to eat?" I asked Adam.

"I'll get something at work," he said without looking at me. "Can you drop Hailey this morning? I could do with getting to work early."

"Okay," I said.

"Good. I'll get going then."

"Everything okay?" I asked.

"Fine." He blew Emily a kiss and left.

Hailey didn't speak to me on the drive to school. She didn't even say goodbye when she slammed the car door.

I got the silent treatment on the way home as well. At least it wasn't just me; she stomped up the stairs as soon as we arrived home, ignoring Ruth and slamming her bedroom door, sending vibrations around the house.

"What's wrong with her?" Ruth asked when I walked into the kitchen.

"I don't think she likes being back at school."

"She'll settle back into it."

"Did Adam tell you she's been asking about moving to Havendon School?"

"I don't think that's a good idea. She needs to keep up with her French."

"Couldn't we find a tutor to teach her French?" I asked.

Ruth moved around the kitchen, tidying things up as she spoke. "I didn't just pick Cromwell School at random, you know. It's one of the best schools in the area and they promised to make sure Hailey kept up with her French. It's the best place for her."

"Except she doesn't seem to have made any friends at school," I argued gently. "She'd like to be with Zac and Imogen. It was nice that she got to know them better over the holidays."

"She can still see Zac and Imogen after school and at the weekends," Ruth said, sounding tired of the conversation.

"I suppose so." Pausing, I searched for a way to fight Hailey's corner but Ruth had headed for the door before I'd found any words.

"I made soup," she told me over her shoulder. "And there's some nice bread. I've got to dash – I've got a meeting up at the church."

"See you tomorrow," I muttered.

Later, after Hailey had ignored my calls to come downstairs, I ventured up with a bowl of soup for her.

She was lying on her bed when I went into her room. She didn't look at me. I placed the soup on her desk.

"It will get better, you know. Give it a week or two and you'll settle back into school. It's just hard when you've had time off."

She rolled over to face the wall.

"You can still see Zac and Imogen," I said.

"You don't even care," she whispered.

"Of course I do," I said, sitting on the bed.

"The girls are so mean to me." She sniffed. "And I hate the teachers. I hate everything about the school." She turned onto her back, tears filling her eyes. "And you won't help me."

"I'm trying." I reached for her hand but she snatched it away.

"Just go away!"

Shakily, I got up and left Hailey's room, then paused on the landing. I was doing the best I could, but it was never enough. Could I do more for Hailey? I felt utterly lost. How was I supposed to know what was best for the girls? And why was I the one who was always worrying? After all, they weren't my responsibility. Adam was their guardian, not me.

Hailey didn't come back downstairs, and Emily was already in her pyjamas when Adam came home.

"Traffic was a nightmare," he told me as he sank onto the couch. Emily climbed into his lap to show off her nails, which I'd just painted sparkly pink. He gave her a weak smile without really paying attention.

"How was work?" I asked.

"Fine. You?"

"Work was fine. Hailey's not been much fun."

"She still on about moving schools?"

"Yes. And you still haven't spoken to Ruth about it."

He looked at Emily. "Do you want me to read you a story before bed?"

She nodded and went to find a book. Adam looked

up at me as he followed her out of the living room. "I'll talk to Mum about it."

"Good. Hopefully you get a better response than I did. She doesn't like the idea."

"There's a surprise."

"Just tell her it's happening. Hailey will be better if she knows she can definitely move in September."

He looked at me impatiently as Emily tugged on his arm. "I said I'd talk to her."

Anxiously, I waited for Adam to come back down. I wanted to clear the air. I assumed his bad mood wasn't just about Hailey's school issues; I guessed it was more to do with our chat the previous evening about his photography. Part of me wished I'd never mentioned it.

Staring out of the window, I watched the sky slowly darken and the street lights at the end of the drive flicker on. I didn't realise I was sitting in the dark until I stood up. Where was Adam?

I went to investigate. Adam was asleep beside Emily. I nudged him awake, encouraging him into our bed, where he fell asleep again immediately. The gentle hum of his breathing filled the room as I waited for sleep to take me too.

Chapter 16

Sarah and I were eating lunch at her desk, as we often did. The bustle of the staffroom didn't appeal to me. Recently, I had little appetite, and today I'd only managed a few bites of my sandwich.

"I had another argument with Adam," I said miserably. "I don't know what's going on with him."

She swallowed a mouthful of sandwich. "I thought things were finally getting better?"

"I thought so too. The Easter holidays were great. It seemed like we were getting somewhere, but the last two weeks have been awful. Hailey is back to hating me and Adam's constantly in a bad mood."

"Sorry." She frowned and reached over to squeeze my forearm.

"It'll be okay." I sighed. I'd been trying to focus on work and not bother Sarah with all my problems, but I wasn't sure how much longer I could carry on with things the way they were at home.

"What were you arguing about?" she asked.

"He's decided we should move to Manchester," I told her, shaking my head at the absurdity of the idea.

"Wow. Was he serious?"

"Who knows! I have no idea what is going on in his head most of the time."

My mind wandered to the previous evening. We'd

been standing in the kitchen, I'd just put Emily to bed, and Adam was cleaning away the dinner things.

"I feel like I spend half my life sitting in the car," he said, stopping to lean against the sideboard. "The traffic just gets worse."

"I know." I took a seat at the table, wondering if I should suggest he set up his photography business again. I hadn't mentioned it since I'd asked him about taking the photos for Angela. It seemed like the perfect solution. For a moment I even wondered if he was going to suggest it himself.

"If we lived in Manchester, I'd be home so much more."

My eyes darted to him, searching his face. Was he serious? He looked back at me, chewing on his lip and waiting for a response.

"We couldn't actually move, though," I said, smiling gently, trying to keep things light.

"It might be worth thinking about. Maybe it would make things easier."

I tried unsuccessfully to read his expression. "Really?" I took a deep breath and tried to calm my nerves. Adam shrugged, as though it wasn't a big deal. "No way," I said, shaking my head. "That's not going to happen. I can't believe you'd consider it."

"It might just take some pressure off me, that's all."

"Well, it might take pressure off *you*," I growled. "But what about the girls? You're talking about moving them, unsettling them again."

"Hailey's not exactly settled now, is she? As you keep telling me."

"Moving is not the answer. What about your mum? We can't do that to her. I won't move, Adam. If you don't want to commute to work, then set up on your own."

His gaze had settled on the floor in front of him. I watched his chest rise and fall before he finally looked up. "Forget I said anything," he said and walked into the living room.

I followed.

"Okay, it's a stupid idea," he said, and reached for the TV remote. "I don't want to spend the evening arguing."

I kept quiet and pulled his arm around my shoulder, snuggling into his chest and hoping to feel more comfort than I did. We sat in front of the TV for an hour before Adam complained he was tired and went up to bed. I had the feeling he just wanted to get away from me. I told myself not to take it personally; he was just having a hard time, that was all.

Without much thought, I left the house, arriving at Tom's place without any recollection of walking there. Even though I knew I shouldn't, I told him everything, pouring out all my worries to him. It wasn't really fair, complaining to him about his son. I didn't have anyone else to tell, though, and I needed to get it off my chest.

Tom always understood, and I felt better for having talked everything through. I didn't feel quite so weighed down when I walked back to our quiet house.

The weight of Sarah's arms around me brought me back to the present and I realised I was crying.

I hugged her for a moment before straightening up and wiping my eyes. "I'm fine," I told her. "Just having a moment. I'm sorry. I'm a barrel of laughs, aren't I?"

"I'm sure Adam wasn't serious," Sarah said. "He probably just had a bad day."

She looked at me with such pity that it made me want to scream. How did I end up such a pathetic mess?

Somehow, I needed to figure out how to fix my life.

Chapter 17

On Saturday, I took Emily swimming. We were mooching around the shops afterwards when I saw a *Star Wars* puzzle and thought of Hailey. I remembered her saying once that she used to like puzzles. I bought it, optimistically thinking it would be something we could do together.

Adam was on the driveway, washing his car when I pulled up beside him. "Want to do mine too?" I asked.

"Sure. How was swimming?"

"Great!" Emily said. "I can swim on my back now too."

"Lying down? That sounds very lazy!"

"It's not," Emily told him seriously. "You have to kick your legs *and* do your arms. It's really hard."

He smiled and ran a hand over her hair. "You wanna help me?" He passed her a sponge and she got to work on my car. I went inside. Hailey was in the kitchen spreading butter on toast.

"Look what I got for you." I pulled the puzzle out of the bag to show her. She said nothing. "I thought we could do it together."

"Puzzles are for kids and old people." She sat at the table to eat her toast and I joined her, taking the lid off the puzzle to look inside.

"It's *Star Wars*, though. You could tell me

everyone's names, educate me a bit."

"Or you could just watch the film," she suggested irritably.

"Do you want to watch it with me?" I asked.

"Not really."

"Let's do the puzzle – it'll be fun."

"Why can't you leave me alone?" She glared at me. "I don't want to do a stupid puzzle with you." She stood up and stormed out of the kitchen, knocking the box as she went and scattering puzzle pieces all around the kitchen.

I bent to pick up the pieces, taking deep breaths and trying not to fall apart. When I'd gathered all the pieces, I opened the back door and shoved the box into the bin, pressing it down heavily and slamming the lid. All I wanted was to get in my car and drive away. Through the window I could see Emily and Adam playing around with the hose, and I couldn't bring myself to cause a scene. Instead I went upstairs and changed into my jogging clothes.

Adam looked vaguely surprised when I passed them outside. With false cheer, I said I needed some exercise. I waved at Emily and took off down the driveway. Jogging had never been so easy. My body may have been complaining but I couldn't hear it. I could only hear the voices in my head, which screamed and raged. In my head, I argued with Adam, shouting the words I never had a chance to say. I begged and pleaded and cried with Hailey. Then I talked everything through with Tom before my head finally started to clear. The anger and confusion disappeared, leaving me alone with my self-pity.

My legs started to burn then, and my poor lungs

wailed at me to stop. I found myself on the trail through the fields beyond the playground. I headed back towards the village and my feet automatically carried me to the pub.

"Hey!" Mike greeted me cheerfully. I perched on a bar stool, thankful the other patrons were occupying the tables in the window away from the bar. "Are you okay?" he asked, his eyes full of concern.

"I need water," I told him, trying to catch my breath.

He placed a glass in front of me. "You look ill."

I held up a hand as he drew nearer to me, then slid off the stool. Quickly I ran, on shaky legs, to the toilets, just making it in time. I lost the contents of my stomach and then crouched on the floor of the cubicle, hugging my knees and resting my head on them. Exercise and stress were clearly not a good combination. I felt weak and jittery.

"You okay?" Mike asked from the other side of the door. I gulped down air and tried to calm myself. "Open the door."

"Just give me a minute," I managed. Silence fell, then Mike's hand reached under the toilet door. I laid mine on top of it, and he gave me a quick squeeze.

"You're not going to pass out or anything, are you?" he asked.

"No, I'm okay now."

"I'll be at the bar."

The quiet creak of the door told me he'd gone and I banged my head gently on the thin wall behind me. After a few minutes, I splashed water on my face and went back to the bar. I sipped the water. Mike disappeared for a few minutes before returning and putting a sandwich in front of me.

"I don't think I can."

"Just eat it," he said. I managed a few bites and felt better.

"Sorry."

"What's going on?" he asked.

"I'm really unfit." I could hear the hysteria in my laugh, and felt like I was going crazy. Mike smiled at me sadly as he dried glasses and placed them on the shelf above him.

Chapter 18

It occurred to me that Hailey had just switched off. I noticed it because I did the same. Drearily, I fought the same battles day after day. It was as though I was sleepwalking through life, and everything around me was background noise. I stopped caring and just went through the motions, wishing my days away. In the evenings I found myself wandering the streets, sometimes sitting and chatting to Tom, or, more often, perched at the bar with Mike.

One Tuesday, I decided to cook scrambled eggs for breakfast, thinking it might make a nice change to toast and cereal.

"I don't like that," Emily told me when I put a plate in front of her.

"Just try it," I said. "You might like it if you try it. It'll make you big and strong."

"Like Uncle Adam?"

"No, like me!" She put a forkful in her mouth, chewed happily then loaded her fork up again.

"I made scrambled eggs," I told Hailey when she walked into the kitchen and headed for the cereal cupboard.

"I'll have coco pops." She pulled out a bowl and shook the chocolate cereal into it.

"We're having eggs this morning," I told her. She

stared at me, challenging me as she moved a spoonful of coco pops to her mouth.

"I want coco pops too," Emily complained, pushing her plate away.

"We're not having coco pops today," I growled, feeling myself losing control.

"*I* am!" Hailey said.

"Me too." Emily reached for the box and I shot forward, snatching it from her.

"I *said* we're not having them," I shouted.

"She can have them if she wants," Hailey said, grabbing the packet from me.

"No, she can't."

The defiance in Hailey's eyes made something inside me snap. I stormed over to the back door, flung it open and hurled the cereal box out onto the patio. "No one is having coco pops!"

Hailey looked amused when I turned back inside. "*I* am." Her slow, methodical crunching of the cereal grated on my every nerve.

"No, you're not!" I picked up the cereal bowl, leaving her holding the spoon in mid-air. Returning to the back door, I flung the bowl out. It smashed against the flagstones and I screamed, a low monstrous sound. I slammed the door, my hands shaking, and turned to see Adam staring at me with a look of anger and disgust.

"I made eggs," I said, as though that might explain everything. Emily's face crumpled. When I moved towards her she wailed, dodging past me to get to Adam. Hailey kept her gaze on the table in front of her. I watched Emily cling to Adam and hated myself. "I made eggs," I said again, bringing a hand to my face as I felt myself falling apart. My legs felt weak and my eyes blurred with tears. "Sorry, baby, I'm sorry." I put a hand on Emily's back. She flinched. Protectively, Adam turned her away from me.

I fled upstairs and heard Ruth's sing-song voice ring around the house just as I made it to the bathroom. Running water into the sink, I splashed my face furiously. Adam's heavy footsteps followed me upstairs.

I'd hoped for some compassion or sympathy, maybe even some understanding, but there was only anger in his eyes.

"What the hell was that?"

"I'm sorry," I whispered, fighting to breathe.

"You're sorry? You just terrified my nieces! What the hell is happening to you?"

"*Your* nieces?" I shouted, grabbing a towel to dry my face. "I thought we were a family. I'm killing myself here, and no one even notices me. I'm living in someone else's house, looking after someone else's kids, and getting everything wrong. I hate this. I hate it! I don't want to live like this!"

His jaw tightened. "What's happened?"

"I need to get ready for work," I told him, hearing Ruth shouting for Adam to hurry up. "You should go too. You'll be late."

He shook his head. "We can talk tonight." He seemed calmer but didn't kiss me goodbye before he left. I'm not sure when he'd stopped doing that.

I called work and told them I was ill and wouldn't be coming in, then waited until it was quiet downstairs before fetching a dustpan and brush to clean up the mess on the patio. Tears streamed down my face as I swept up the broken cereal bowl.

Then I took the car up to Tom's place. Where else would I go? The words tumbled out of my mouth as soon as I got there. I prattled like a crazy person, telling him how hard everything was and that I couldn't cope. That I didn't want to be there. I yelled at him that I wanted to leave.

"Tell me what to do," I begged. "If you tell me to stay, I'll stay." I needed to hear him get angry with me, to shout at me and tell me to pull myself together, to tell me I should stay no matter what. He didn't, though, and I left feeling even angrier. I was angry at Tom now as well as Adam and Hailey and Ruth. Becky and Will too – I was furious at them. How dare they die and ruin all our lives?

Aware that I was shaking and couldn't see for crying, I abandoned the car. Keeping my head down and walking quickly, I made it to the back door of the pub. I banged heavily on the door until it finally opened and I fell into Mike's arms.

"I didn't know where to go," I told him. I couldn't catch my breath. My legs went from under me as everything went blissfully dark.

"Do you ever eat?" Mike asked. I opened my eyes and found myself lying on his couch. He gave me a glass of water and I sat up to sip it.

"What's going on?" he asked.

"Sorry," I sniffed, wiping at the tears which wouldn't stop flowing. "I need to leave but I don't know how."

"Leave Adam?"

"Adam, the village, that house, the kids …

everything."

"Why now?"

"I thought things would get better, but they're just getting worse."

He nodded. "I don't want to encourage you to leave, but you need to do something. You've lost so much weight I'm worried you'll fade away, and you're miserable. You need to look after yourself for a while. What's with the fainting?"

"I just didn't eat today, and I'm so tired. I screamed at the girls, threw stuff…" I paused and fresh tears appeared. "Adam looked at me like he hates me. I went to talk to Tom…" I paused again but Mike barely reacted. He certainly didn't look surprised. "Don't tell Adam; he wouldn't like it."

"I'm going to make you a sandwich. Are you going to work today?" He nodded his approval when I told him I wasn't. "Good. Eat something and sleep for a while. Everything will be clearer then."

When I woke an hour later, Mike was gone, and I left the pub by the back door. I retrieved my car and sent Adam a quick message telling him he'd have to pick Hailey up from school. I'd be home late. Then I left the claustrophobic village of Havendon and drove to Manchester.

Hannah Ellis

Chapter 19

I parked in a multi-storey car park in the centre of Manchester, and went into the first hairdresser I found. After waiting twenty minutes on a leather couch, a stylist introduced herself as Marina. She sat me in front of a mirror and asked me what I wanted. I gave her vague instructions to cut a lot off and make it look nice.

She did as instructed, and I nodded my approval when she held up the mirror to show me the back. My dark hair bounced with volume and fell in layers to just above my shoulders. It was suddenly glossy and healthy again, framing my face. It felt good to admire my new look in the mirror. I couldn't remember the last time I'd done anything for me. I'd taken to scraping my hair back into a ponytail and not really caring about my appearance. As I studied my reflection, Mike's comment about my weight came to my mind. My clothes had been a little looser recently, but I didn't think it was noticeable to anyone else. My cheekbones looked suddenly pronounced. I told myself it was probably the haircut, and got up to follow Marina to the till.

After that, I found a place to get my nails done and then took my time wandering around the shops, trying on clothes at random. I found that I fit easily into a size 8, where I'd previously been a solid 10 to 12. After purchasing a pair of jeans and a couple of tops, I tried on a pretty summer dress, buying it even though it seemed extravagant. I lived in work clothes or jeans and T-shirts, my reduced hours meaning that I didn't have extra cash to splash on anything unnecessary. I hadn't gone shopping for anything other than essentials for a long time.

Finally, I found myself in the children's section of Debenhams, where I picked out outfits for Emily and Hailey. Ruth had always taken them shopping when they needed anything new, and it only occurred to me now that it might be a fun thing to do.

When I got bored of shopping, I took myself to the cinema and sat in a near-empty theatre watching a romantic comedy, a sad smile on my face. I'd checked my phone once, early in the day, needing to be sure Adam had seen my message and would be there for Hailey. His text messages had been angry enough that I chose not to listen to the voicemails he left. Instead, I left my phone on silent, buried deep in my handbag.

I arrived on the doorstep of my friends' beautiful old Victorian house early in the evening. I'd met Chrissie and Matt on *A Trip to Remember*; we were three strangers, thrown together along with four others to spend a week in the Spanish sunshine. I'd only taken part in the TV show on a whim, in a moment of madness after losing my job, and the bond I'd developed with the others on the show had been unexpected.

The friendships we'd formed would last a lifetime. I knew I would always be welcome in their homes and their lives, regardless of how much time had passed without us speaking. Nonetheless, as my hand hovered over the bell, I felt guilty that I'd not been in touch for so long. Worse, I'd forgotten to return calls and messages. Since Hailey and Emily had arrived in my life, I'd let my social life and friendships fall by the wayside.

"Hey, stranger!" Matt greeted me warmly with a huge smile and an even bigger hug. He was tall and well built, and his hugs always made me feel small.

"I've missed you," I said, feeling unexpectedly sad.

"Chrissie!" he shouted, drawing me in and closing the door behind me. "Come and see who's here."

"Oh my God!" Chrissie beamed as she walked out of the kitchen. Her ginger hair was pulled back into a ponytail, loose strands spiralling around her face. "I thought you'd fallen off the planet. You could return my calls once in a while." She looked at me seriously for a moment. I apologised. "Okay, you're forgiven! Are you staying for dinner?"

"I'd love to," I said, following her back to the kitchen.

"It's nothing exciting," she warned. "Just pasta. What are you doing in town?"

"I've been on a little shopping spree," I told her.

"Aw, you left poor Adam babysitting while you've been off having fun?" Matt said.

"Something like that." I ignored the look the two of them exchanged. "Do you think I could crash in your spare room tonight? I don't think I can face the drive back."

They exchanged another look and neither of them spoke.

"What?" I asked.

"Of course you can stay," Chrissie said.

"What's going on?" Matt asked, leaning against the sideboard while Chrissie busied herself filling a pan with water. He raised his eyebrows when I looked at him questioningly. "Adam called both of us today. I promised to let him know if you turned up here."

Chrissie eyed me sympathetically, and I felt guilty for getting them caught in the middle of things.

"I just needed a break."

"Call him and tell him where you are at least," Matt said.

"It's fine. I messaged him earlier. He's not expecting me home. I'll call him later," I promised.

"Fine!" Matt put an arm around me and squeezed me affectionately. "You should come round more often; it's nice to see you. I'm going to jump in the shower before dinner."

"Your hair looks nice," Chrissie said, pulling a bottle of wine out of the fridge.

"Thanks. I just got it cut. Do I look like I've lost weight?" I blurted. She laughed as she poured the wine, then handed me a glass.

"Oh – you were serious, weren't you?"

"Yeah." I clinked my glass against hers, taking a sip.

"You're tiny," she told me. "If you want me to be honest, I don't think you look healthy – but there's a chance I'm just jealous! Let's sit in the living room while the pasta cooks." I followed her through, noticing the bridal magazines balanced on the arm of the chair.

"Oh!" I glanced from the magazines to Chrissie. She held up her left hand to show me her delicate engagement ring. "Congratulations!" I hugged her. "That's amazing." I plastered a smile on my face and ignored the pangs of jealousy that stabbed at my chest.

"I would have told you if you'd returned my calls. You missed a good party."

"Sorry," I said, sheepishly. "I'm a terrible friend."

"Yeah," she agreed cheerfully. "But you're forgiven."

"Fill me in, then," I said. "Have you set a date? How did he propose?"

I listened intently, smiling in all the right places and hoping she didn't feel the envy that permeated my every fibre.

Matt interrupted us ten minutes later, his phone in his hand, and thrust it at me. "I didn't call him; he called me."

"Thanks," I said. Chrissie discreetly scuttled off to the kitchen.

"Why aren't you answering your phone?" Adam demanded. I resisted the urge to hang up, knowing he'd only call back. The problem was, that I knew I didn't have a reasonable answer to his questions.

"I just needed some time to myself."

"I have to work!" he said angrily. "I can't just drop everything to pick Hailey up without any warning."

"I messaged you this morning. That was a fair amount of warning."

"I had to leave in the middle of a job," he told me.

"She is *your* niece," I told him calmly.

"Is that what this is all about?" he asked, tiredness creeping into his voice.

"No, it's only a part of it."

"Just come home and we can talk."

I imagined him pacing as I told him I was going to stay the night with Chrissie and Matt.

"Can you just think about the girls for a minute?" He spat the words at me fiercely. "You scream at them this morning, and then you disappear and don't come home. They don't understand what's going on. Neither do I."

Telling me to think of the girls didn't sit well with me. After so long of only thinking of the girls, I refused to let him make me feel guilty for having a day to myself. "I'll see you tomorrow." I hung up and wondered if that would end up being a lie.

"Everything okay?" Matt asked, returning from the hall, where he'd been hovering.

"Fine, thanks," I said, passing him his phone.

We ate from trays on our knees and spent the evening chatting and reminiscing. They filled me in on their wedding plans, their jobs, their lives – which were hurtling forward while mine stood still. I drank half my wine before stopping, in case I turned into an emotional wreck and blubbed to Chrissie and Matt.

I managed to push thoughts of Adam and the girls from my mind until I went up to bed. It was strange not to look in on the girls before I turned in. Weirder still that I crawled under the covers knowing that my favourite five-year-old wouldn't intrude on my space during the night. I was suddenly free – but felt anything but.

Climbing back out of bed, I fumbled in my bag for my phone, and read the last message from Adam. It told me he loved me and asked me to come home. I left a note in the kitchen and crept out into the night to make the drive home in the darkness.

The house was still when I eased the door open. I'd expected Adam to be on the couch, but there was no sign of him. Our bed was empty, so I glanced into the girls' rooms, only to find more vacant beds. I wondered briefly if they'd gone to stay with Ruth. Hearing muffled voices, I followed the sound downstairs and through the kitchen to the back door.

Three faces turned to look at me when I opened the door. Emily's damp eyes glistened in the moonlight and she clung to Adam, in the exact same position she'd been in when I last saw her. Adam's eyes flashed with relief.

"We don't know which one's Mum," Hailey told me sadly. She was leaning against the house, peering up at the sky.

Emily reached for me and I took her from Adam, savouring the feel of her arms around my neck.

"The three stars are right there." I pointed them out to her. "See? The one in the middle."

"Where's Daddy?" Emily asked.

"Just to the left." I moved my arm accordingly, peering up at the clear sky with them.

"What about Grandpa Tom?" Hailey said.

"He's there." My voice caught in my throat. "Just to the right."

Adam moved behind me, his arms encircling Emily and me, and his head resting on my free shoulder. I took his hand and held it tightly over my heart as I pulled him closer to me.

Chapter 20

We never got around to talking things through. Adam made a brief effort to be more attentive and Hailey seemed to soften slightly. Swept away with the monotony of life, we slipped back into our routines.

It was a Tuesday afternoon and I was just leaving work when I got a phone call from Hailey's school saying there'd been an incident, and I had to go to the main office when I collected Hailey.

I walked against the flow of school kids and through the main doors of the old stone building. Ivy crept around the entrance and I pulled myself up to my full height, trying not to be intimidated by the place. I walked down the long corridor to the office and knocked on the door.

Charlotte Bainbridge, the tall, blonde, head teacher, greeted me and I reached to shake Mrs Chapman's hand. She was Hailey's form teacher. Hailey sat slumped in a chair and didn't look up. I took a seat beside her.

"Sorry to call you in like this," Mrs Chapman said. "But we thought it was better to deal with this immediately."

"Okay," I replied uncertainly. 'What's happened?'

"We had an incident in the last lesson today. Hailey got into an argument with three other girls."

I nodded and waited for her to go on.

"We were concerned by how aggressive and abusive Hailey became."

"Okay," I said, feeling apprehensive. "What were they arguing about?"

"The other girls said that Hailey started shouting at them for no reason," Mrs Chapman said. "I have to say I was shocked by her outburst."

"I don't think Hailey would shout at anyone for no reason." I looked from the teachers to Hailey, who kept her head down.

"Hailey told me the girls were annoying her," Mrs Chapman said, glancing at the head teacher with a look of impatience.

"Well, what were they doing to annoy her?" I asked.

Mrs Bainbridge sat up straighter. "The girls said they weren't doing anything and that Hailey simply – in their words – flipped out."

I shook my head, trying to make sense of what had happened. "So what did Hailey say to them?"

The teachers glanced at each other and Mrs Chapman shifted in her seat. "We're not sure, but it was clearly offensive."

"I'm sorry, I'm confused. You're not sure what she said? I thought you'd seen what happened?"

"Hailey was speaking French when she had her little outburst," the headmistress told me.

A laugh escaped me before I could stop it. "So you're telling me that you don't actually know what Hailey said to the girls? You have no idea if she was being offensive. And you don't seem to know what the girls did to upset Hailey in the first place."

"The three other girls involved all said this was an entirely unprovoked incident," Mrs Chapman said.

"I'm sure they did!" I looked at Hailey and squeezed her hand. "What happened, Hailey?"

She didn't say anything, so I asked again.

"They're always mean," she mumbled. "I told you before."

My chest tightened as a tear dropped from her cheek onto her skirt. "Tell me what happened today." I pulled her chin gently, forcing her to look at me and willed her to talk, to give me some ammunition.

She kept her eyes on me when she spoke, trying unsuccessfully to control her emotions. "They always call me a frog and tell me I should go back to France. They say mean things to me all the time. They try and trip me, and shove me when I walk past them." She swallowed hard and her chin wobbled. "Today they called me an orphan frog. An ugly orphan frog. I'd just had enough of them, so I shouted at them to stop." She looked down again. I swallowed the lump in my throat, clinging to her hand as I turned back to the teachers, who squirmed in their seats.

Mrs Chapman frowned uncomfortably. "I'm sure they wouldn't say something like that."

"So you're saying Hailey's lying?" I raised my voice slightly and felt my heart beat faster.

"The other girls all said—"

"They would all say the same thing, wouldn't they? They knew they'd be in trouble. They were bullying Hailey!" I shouted, struggling to keep my voice even.

"I think we should just calm down a bit," Mrs Bainbridge said, her voice condescending.

"I'm sorry, but I don't think that's going to be

possible," I told her. "Where are these other girls now?"

"We addressed the issue with the girls and they've gone home."

"Were their parents called in?"

"No," Mrs Chapman said. "But I'm sure if you'd witnessed Hailey's behavio—"

"Behaviour caused by bullying which you've failed to pick up on, and are now unwilling to acknowledge?" I took a deep breath. I was so angry: at the teachers for not seeing any of this and at myself for not listening to Hailey when she told me that the other kids were mean to her.

"I assure you we take bullying very seriously," Mrs Bainbridge said.

"The reason we're paying a fortune for Hailey to attend this school is because you convinced us you were best equipped to deal with her situation. As well as supporting her emotional needs, you also agreed to support her language abilities. I don't feel that you're supporting her at all, and today it seems as though she's been punished for speaking French…"

"That's not the case at all," Mrs Bainbridge told me. "We have a private tutor specifically to support Hailey with French."

"And when does this extra tutoring happen?"

The teachers glanced at each other, looking slightly confused. It was Mrs Chapman who spoke. "Hailey has three tutoring sessions a week."

"Yes, but when do they take place? What is she missing?"

"She does it during break-time," Mrs Bainbridge informed me.

"So she *is* penalised for her language abilities. She misses three breaks a week." I'd known about this, and had an issue with it for a long time, but had never had a chance to voice it, since Ruth didn't think it was a problem. "I've also spoken to the school before about Hailey's lack of friends, and you told me everything was fine and it may just take some time for her to settle. But that's clearly not the case." I stood up, needing to get out before I lost control and started shouting abuse at them. If only I could shout at them in French, like Hailey had!

"Mrs Lewis, if you could please sit down, we can get to the bottom of things."

"It's *Miss* Mitchell," I corrected her, "and I'm afraid I'm going to have to leave. I don't think we're going to get anywhere with this today."

"Miss Mitchell…"

"You've let a vulnerable child be bullied…" My voice was rising steadily. "And instead of investigating the matter properly, you've assumed she's in the wrong. It seems that it's not just the kids who are bullies around here. Come on, Hailey." I pulled her gently out of her chair and ushered her into the hallway, ignoring the teachers' protests. Hailey slipped her hand into mine and we walked quickly down the hall and out into the fresh air. We were halfway across the playground when she tugged on my arm to slow me down.

I turned to look at her tear-streaked face.

"Thank you for sticking up for me."

"Of course I would stick up for you," I snapped, my emotions taking over. "What did you think I would do? I will always stick up for you, and maybe if you could stop hating me for five minutes you might see that."

"I don't hate you." Her words were garbled by her sobs. "I asked you if I could change schools and you said no."

"I said you could move in September."

"I told you that was too long," she cried. She had – she'd told me exactly that and I'd ignored her concerns, hushed her protests. I should have listened to her and found out what was really going on.

"I'm sorry," I said. "I'm so sorry."

"I want my mum," she sobbed, wrapping her arms around my waist. "I just want my mum."

"I know," I said, holding her and stroking her hair. "I'm sorry. I didn't know what was going on. I didn't know it was that bad."

"Gran said I can't move schools. Even in September. I asked her and she said no."

"It's not your gran's decision," I told her. "I'll talk to Adam again. I'll sort everything out, I promise."

An arm around her shoulder, we walked to the car. I glanced at her in the rear-view mirror when I started the engine. "We'll get you into Havendon School," I told her. "You'll be with Imogen and Zac and you'll make loads of new friends too."

"I want my old friends," she said and I turned to see fresh tears overflow from her eyes.

I reached back and squeezed her hand. "I know. I'm sorry."

She'd kept in touch with a couple of girls at first. There'd been postcards and letters, but they grew less and less frequent until they had stopped altogether. "I'll fix things," I told her. "It'll be okay."

We drove in silence. When I looked back, Hailey was asleep, her head against the window. I pulled up in front of Angela's house and got out, leaving Hailey asleep in the car.

"I need your help," I told Angela when she opened the door, my voice quivering.

"Come in." She put a hand out to me, concern on her face.

"I can't; Hailey's in the car. How long would it take to get her in to the local school?"

She stepped outside and put a hand on my arm. "What's happened?"

"She hates the school. I think she might be being bullied. I can't send her back there."

"Okay." Angela looked me in the eyes and I took a deep breath, trying to calm myself. "All the local kids are entitled to a place in the local school. Everyone expected Hailey to go there. They'll gladly take her."

"She can't go back to her school," I said, crying. "I can't send her tomorrow."

"Take her to Dr Griffin," she said quickly. "Get her to agree she's unfit to be in school this week. Then call Mrs Godfrey at Havendon Juniors. You'll just need to transfer her records and she'll be able to start immediately, I'm sure."

"Okay," I sniffed. "Thank you."

"Does Ruth know?" she asked.

I wiped my eyes and shook my head.

"Adam?"

"No." I laughed bitterly. "I'm in for a fun evening!"

"You know where I am if you need me."

I thanked Angela again and hurried back to the car, feeling determined.

Hannah Ellis

Chapter 21

"You're late," Ruth called when we walked through the front door. She was in the kitchen. The house was filled with a strong fishy aroma. Ruth made fish pie about once a month and nobody liked it.

"Hi," I said, walking into the kitchen, ignoring her comment about us being late. "Hey, Emily." I ruffled her hair.

"I've made fish pie," Ruth said. "And I don't want any arguments, Hailey. We're all eating it."

"Hailey doesn't like fish pie," I said as Hailey hovered quietly in the doorway.

"It's good for her," Ruth said.

"I don't like it either," Emily complained.

"I'll just make some pasta for the kids." I managed to sound confident and pulled a pan out of the cupboard.

"I've already cooked." Ruth took the pan from me and put it away. "We'll all eat fish pie."

"I just won't eat," Hailey said calmly. "I'm going to my room."

"You have to eat," Ruth called after her. "Come back down here now."

"Leave her," I said, reaching for the pan again and filling it with water.

"They need fish in their diet," Ruth said, raising her

voice slightly.

"Not tonight they don't."

"So I spend the afternoon cooking and you just waltz in and say no one has to eat it?"

"Yes. I have waltzed into *my own home* and told the kids they don't have to eat something I know they don't like." I glanced at Emily, who had her head in a colouring book.

"You know, it would be nice if you could show a little bit of appreciation for all I do around here," Ruth said.

"Thank you for cooking," I said through gritted teeth. "But I think we just need a bit of space tonight."

"Excuse me?"

"We need some time to ourselves."

"You're kicking me out of my own home now?"

"No, I'm not." I wanted to tell her that it wasn't her home, but I wasn't feeling that brave. "I'm just asking for some space, that's all."

She glared at me as though she couldn't believe her ears. "Well, I won't stay where I'm not wanted." She kissed Emily on the top of the head before storming out of the house. I resisted the urge to chase after her and apologise.

"So we're not having fish pie?" Emily asked, looking at me with her big blue eyes.

"No, sweetheart. Not tonight."

Adam had arrived home by the time the pasta was ready. "I've had Hailey's head teacher on the phone," he said, kissing me on the cheek. "What happened?"

I glanced meaningfully at Emily. "I'll tell you later."

"Fish pie night?" he asked, turning his nose up.

"No, pasta."

He eyed the fish pie on the counter suspiciously. "Where's Mum?"

"I told the kids they didn't have to eat fish pie, and she left."

"You've not upset her, have you?"

"Probably," I said.

"She's only trying to help."

"I know, and I'm very patient with her – not that anyone notices – but I ran out of patience today." I turned to Emily. "Run up and tell Hailey dinner's ready, will you? Tell her it's pasta," I added as she walked out of the kitchen. I cleared Emily's colouring books away to set the table.

"Hailey says she's not hungry," Emily told me when she reappeared. I put three bowls of pasta on the table and took a fourth upstairs to Hailey.

"Tell her to come down and eat," Adam shouted after me.

I sat down next to Emily when I returned, and felt Adam's eyes on me. "You should've told her to come down."

"She had a bad day," I said.

I put my head in Hailey's room after I'd put Emily to bed. She was curled up on her bed, her eyes closed. I picked up the untouched pasta and went down to talk to Adam. He muted the TV when I walked in the living room.

"What happened?"

I sank onto the couch beside him. "Some girls were picking on her and she shouted at them in French. It was three against one, so the other girls got away scot-free while Hailey got into trouble."

Adam massaged his temples, looking as though he had the weight of the world bearing down on him.

"She needs to move schools," I told him.

"Mrs Bainbridge thinks you over-reacted. That you said Hailey was being bullied and they weren't doing anything about it. She says it was an isolated incident."

"Well, she would say that," I snapped. Adam eyed me wearily and I tried to keep my cool. "Maybe I did over-react. I'm not sure."

"Lucy, she can't change schools because a couple of kids were teasing her."

"She's miserable," I said, trying my hardest to stay calm. I needed us to talk about this without it turning into an argument. "And I think it's more than just harmless teasing – but even if it's not, I still think she should move schools. Something's not right."

"She can't just move schools with no notice. Besides, it's not long until the summer holidays. It doesn't make any sense to move her now. And Mum's not going to agree to her moving schools so close to the end of term. She's paying a fortune to send her to that place."

"It's not up to Ruth. You're her guardian. It's your decision."

"Then we'll go in and talk to the teachers. See what we can do to make things better." He picked up his beer. Anger boiled inside me. How could he be so flippant?

"That's not good enough," I told him firmly. "Those girls are horrible to Hailey. They call her ugly and an orphan. And it wasn't just today; it's every day. I don't know whether you want to classify it as teasing or bullying, but Hailey's had enough to deal with. Don't make her suffer any more."

"I'll go in with her tomorrow. I'll talk to the teachers and find out what's really going on." He reached for the remote again. "I'm not just taking her out of school."

Maybe I was over-reacting but I couldn't let it drop. Hailey needed me on her side and I was determined to fight for her. "I spoke to Angela and she says they'd accept her in the local school immediately. She said we could take her to Dr Griffin and get her a sick note for this week."

"You spoke to Angela before you spoke to me?" he asked, his voice tinged with anger.

"I just wanted her advice. I only asked if we'd be able to get her into the local school. She's the school nurse; she knows about this stuff."

"You're jumping way ahead of yourself." He rubbed his eyes wearily. "You can't just decide she needs to change schools. We need to get to the bottom of things properly."

"But I hate seeing her so miserable. She'll do better at the local school."

He leaned back into the couch. "What's really going on?"

"What do you mean?"

"I think Hailey's given you a sob story because she knows you'll do anything to get her to like you…"

"Are you serious?" I shot at him. He took my hand.

"I know she gives you a hard time, and I know it's difficult for you to deal with."

I pulled my hand from his. "It's not about me. I

can't believe you'd say that."

"I told you, I'll talk to Hailey tomorrow. It would be nice to come home and be able to relax."

I clenched my teeth. "I'm sorry," I said, my voice full of sarcasm. "I'll leave you to relax. How rude of me to bother you with concerns about the kids in the evening."

"Lucy," he called weakly as I walked out of the living room. He didn't bother to follow me, so I tidied up the kitchen, holding my breath when I put the pungent fish pie in the fridge. I'd deal with it with later. I made a cup of tea and sat at the kitchen table to drink it.

"I'm sorry," Adam said when he finally joined me. "I'll talk to Hailey. If she really wants to change schools, we'll make the arrangements for September. I'm going to go to bed."

I turned away when he tried to kiss me.

"Surely you didn't think I'd agree to let her change schools next week?" he said.

I got up and put my cup in the sink. "Goodnight," I said, forcing myself to kiss him. Anything to get him out of my sight.

"Are you coming to bed?"

"I'm going to watch TV for a bit," I told him. "I won't be long."

I waited twenty minutes – certain he'd be asleep by then – then opened the front door and went out into the brilliantly clear night. I felt better as soon as I'd left the house.

Not feeling like going to Tom's grave, I made for the pub.

"Are you still open?" I asked Mike. I'd peered in

the window and seen the place was empty. He was busy cleaning up.

"Not really, but come in anyway."

"Sorry, I thought I might be in time for a quick drink. I don't want to be in the way…"

"Help me clean up and I'll have a drink with you." He threw me a damp cloth and told me to wipe down the tables. I worked my way methodically around the room, wiping tables and straightening chairs like I'd seen Mike do. I was rewarded with a glass of wine, and sat at the bar to drink it.

"Everything okay?" Mike asked, sitting beside me with a pint.

"Yeah."

"It's okay to say no."

"No, then!" I said. "Everything isn't okay." I took a long sip of wine. "Life feels like a constant battle at the moment."

"That's understandable. It's a crap situation you found yourself in."

"I think Hailey should change schools, but Adam thinks she's fine where she is."

"I never understood why she didn't go to the local school in the first place," Mike said.

"Because Ruth thought she'd be better off in a private school."

Mike nodded and didn't comment further.

"Ruth will go mad when she hears I want her to change schools. She's always there, always around the house making comments and looking at me like I'm useless."

"I'm sure she doesn't mean it."

"I know she doesn't mean it," I said curtly. "And

she's been through so much. It's been so hard for her. I know all that, but she's still driving me crazy!"

"Hang in there – things will get better."

I wished he was right. When the girls came to live with us, I told myself it would take a year. We would have an awful year, that was inevitable, but then things would gradually settle down and get better. It had been eighteen months – and I was still waiting for things to get better.

"What's been happening round here?" I asked in a bid to change the subject.

"Are you asking me to break my bartenders' code of confidentiality?"

I laughed. "Is there such a thing?"

"No, not really," he said. "Let's see … I had to escort George home at the weekend after he came in for a quick birthday drink. I got an earful from Liz when I brought him home. Apparently it was my fault he drank too much." He raised his eyebrows and I laughed.

"What else?" I asked, taking another sip of wine. He launched into a rundown of the village gossip. It was nice to sit and laugh, and I actually felt myself relax, which was rare. I left feeling happier about the world, having momentarily forgotten my problems at home.

Chapter 22

That night, I didn't get nearly enough sleep and the sound of my alarm made me want to cry. Adam groaned beside me and I silenced the alarm, sitting up. It was the usual routine: I'd get showered while Adam snoozed on, then I'd go down and get started on breakfast and lunches.

Hailey was already sitting at the kitchen table in a pair of jeans and a T-shirt.

"Did you talk to Uncle Adam?" she asked, looking fragile. I wanted to settle her on the couch, tucked safely under a blanket with a cup of hot chocolate and her favourite TV shows.

"Yeah. We're going to see what we can do," I replied vaguely. She looked at me, her eyes huge, begging me to help her. I was going to let her down again and she would never forgive me.

"I don't have to go back there, do I?"

"You'll have to go this week and then we'll try and sort something out for next week." I hated myself. I was buying time and she knew it.

"Please don't make me go." A tear ran down her cheek and my heart broke for her. Then Emily wandered in, looking half asleep. Automatically, she sat at the table and I put a bowl of cereal in front of her. My mind raced, trying to figure out how to help

Hailey.

"Morning." Ruth came in, the tone of her voice telling me she was still angry with me. She looked at me for too long, no doubt expecting an apology. I was silent.

"Why haven't you got your uniform on, Hailey?" she asked finally.

"She wasn't feeling well," I answered. Ruth moved and put a hand across Hailey's forehead.

"You seem fine," she declared. "Go and put your uniform on. You don't want to be late."

Hailey looked at me and then moved dutifully out of the kitchen.

"She hates that school, you know?" I sat next to Emily and tried to act casually.

"Some kids just don't like school," Ruth replied. "She'll get over it."

"She's getting bullied."

"Don't be silly," Ruth said, a look of impatience flashing over her face. "It's a great school."

"She should be at the local school. Maybe then she'd have some friends and be happier."

"Will you just stop!" She turned and glared at me. "It seems that all you want to do at the moment is stir up trouble."

"I want Hailey to be happy," I told her firmly.

Adam came in. "I'll talk to Hailey about school."

"There's nothing to talk about," Ruth said. "She's in the best school in the area and she's staying where she is."

"Even if she's miserable and the kids are calling her an orphan and telling her to go back to France?"

"What's an orphan?" Emily asked. There was

silence.

Hailey appeared in the doorway, wearing her uniform, tears running down her cheeks. "I don't want to go to school."

"You can't just not go to school because you don't like it." Ruth's voice was condescending, and it grated on me.

"They're really mean to me," Hailey cried.

Adam moved over to her and wiped the tears from her cheeks. "I'll come in with you today and talk to your teachers."

"Lucy?" she said quietly, desperation in her voice.

"I don't think she should go today," I said.

Ruth clicked her tongue, huffing. "Of course she has to go to school."

"No, she doesn't. She can stay home today and we can decide what to do next."

"She's going to school," Ruth told me firmly. "And it's not really anything to do with you."

"Excuse me?"

"These aren't your decisions to make."

I took a deep breath, telling myself to focus on Hailey and not let Ruth get to me. I could rise above her. I moved to stand beside Hailey, putting a hand protectively on her arm.

"I could take her to the doctor and get her a note," I said to Adam. "Just let her stay at home until we sort things out."

Ruth jumped in, her tone suddenly fierce. "You're not taking her anywhere. Adam and I can deal with this. It's a family matter."

"Mum!" Adam snapped. I stood frozen to the spot, unable to believe what I'd heard. "Hailey, get in the car," Adam said. "Everyone else, calm down."

"Adam." I followed him out to the car and watched Hailey climb into the back. "Don't make her go today."

"Back off," he fired at me, his anger taking me by surprise.

"So *you* think this is none of my business too?"

"I didn't say that." His face softened and he leaned against the car. "Of course it's your business. Mum was out of line. I don't know what to do about Hailey, but everyone shouting at each other won't help."

"Please don't make her go back there," I said, taking his hand. "I feel like I never really know what I'm doing with the girls. But today I *know* what to do and you're not listening to me. She needs to change schools. Immediately."

"I told you I'd talk to her," he said gently. "I'll talk to her teachers."

"That's not enough," I snapped. "She's been through so much – don't make her go back there."

"I'm doing the best I can!" he said, his voice full of frustration.

"Fine!" I said, realising I was losing the battle. "Talk to the teachers. But I'm coming with you. I need to be involved. I want to be there for Hailey."

"Okay," he agreed. "But you need to stay calm."

"I will. I'll follow you," I told him. "I'll meet you there."

Hurriedly, I finished getting ready and kissed Emily goodbye, avoiding looking at Ruth. In the car I called work to say I'd be late.

When I arrived at the school, Adam was pacing the

pavement. He opened my passenger door when I pulled up behind his car. "Is Hailey okay?" I asked. He climbed in the car beside me and put his head in his hands. I rested my hand on his back.

"Can you take her home?" he asked.

"What happened?"

"I didn't realise how bad it was." He looked at me, his eyes sad. "She's hysterical. She won't get out of the car. You were right; she can't go back there. We'll get her into Havendon School."

I nodded through my tears. "I feel like we've let her down. We should have seen this earlier."

He drew me to him and I relaxed a little in his arms.

"We can still fix it," he told me. "She'll be okay. Take my car home. I don't think she'll get out. I'll go in and talk to the staff."

I nodded and we got out of the car, exchanging keys. He kissed my cheek and walked towards the school.

"Are you okay?" I asked Hailey when I got into the driver's seat. She was deathly pale and her eyes were red and puffy. "I'll take you home," I told her when she didn't reply. We drove in silence. She moved slowly from the car to the house without a word. I sat her on the couch and put the TV on before I went into the kitchen to make her a chocolate milkshake – her favourite.

"Thanks," she said when I put it on the table in front of her.

"Everything will be okay, you know." I sat down beside her and she leaned against me. I pulled her to me and held her tightly while she cried.

When Adam arrived home, we slipped outside to

chat to avoid being overheard. I'd forgotten all about work until Adam asked if they were okay about me not coming in.

"Oh!" My hand shot to my mouth. "I completely forgot to call them again. I rang them to say I'd be late."

Adam glanced at his watch. "Why don't you head in now? I'll be okay with Hailey. I spoke to Dr Griffin. She'll see her this afternoon. I'll have to ring Havendon Juniors and see when we can get her in."

"I feel like I should be here," I told him. "But I'm not sure how understanding Mrs Stoke will be if I miss work again."

"We don't both need to be here."

"What about the rest of the week?" I asked.

"I guess we can't leave her with my mum," he said, running a hand through his sandy hair. "I'll have to go down and talk to her later."

"I think one of us should be here with Hailey this week."

"The studio wasn't impressed about me not making it in today," he said. "I can probably wrangle tomorrow, but I'm not sure I can push it beyond that. I don't want to risk losing contracts with the studio. They've been good about everything with the kids but I daren't take too much time off."

"I wish you'd give up the studio work," I said without thinking. "It would be so much easier if you worked locally."

His eyebrows shot up. "You really want to discuss that now?"

"No." I sighed. "I'll shut up."

"We need the money," he reminded me.

"I know," I said, taking a seat on a weathered-looking patio chair. "You take tomorrow off and I'll see what I can do about the end of the week."

"Thank you."

"We really messed up," I said, dropping my head into my hands. "We should have listened to her before."

"She'll be okay," he said, squeezing my hand.

I pulled away from him and looked up, surprised he could be so blasé. "We messed up. And I'd like her to be more than okay. I want her to be happy. I want us all to be happy – but we're going wrong somewhere."

He frowned at me. "It's a difficult time. But we're doing the best we can, aren't we? There's no point torturing yourself."

"I'm not torturing myself, but I don't think this is a happy home for anyone and we need to do something about that." Tears stung my eyes but I could still see the confusion on Adam's face. He genuinely thought everything was all right. Was it me who was just expecting too much? "Sometimes I hate being in the house," I told him honestly. "It feels like the walls are going to close in on me."

He smiled then and I wanted to hit him. "I think most parents feel like that a lot of the time."

"It's more than that," I said, tears falling down my face. "I'm exhausted. I feel like whatever I do is wrong. I'm trying really hard and then your mum goes and says things like she did today to make me feel like I'm not even a proper part of the family."

"She didn't mean it," he said dismissively. "She was just upset."

"Fine," I said, realising he was never going to see it

from my point of view. I was too tired to argue. "It doesn't matter."

"You're as much a part of this family as anyone," he said. "And you definitely have a say in the kids' lives." He looked serious. "You know I'd be lost without you, don't you? I love you."

"I know," I said, feeling defeated. "I'd better check on Hailey and go to work."

Chapter 23

Adam said Serena Griffin was brilliant with Hailey. I'd met her a few times before and she was always a calming presence. She agreed that Hailey should have the week off school and advised Adam to inform Hailey's counsellor about the bullying. When he expressed concerns about Hailey's counselling, Dr Griffin suggested finding someone new. Perhaps Hailey just didn't click with Mrs Miller, she said, and she would make more progress with a different counsellor.

Adam met the head teacher at Havendon Junior School, who was both accommodating and supportive, agreeing that Hailey could start the following week.

It was a week of paperwork and phone calls, but we got through it. Hailey was quiet and withdrawn, but seemed to relax when she realised she was finally going to change school.

When I'd walked into work late on Tuesday morning, I'd made my way straight to Jean Stoke's office. I apologised for being late and had intended to ask for the rest of the week off. However, her manner was unfriendly: she gave me a lecture about my commitment to the job, hinting that unless things changed I wouldn't have a job there the following school year.

She made it impossible for me to request more time off, and after apologising profusely, I scurried out of her office with my tail between my legs.

Adam ended up taking the week off work, and I was glad. He needed a break and Hailey needed the time with him. They spent most of the week lazing in front of the TV, which was good for both of them.

Guilt niggled me constantly. If only I'd spent more time with Hailey and found out sooner what was going on, I could have saved her so much stress.

When there was no sign of her on Saturday morning, I ventured up to her room, knocking lightly before pushing the door open. She was sitting at her desk, her back to me. She pulled out her earphones and turned to me.

"Are you okay?" I asked.

"Yeah," she said, swivelling in her chair. "Can you help me with this?"

I nodded as I walked over and smiled when I saw the *Star Wars* puzzle pieces spread over her desk. "I thought I'd put that in the bin."

"I found it and took it out," she told me, looking me in the eyes. "I'm sorry."

She moved over and I perched on the chair beside her, poring over the puzzle. "It doesn't matter."

*****

Adam took Hailey to school on Monday morning and rang me at work afterwards to tell me it had all gone well. She'd gone in happily with Imogen and Zac. His phone call did little to put my mind at ease, however, and I spent the whole day worrying about how her day was going. I needed things to go well for her. It seemed like we were fighting one battle after another, and I just needed something to go right for once. When I arrived at Havendon Juniors that afternoon I had time to spare. I sat in the car and pulled out my phone, needing to kill time before the bell went.

"This is a surprise," Chrissie said when she answered. "What did I do to deserve a phone call from you?"

"Thanks. Make me feel like an awful friend, why don't you?"

"So you're calling to find out how I am and see what's happening with me?"

"Yes," I said confidently. "How are you?"

"Fine, thanks, but I'm too busy for small talk. What do you want?" She laughed when I hesitated. "Oh come on, we both know you need something. Spit it out."

"Sorry! I'm actually looking for a new grief counsellor for Hailey, and wondered if you can recommend someone. I've searched the internet and I've got a list of names but I don't know how to choose one." Chrissie was a social worker. I was hoping she'd have some connections – or at least be able to point me in the right direction. My search had left me feeling confused. I wanted to pick the best counsellor for Hailey.

"Is Amelie Bright on your list?"

I glanced at the piece of paper in my hand. "Yes, but I already tried her and the receptionist said she's not taking new patients at the moment."

"That sounds about right. But she's the best. I can give her a call. Our paths cross frequently. I'd say she's a friend, but she's a psychotherapist and that's not really the kind of friend I want, if you know what I mean…"

"Not really."

"Never mind. She's amazing. I'll fill her in on Hailey and see if she'll take her on."

"That would be brilliant."

"No problem. I'm fine, by the way! Life is good. Nice of you to check in with me!" I heard her laughter down the line before she hung up, leaving me sitting in the car, smiling. I got out and moved to the school gates, mingling with the other parents.

"Imogen was so excited about Hailey starting," Karen said when I found her and Angela in the crowd.

"I hope the first day went well," I said nervously.

"She'll love it." Angela smiled at me. "Was Ruth okay about it?"

"She seems to be warming to the idea. Once Adam had made the decision and she realised it wasn't up for discussion any more, she was surprisingly all right about it."

Ruth hadn't apologised for what she'd said to me, but she seemed to be making some effort to be nice to me and I took that as an apology, certain it was as close as I would ever get to one. I moved my gaze from the school to Angela and Karen, who were smiling at me supportively. "I'm still kicking myself that I didn't insist she moved schools earlier," I told them.

"Don't be too hard on yourself," Karen said. "Hindsight is a wonderful thing."

There was a sudden buzz as the school doors opened and groups of kids came bustling out. My chest tightened at the sight of Hailey with Zac and Imogen, smiling and laughing as they walked towards us. I swallowed the lump in my throat and blinked back tears. Hailey wouldn't thank me for blubbing at the school gates.

"Hi!" She greeted me with a smile and I thought of all the miserable times I'd picked her up from her old school.

"How was it?" I asked as she walked beside me to the car.

"Awesome!"

I managed a nod. I made it into the car before I let out a sob and pushed my palms into my eyes in an attempt to hold back the deluge.

"Oh God, what's wrong?" Hailey asked indifferently.

"I'm just sorry you didn't move schools sooner." I sniffed.

"It's not really your fault, is it?"

"I could've done something."

"You did. Eventually. Can you just drive me home? I don't want my friends to see you crying."

"Sorry," I said, attempting to pull myself together.

"You're so pathetic," Hailey told me when I started the engine. I turned and caught her smile and we both laughed.

Hannah Ellis

Chapter 24

It was odd to pick Hailey up without the usual feeling of dread – and stranger still to be greeted with a smile. A week went by. I wondered how long it would take for me to get used to it: for her smile to seem normal and not a novelty.

I didn't ask how her day was any more. I didn't need to; she'd launch into a full account as soon as we got in the car. She told me all about the other kids in her class: the ones she liked, the ones she didn't like, the class clown, the teacher's pet – I knew them all. It was less than a five-minute drive from the school to our house and I wished it were longer. I could've driven around all evening listening to Hailey chatter away.

Thanks to Chrissie's connection, I managed to get Amelie Bright to take over Hailey's counselling. She was based in Manchester but did one day a week in a clinic in Brinkwell, and agreed to fit Hailey in on Wednesday evenings. Adam took her to the first appointment and I found myself increasingly anxious while I waited for them to come home. Now that Hailey was doing so well at school, I was nervous of anything which could potentially unsettle her. I needn't have worried.

"How was it?" I asked when they walked in. I

stopped stirring the pasta sauce, which I'd been using as a distraction, and turned to talk to them.

"She's nice," Adam said, joining Emily at the table.

"Was it okay, Hailey?" I was practically holding my breath as I waited for her verdict.

"Amelie's cool," she told me casually. "Much nicer than annoying Mrs Miller. Is dinner ready?"

"Yeah." I had a smile on my face when I pulled out plates and piled spaghetti on them.

The girls sucked up the spaghetti, laughing as Adam did the same. I caught his eye and smiled. He was in a good mood for once, so I decided I'd take advantage of it and talk to him about doing my teacher training.

I waited until the kids were in bed and we were sitting on the couch.

"I've been thinking about work," I said. "I think I'm going to do my teacher training next year. I don't want to put it off any longer."

He muted the TV and turned to me. "I thought you were happy at St Jude's."

"I'd stay at St Jude's. I can do my teacher training with them – that was the original plan. I'll probably have to do a lot of sweet-talking – I'm not exactly the favourite member of staff at the moment, but I think I could manage it."

"So what would that mean? More hours?"

"Yeah. It won't be easy, but I want to teach and I don't want to keep putting it off."

"What about Hailey?"

"She could walk back from school. Ruth would be here for her when she gets home. Other kids her age get themselves home. We live in a village and everyone looks out for each other. I don't think it would be a problem."

The school was on the road out of the village, only a ten-minute walk from the infants school where Emily went, so theoretically Ruth could pick both girls up – although I couldn't imagine Hailey thanking us for that.

"But we'd be relying on Mum more. I thought you wanted her around less, not more."

"I don't have a problem her being around to look after the girls; I just don't like that she seems to be here to check up on me all the time. I don't think she'd mind staying with the girls a bit longer in the afternoon."

"I don't know. It feels like everything is just settling down and it's going to disrupt things again."

I felt my throat getting tighter and wondered whether he was right. Wouldn't it be better to just keep the peace at home? Did I have the energy for teacher training, or for a full-time job? Even talking to Adam about it felt suddenly too much for me, so maybe I was overestimating myself.

"I don't even know if Jean would agree to it. She's not very happy with me after all the time I've missed."

"It's up to you." He turned back to the TV. "I guess we'll figure things out, if it's what you really want."

"But you'd rather I didn't?"

He frowned and gave me his usual annoying shrug, signalling he didn't want to discuss it further.

"So you can't be supportive?" I asked.

"Yes. I will be supportive," he managed, sounding anything but. He handed me the remote and walked out of the room.

As his footsteps receded up the stairs, I stared blankly at the TV for a while, waiting for him to fall asleep.

"You've got great timing," Mike told me casually when I walked into the deserted pub. "I was just about to lock up."

"Do you mind?"

"No. Do the bar," he said, throwing me a cloth and pointing to a bottle of spray cleaner. He locked the door behind me and I enjoyed wiping down every surface I could find while Mike cashed up the till. I'd worked up a sweat by the time I'd finished. When I looked over, Mike was leaning against the bar, watching me with a smile on his face. "Why don't you tell me what's going on?"

I brushed the hair out of my face with the back of my hand and wiped my chemical-smelling hands on my jeans before taking up position at the bar, exchanging my cleaning supplies for a glass of crisp white wine. I took a long sip, savouring the taste.

"I was thinking about my career. I've always wanted to be a teacher, but now it seems selfish of me to want that. I don't know what to do."

Mike pulled up a stool beside me, a pint of lager in his hand. "What does Adam think?"

"He's not thrilled by the idea."

"You need to have your own life too, besides Adam and the girls. You'll go mad otherwise."

"That's the thing – I feel like I am going mad half the time. My life seems so unreal sometimes. I feel that if I do my teacher training, I'd get a bit of my old life back. It'd be like I haven't lost everything." I stopped and looked at Mike, hearing how I sounded. "That came out wrong," I told him. "Of course I didn't lose everything. But sometimes I feel like I have no control any more. I'm just being swept along with it all."

"You certainly gave up a lot."

"I feel like I gave up the most," I said, resentfully. "Maybe that's what makes me want to get on with my career. I'm jealous that Adam still has his career. Plus he gets all the credit. He's the hero of the tale, taking on his nieces and working himself to the bone to provide for them."

"Well, aren't we bitter this evening?" Mike said. I sipped my wine. "But that's not the story I hear. If I were to listen to gossip, which I don't, of course, I'd tell you that you're practically Superwoman in your little story."

"Really?" I don't know why it mattered, but it did. He nodded and I placed my drink down with a shy smile.

"Adam gave up a lot too." Mike glanced around at Adam's photos which hung around the pub. "It can't be easy to get so close to your dream and then walk away."

"I tried to get him to go back to it, but he won't."

"That's understandable."

"Is it? I don't really get it." I shook my head, not wanting to discuss it. "Anyway, tell me something fun. How's the internet dating? Have you met up with anyone yet?"

"Not yet. I'm still working up the courage. I've been talking to one woman a lot. Maybe I'll ask her out."

"You should. It would be good for you to have something else in your life besides this place."

"Maybe," he said vaguely.

Mike would make someone a great boyfriend. He was good-looking and funny. There was an easy charm about him, and he was comfortable to be around. He always seemed to know the right thing to say.

I finished my wine as Mike reached the bottom of his pint, and decided it was time to head home. "Thanks for the drink and the chat."

"Any time," he told me, unbolting the door and pulling it open for me to slip back out into the night.

Chapter 25

Every day at work, I thought about talking to Jean Stoke about the teacher training programme. My conversation with Adam played on my mind and I wondered whether I should give up the whole idea of teaching. Things were strained between Adam and me, and I wasn't sure I wanted to rock the boat any further. Especially now that Hailey was finally settling and the girls were doing so well. Every afternoon I left work promising myself I would make a decision and talk to Jean the following day. I wanted to talk to Adam about it again, but he was always so tired and distant in the evenings that I never felt like bringing the subject up. I'd need to make a decision soon; the school year would be over before I knew it.

It was a Tuesday and again I'd kicked myself for walking out of work without making it to Jean's office. However, it was my birthday, so I had a good excuse. Tomorrow, I told myself, definitely tomorrow.

The atmosphere in the kitchen at dinnertime was awful. I sat at the table with the girls while Ruth paced up and down, occasionally craning her neck to look out the window and down the drive for Adam. The disappointment on Hailey's face was killing me. I suddenly hated Adam.

"Let's just eat," I said to Ruth. "The kids are hungry."

I, on the other hand, had no appetite. I just wanted the day to be over.

"He'll be here any minute," Ruth said, her voice anything but confident. "I spoke to him yesterday. He said he'd be home early for dinner, and then he was going to take you out to the pub."

It wasn't the most romantic of plans anyway – hardly any effort for him really, but still he couldn't manage it.

"He wouldn't forget your birthday," Ruth said firmly. I wanted to cry. It wasn't as though I was the sort of person who made a big fuss about birthdays; I didn't need to spend a whole weekend celebrating, but I did like the phone calls from my friends and family and I enjoyed eating cake with those closest to me.

Adam had rushed out in the morning, complaining he was late for work. I'd had phone calls throughout the day from my parents and my little brothers, and a few of my friends. I hadn't heard from Adam all day and every time the phone rang I'd expected it to be him. All day, I expected him to remember and call me in a panic.

That hadn't happened, though, and now he wasn't even going to make it home for dinner. I stood up, needing to do something. "We should just eat. He must have been held up."

"Why isn't he answering his phone?" Ruth grumbled. Her face fell when I looked at her, and I hated him even more because I knew what she was thinking.

"He's fine," I said and moved closer to her to

whisper, "Nothing has happened. He'll be home soon."

Her hands shook as she tried to call him again.

"Stop," I said gently and took the phone from her hands. "His phone is switched off. He probably forgot to charge it. I'll ring Carl and find out how late they have to work."

I grabbed my phone and rang Carl. He answered after a few rings, sounding surprised but happy to hear from me.

"I bet you don't really want to talk to me, do you?" he said.

"Is Adam around?" I asked.

"Somewhere," he said. "Hang on."

I moved the phone away from my mouth. "He's fine," I told Ruth. "Just stuck at work."

"Hi," Adam's voice came down the line. "Everything okay?"

"Yeah. We were just waiting for you for dinner, and you didn't answer your phone."

"Sorry, the battery must be dead. Work's crazy but I should be leaving soon."

"Okay," I said. "No rush."

I hung up and moved to dish up the lasagne Ruth had made. There was a chocolate cake standing next to it that Emily had helped decorate. The three of them were looking at me when I turned around with plates of food.

"He's running late," I said quickly, trying desperately to hide my pain. "We'll eat without him."

"He's not coming to the party?" Emily asked.

"Nope," I said, setting a plate in front of her. "Just us girls. Which means more cake for us," I added.

I longed for the days when I only had myself to worry about. What a treat it would be to storm up to bed and be miserable in peace, but I had to keep the cheerful 'I don't care' act going for another couple of hours until the girls were in bed. Ruth wasn't helping matters. Her silence was unnerving.

I tucked into my lukewarm lasagne and told the girls to do the same. Hailey glared at me but didn't say anything. She slowly started to eat. Emily told me all about how she'd helped with the cake. She'd made me a card too, and a necklace of green beads, which hung around my neck. Ruth had given me a pair of slippers and some bath products.

Emily's chatter filled the air, and for most of the meal I managed to push thoughts of Adam from my mind. I blew out my candles and we moved in to the living room to eat cake in front of the TV. I cuddled Emily on the couch until CBeebies was over for the day.

"Shall I put Emily to bed?" Ruth asked.

"No, it's fine," I said. "Say goodnight to Gran, girls, and go and get ready for bed. I'll be up in a minute."

Hailey ushered Emily up the stairs and Ruth turned to me. "I can't believe he's still not home," she whispered.

"It doesn't matter," I told her feebly. "Thanks for dinner and my cake."

"You're welcome." She hugged me, and I thought I was going to cry. "I'll kill him," she said fiercely when she moved away.

"After I do," I said, managing a smile. "See you in the morning."

I forced myself up the stairs and helped Emily finish getting ready for bed, sitting with her until she fell asleep.

"Don't stay up too late," I told Hailey when I looked in on her. She had her earphones in and a magazine on her lap.

"Lucy," she called when I started to walk away. "Are you okay?"

"Fine," I said. "I'm tired. I'm going to go to bed too." I left her and went to put my pyjamas on and crawl into bed. In the silence, I listened for Adam coming home and debated what to say to him. A part of me didn't want to say anything at all: being so angry with him was exhausting, and arguing with him was so much effort.

"Lucy?" Hailey's voice interrupted my thoughts and she edged into the room to perch beside me on the bed.

I saw the tears in her eyes and sat up. "What's wrong?"

She shook her head and held her hand out. "I made you this. You probably won't like it. It's kind of stupid…"

"I love it," I told her, taking the friendship bracelet from her. I remembered Ruth buying her a kit and she'd complained to me that she used to make friendship bracelets when she was seven and they were just for kids. "Tie it on for me," I said, holding out my wrist. She tied a knot and I held out my arm to admire the greens and blues. "Thank you."

"You're welcome." She leaned over and gave me a big hug. "I'm sorry Uncle Adam forgot your birthday."

"Don't you be sorry," I said. "He'll be sorry enough for himself when I see him!" I tried to make light of it but the tears that fell down her face told me she wasn't fooled. "It's okay," I said, squeezing her hand.

"Is it?" she asked, her big green eyes regarding me intensely. I couldn't defend Adam's behaviour to Hailey; I didn't want her to think it was acceptable.

I shook my head and swallowed the lump in my throat. "It's not okay," I told her and pulled her to me for another hug. I didn't know how to explain things to her because I didn't understand them myself. My relationship with Adam was falling apart. Forgetting my birthday was just another way he'd let me down. I was becoming the sort of woman who would put up with anything. What could I do, though? It would be so easy if it was just the two of us. I could walk away and never look back. But there were kids involved. I was trapped.

"Sorry you had a rubbish birthday," Hailey said, pulling away from me.

"It wasn't all bad," I said, glancing at my bracelet. "You'd better go to bed. Don't worry about Adam and me, okay?"

She smiled and walked out of the room. I switched off the bedside lamp and was just nodding off when I heard the click of the front door closing. A floorboard creaked at the top of the stairs and I heard mumbled voices before Adam came into the room.

"You're already in bed?" he said, when the light from the hallway flooded in. I sat up and turned on the lamp. He took his wallet and phone out of his pockets and put them on the dresser. "Any idea why Hailey waited up especially to tell me she hates me?"

"She's upset you forgot my birthday," I told him and watched confusion flash across his face. There was a moment when I thought he was going to correct me. Tell me it wasn't my birthday today. Then he closed his eyes and swore softly, dropping onto the edge of the bed. "I'm sorry," he said when he finally turned to look at me. "Work was crazy. I had such a bad day…"

"Me too," I said bitterly.

"I'm so sorry," he said again. "I can't believe I forgot."

"How *did* you forget?" I asked. "Your mum spoke to you about it, and Emily's been wittering about it for ages. It's not like no one's mentioned it!"

"I know," he said pathetically. "I just lost track of the days. I wasn't thinking…"

"You weren't thinking about me," I said miserably. "Which sums up our whole relationship, doesn't it?"

"Of course I think about you." He dropped his head into his hands and I almost felt sorry for him; there was no way he could win this argument. He'd really messed up this time. "I'll make it up to you," he said, looking me in the eye.

Turning away from him, I switched off the light and lay on my side. I listened as he undressed and got into bed beside me.

"I'm sorry," he whispered in the darkness. We lay silently, and neither of us fell asleep for a long time.

Chapter 26

Adam wasn't beside me when I woke. Glancing at the clock, I realised I was running late. I vaguely remembered hitting the snooze button a couple of times. Bickering voices drifted up to me when I headed to the bathroom, but I ignored them and showered quickly.

"I overslept," I told Ruth when I finally walked into the kitchen, taking the coffee she handed me and sitting down for some cereal. "Thanks for doing the sandwiches."

"Can you drop me at Zac's this morning?" Hailey asked, getting up from the kitchen table. Adam was sitting opposite Emily, sipping a coffee.

"Yeah, but I need to leave soon," I said. Since she didn't like being early for school, Adam or I would sometimes drop her at Angela's and she'd walk from there with Zac and Imogen. On other days she'd walk down to the village with Emily and Ruth, then continue alone, usually finding friends to walk with along the way.

"I'll be ready in two minutes," she told me, hurrying upstairs.

"Don't forget to brush your teeth!" Ruth and I shouted after her at the same time.

"I'll see you this evening," I said a few minutes

later, running a hand over Emily's hair. "Have fun at school."

Adam stood when I walked past him and took my hand, pulling me to him and kissing me on the cheek.

"See you later," I said with a weak smile.

"I'll be home early," he told me.

I didn't respond, just headed off to work, dropping Hailey on the way.

For once, Adam kept his word and arrived home from work at a reasonable time. Ruth left when he came in, falsely believing we needed time alone. She'd asked if we wanted her to stay with the girls so we could go out, but I'd declined her offer. She was finally trying to give us some space but – ironically – I didn't want it any more. I'd have preferred it if she'd stayed for dinner. I had no desire to be alone with Adam, and the girls weren't enough of a buffer.

"Happy belated birthday!" Adam said cheerfully after Ruth left. I stopped dishing up dinner and turned to face him. I took the small jewellery box he held out and for a moment was transported back to a time when such a box would have thrilled me. Before the girls came to live with us, I'd often imagined him proposing – and had been ecstatic at the idea. I swallowed, praying it wasn't a ring, and relaxed when I flicked open the lid to see earrings – little studs in the shape of flowers.

"Thanks," I said, kissing him on the cheek and then holding out the box to show the girls as they crowded around me. I put them aside. It was too little too late. Even when he knew he was in my bad books, he couldn't manage to think of something special or personal. The shop assistant had probably picked those out for him. I glanced at my bracelet from Hailey and thought of my tacky beads from Emily; the girls had definitely won when it came to giving me jewellery. The girls chatted over dinner and, when I put Emily to bed, I snuggled in beside her, and woke the next morning in the same position.

As the week continued, Adam and I fell into a routine of polite conversations and awkward silences. When I sat on the couch with him on Saturday evening I was exhausted and in no mood for an argument.

"How long do you plan on giving me the cold shoulder for?" he asked casually.

"I don't really know," I said flatly.

"I forgot your birthday and I apologised. I don't know what else I can do."

"It's not just the birthday," I told him. "It's so much more."

"Like what?" he asked defensively.

I took a breath and searched for some energy. Had he really no idea? "Everything," I said. "I'm miserable. We're falling apart and I hate that the kids are watching everything we do. We're setting a really bad example."

"What?" He sounded confused. He genuinely didn't seem to see things the same way I did.

"Our life has become about getting through the day or the week, or the month. I hate that. I want us to plan ahead and set goals. I want to follow our dreams!"

"Is this about the photography again?" he asked, the muscles along his jaw tensing.

"Yes," I said. "Among other things."

"We've already talked about this. I don't know why you keep pushing me."

"Because I'm your girlfriend," I said, raising my voice. "Why shouldn't I push you? And why won't you push me? Or at least support me. I told you I wanted to do my teacher training and you brushed it aside. You weren't supportive at all."

He shifted in his seat and I wondered whether he was going to walk away. "There's more to think about than what *we* want," he said. "We have to think about what's best for the girls, and that means sacrificing some things."

"It doesn't have to," I said. "Things aren't as simple as they used to be, but it doesn't mean we have to give up on the things we want out of life. The girls should look up to us and see they can do whatever they set their minds to."

"Do the teacher training then," he said. "I thought you were going to anyway."

"I will," I told him, battling my emotions. "It would just be nice if … Never mind."

More than anything, I wanted him to be supportive of my career, but I was fighting a losing battle. He was so hard to talk to and every time I tried I ended up more frustrated. I got up and went into the hall, needing to escape. "I'm going for a walk," I told him. "I need some air."

I ignored the puzzled look on Adam's face and left.

Chapter 27

As May crawled on, the evenings began to draw out. It made such a difference to the day. The girls played outside after school, they'd starting going to friends' houses sometimes for dinner, or they'd have friends over to us. I liked to clean the kitchen to the sound of the kids playing outside. Even the sibling bickering was bearable when they were out in the sunshine.

It was Wednesday and Adam had taken Hailey to her counselling session. They joined Emily outside when they got home and I was watching them out of the window, the three of them laughing. I hated the fact that it made me angry. Why could those little girls make him laugh, but I couldn't? Not that I ever tried any more. We lived parallel lives, with the kids between us, keeping us together.

I knew that if I went out and joined them, Adam's smile would fade and he'd make an excuse to go inside. These days there was always an atmosphere between us.

When they came in, we went through the motions of getting them up to bed, the kids' chatter masking the fact that Adam and I didn't speak to each other.

The girls were tired and fell asleep quickly. Coming downstairs, I found Adam on the couch, a beer bottle in his hand, staring at the TV.

He didn't notice me and I went to the kitchen, sitting at the table with a glass of wine and staring into space.

Again, I didn't bother to wait until Adam was asleep before I made my way out of the house. I'd stopped caring what he might say. I didn't even fully register that I was going out until I heard his voice. My hand was on the door handle.

"Where are you going?" he said, startling me.

I felt the guilt course through me, and at the same time chastised myself because I had nothing to feel guilty about.

"Just a walk around the village," I lied, almost without hesitation. "A bit of fresh air before bed." I turned to leave, only really caring about getting away from him.

"We live in a village," he said angrily. "People talk. I know you're going to see Mike."

I found myself strangely relieved that he only knew about my visits to the pub. Adam thinking I was cheating on him with the barman seemed better than him finding out I spent a lot of time complaining about him to his dead father. All those evenings I'd spent telling Tom that I didn't know how long I could keep going, that I would probably leave his son soon. I thought that if I talked to him enough, I'd eventually hear him telling me not to go. I thought he'd tell me I had to stay – because I'd promised him I would.

If the last words I'd spoken to Tom hadn't been a promise to stay by Adam's side, would I still be there? A part of me knew I needed to break that promise before the promise broke me.

Looking up at Adam, I couldn't find any words. I couldn't bring myself to argue with him. Couldn't find it in me to protest my innocence.

"I just need some air," I said. "I won't be long."

Under the light of the street lamps I took my usual route, walking quickly into the village and then up the hill to the graveyard. I sat with my back against the cool marble of Tom's headstone, exhaustion finally enveloping me as I told him I'd come to say goodbye.

Hannah Ellis

Chapter 28

I woke abruptly. The marble had numbed my cheek, and it took me a moment to remember where I was. I shivered on the cold ground and jumped with fright at the figure looming over me.

Adam bent down to me.

"I've been looking all over for you," he said gruffly. He didn't sound relieved to have found me. "What are you doing here?" He didn't wait for an answer, but pulled me up and led me across the churchyard, back to the street.

Tension radiated from him. Fear crept over me. Under the streetlight I was shocked to see blood staining his cheek.

"What happened?" I demanded, stopping and turning Adam to face me.

His eyes flashed with anger and he flinched when I moved my hand to his grazed cheek. "I had an argument with Mike."

"Adam! What have you done?"

"What did you expect?" he growled. "You're sneaking around with the local barman – who happens to be my friend! – and you think I'm not going to say anything? What the hell, Lucy!"

"Oh God, Adam, it's not like that." My heart was pounding. I took a step away from him. How on earth had we come to this?

"Don't lie to me!" His voice was loud and angry, but I saw the hurt in his eyes and felt sorry for him. For both of us. I'd never imagined our relationship could become such a mess. We had been so solid, once upon a time.

"I'm not lying!" I yelled, exasperated. "There's nothing going on between me and Mike."

He eyed me with contempt. "I don't believe you."

There was silence. I only found my voice when Adam turned to walk away.

"Mike was with me," I said, my voice quivering with emotion. "When I found your dad."

Adam's eyes softened at the mention of Tom, and I realised I should have told him long ago. He'd never asked for details about that day, and I had never offered them. It was hard for me to re-live.

Becky and Will had been in a car accident. They'd both died instantly. Thank God the girls hadn't been with them. We'd all gone to France but Tom and I flew back after the funeral. Adam and Ruth stayed in France, packing up the house and dealing with a mountain of paperwork. There was so much to do and every tiny detail was heart-breaking.

Tom had been unwell; he'd fainted after the funeral. Ruth had insisted it was all too much for him and he should go home. We could get the girls' rooms ready and Tom would go to see Dr Griffin for a check-up. When we got home he had, reluctantly, seen the doctor and been given the all-clear. We were told he'd just fainted due to shock and grief.

"Mike was passing when I left the house that morning," I told Adam, my voice shaky. "He said he'd come and see Tom, ask if he could do anything to help. I don't know what I would have done if he hadn't been there. He took over, called the police and dealt with all the formalities." I had been numb, sitting beside Tom's body, unable to believe he'd gone. He'd had a massive heart attack ... but he looked so peaceful sitting in his favourite spot on the couch. All I could think was that I'd have to ring Adam and tell him he'd lost his dad as well as his sister and brother-in-law. It was too much. How could life be so cruel? It had seemed surreal. "Mike helped me out of the house when my legs refused to work," I whispered. Adam didn't need to hear the whole truth: that when the gentle persuasion of the police officers didn't work, Mike had dragged me, sobbing and hysterical, from Tom's side. He'd helped me home and then held me while I cried.

"He sat with me when I called you in France to tell you what had happened, and stayed with me until you came home. He put food in front of me and insisted I ate." I paused, blinking back tears as I waded through the memories. "And then you were home with the girls, and he was gone, and I had to be the one to make sure that people ate, to see that everyone was all right. Mike asks if I'm okay. He can see I'm *not* okay. He's only ever been a friend to me, I promise." I still hated that Mike had seen me fall apart the way I had. For a while, I'd avoided him – partly because I was embarrassed and partly because seeing him brought back memories that I'd rather keep buried.

"I didn't know all that," Adam said.

"Nothing happened between us!" I needed that to be clear – mainly for Mike's sake, since I'd be gone soon and he'd have to deal with any backlash. "I wasn't sneaking around with him. I just needed a place to go sometimes. Somewhere to escape to. We're falling apart, Adam, but it's nothing to do with Mike. We don't talk any more, not without sniping at each other. I'm so unhappy and you either don't see it or you don't care."

"Of course I care," he said gently, taking a step towards me. "I love you so much. I couldn't cope without you, you know?" He moved his hands to my face and kissed me softly, sending ripples of desire around my body. My head spun and the thoughts that had been so clear a few minutes earlier were suddenly jumbled and confusing. Grief, and the sudden responsibility of his nieces, had taken the happy-go-lucky man I'd fallen in love with and made him darker. He had an edge to him that he hadn't had before – and I hated it. For that moment, as he embraced me, I felt my old Adam come back. The kind, caring person I'd thought I would spend my life with. The voice inside me told me to stay and work things out.

When we arrived home, Ruth slipped out of the front door without a word. She gave Adam a quick hug, but didn't mention the cut on his cheek.

I checked on the girls and then went to Adam, who was sitting on our bed. "They're fast asleep," I told him. "We need to talk."

"I know," he said, reaching for me. "Tomorrow."

"Is Mike okay?" I asked, my eyes drawn to the wound on Adam's cheek. He'd cleaned it and it was only a small cut.

"He probably has a black eye, and he's pretty

angry, but he'll be fine. I'll go and see him tomorrow and clear the air."

"What happened to us?" I asked drearily.

"We're okay," he said confidently. "We'll get through this. Everything will be fine."

I didn't have the energy to argue. When he kissed me, every part of me responded. We made love. I clung to him and remembered how life used to be – and how much I had loved him.

The minutes on the digital clock behind Adam ticked slowly by. I spent the night watching him sleep. At the first hint of light, I drew the curtains open a crack and opened the wardrobe. I found a duffel bag at the bottom and quickly shoved in some clothes. Then I found a smaller bag and hastily packed make-up, my few bits of jewellery, a hairbrush, perfume – anything I saw.

"Hailey." Gently, I nudged her awake. She blinked up at me. "I have to go away for a while."

"What do you mean?"

"I'm moving out," I said sadly.

Her eyes snapped open and she reached for my hand. "No!"

"I have to. I'm sorry."

"Please don't." Tears welled in her beautiful big eyes and I needed all my resolve not to change my mind.

"Look after your sister. Give her lots of cuddles."

"Why are you going?" she asked.

"Not because of you." I wiped a tear from her cheek. "I only stayed so long because of you. I love you both so much, but I have to figure some things out and I can't do that here."

"I'll see you again, won't I?"

"Yes, of course." It broke my heart that she needed to ask. "I love you. Don't forget that." I hugged her tightly and kissed her cheek before slipping into Emily's room. I couldn't wake her, couldn't face seeing the confusion in her eyes. I laid a kiss gently on her blonde hair and went back to wake Adam.

"Morning," he groaned.

"I'm sorry," I said.

"What's wrong?" He sat up and looked at me before noticing my bags in the doorway. "What's going on?"

"I have to leave," I said. "I'm sorry." I kissed him and moved swiftly to the door. I picked up my bags and ran down the stairs, ignoring Hailey, who was hovering in her bedroom doorway.

"Lucy!" Adam followed me. "What do you mean you're leaving? You can't just leave. I'm sorry I jumped to conclusions about Mike. I should've talked to you. Just stay and we can talk! We'll sort everything out."

"I'm sick of waiting for you to talk to me. I can't do it any more."

I managed to stay calm and cool – to the point that I felt heartless. If I didn't move quickly – if I stopped to look around – I wouldn't be able to leave. So I got in the car and drove away without looking back.

Part 2

Hannah Ellis

Chapter 29

"I would've been out of there long ago," Chrissie told me. She'd had a few drinks and the wine had loosened her tongue. She and Matt had happily offered me their spare room when I turned up on their doorstep again.

"No, you wouldn't. You wouldn't just leave Matt if things didn't go to plan."

"I don't think I could take on someone else's kids – especially in such a new relationship. You and Adam had only been together for eighteen months when his sister died. I don't think many relationships would survive that."

"I didn't really have a choice," I said, taking a sip of wine. "I couldn't just leave him."

"No one would've blamed you."

"But I loved him. I couldn't leave. And then later I couldn't leave the girls." Thinking of the girls made my chest feel tight. I thought that leaving Adam would be like ripping off a plaster, but now I wasn't sure the stinging would ever go away. In the two days since I left, I'd been consumed by guilt and doubt. Should I have tried harder with Adam? Part of me knew I could have done more, but I'd lost my ability to think clearly. In the end I'd been consumed by the desire to leave. I hadn't tried harder because I hadn't wanted to. Maybe our relationship had been doomed from the moment Becky died.

"So why now?" Chrissie asked.

"Adam's changed," I told her, pulling my legs up under me and curling into the comfortable chair. "We've both changed. We were angry with each other all the time. I hated being in the house. It was stifling. Being around Adam was a constant battle. I couldn't see any end to it."

"So you don't love him any more?" She stared at me, trying to understand. I didn't know how to answer. Did I love Adam? Not like I used to. I think I was probably just clinging on to what we used to have. The Adam I lived with didn't seem like the Adam I'd fallen in love with.

"No," I told her after a pause, realising when I said it that it was the truth. "Everything is such a mess. I used to be so sure that I'd marry Adam and be with him forever … but, now when I look at him, I don't feel anything. Nothing good, anyway."

"I think you did the right thing," Chrissie said confidently. "You shouldn't have to sacrifice your dreams for someone else's kids. I always thought it was odd that Adam let you be the one to cut back on your work to look after the kids while he carried on as normal."

"I didn't mind. Plus, it made sense. I could work part-time; he can't. And he earns more than me. We fell into these roles and that was fine, I guess. Once the kids had been with us a while, it didn't matter who the blood relatives were – not to me, anyway. They were my family. And, in the end, the kids weren't the reason I left. Adam and I couldn't communicate any more. Our relationship just wasn't strong enough to take everything that had been thrown at us."

"Hmm," Chrissie mused. She didn't understand and

I couldn't expect her to. "It always seemed weird to me." She finished her wine and went to pour more. I declined, not thinking it safe to drink too much in my emotional state.

"Anyway, tell me about your wedding plans…" I prompted.

"Don't think I don't know you just want to change the subject!" The wine sloshed around her glass as she laughed. "But, okay … we have a date now – the fifth of July next year. We booked the venue. I showed you pictures, didn't I?"

I nodded. The hotel was at the other side of Manchester, and had the most beautiful gardens.

"Matt's mum's driving me mad with her crazy suggestions. I wish she'd just keep out if it."

"It's nice that she wants to be involved."

"I disagree!" Her phone buzzed, and she reached for it. I listened while she chatted to Matt, and heard her agreeing to meet him. "Right…" She hung up the phone and stood up, looking at me. "Let's get changed and go and meet the gang. Matt's at Dylan's pub and Ryan's there too. Let's go!"

Ryan and Dylan had been on the TV show with us and we used to spend a lot of time in Dylan's pub, the Fox and Hound. His dad, Jack, owned it really, but it was always Dylan's pub to us.

Normally I would have loved to catch up with the old gang but today all I felt like doing was curling up into a ball and hiding from the world.

"I was thinking of going to bed soon," I said. "I'm not up to a night out."

"Don't be daft – it's just a couple of drinks with the boys. It'll be fun. You need to get your mind off everything. I'm not taking no for an answer!"

I realised I wasn't going to win this battle. "I'm not staying long," I said.

"Yes!" She grinned at me and wobbled when she left the room to get changed.

As soon as Dylan embraced me, I was glad that Chrissie had persuaded me to go out. Dylan's pub was so familiar, and it was good to be in the company of old friends. I spotted Jack, Dylan's dad, and went around the bar to give him a quick hug. Jack was a sweet man and it was immediately obvious that he and Dylan were father and son: they both had a hint of red in their sandy-brown hair, and kind brown eyes. Jack greeted me warmly, as always, and I went to sit at a table in the back corner where Matt was chatting to Ryan over a pint.

I hugged them both excitedly and felt suddenly giddy; it was good to be out with the old gang. "We don't have privileges in the back room any more?" I asked.

"They're renovating," Ryan told me. "But we actually lost privileges when we stopped being recognised."

"Every silver lining has a cloud, I guess."

"I miss the old days," Chrissie said, taking a seat next to Matt. "We had so much fun."

I smiled, thinking of our brief flirtation with fame. After we'd been on *A Trip to Remember*, we were thrust into the media spotlight for a while. We used to hide out in the back room of the pub where we wouldn't be hassled by members of the public.

"We didn't have a care in the world, did we?" I

said.

"I think those glasses might be slightly rose-tinted," Matt said. "As I recall, you didn't have it that easy back then. Remember how the whole world hated you?"

"Well, apart from that!" I hadn't been portrayed in the best light on the show, and public opinion of me was pretty low for a while.

"That was nothing, though, was it?" Ryan commented. "Not compared to the way life slapped you around the face later … Stuck looking after someone else's sprogs. You really don't have the best luck, do you?"

"It's nice to know you've not changed, Ryan!" I raised an eyebrow at him and sipped at my drink. Ryan was the baby of our group. He'd only been twenty when *A Trip to Remember* was aired, and he was young for his age. Now, he had the same baby face as when I'd first met him, and still insisted on smothering his dark hair in gel so that it stuck straight up. He looked like he could be in a boy band.

"What?" he asked when everyone glared at him. "I only said what everyone else was thinking."

"Tact never was your strong point," I said.

"Well, it was pretty shitty, wasn't it? But I heard you finally came to your senses, anyway…"

"Shut up, Ryan." Dylan took a seat beside me and gave my hand a quick squeeze. I'd always found Dylan's presence reassuring.

"When's Kelly back from Australia?" I asked. Kelly and Margaret had also been on the show with us, and Kelly was currently in Australia with Margaret, who lived there. She'd got a year's holiday visa and had given up her waitressing job for the warmer climate.

"I think she's still got six months," Chrissie said. "She'd stay longer if she could extend her visa. She says being a waitress is much more fun at a beach bar."

"I bet she finds herself a poor unsuspecting surfer dude to marry and stays there," Matt said.

"Maybe I should go out and visit them in the school holidays," I said.

Chrissie looked at me seriously. "You should. You'd have a great time."

"I'm not sure my savings would stretch to it. I'll just spend the summer in here propping up the bar instead." I tried not to think about the fact that I should be spending the summer with the girls. I'd have to talk to Adam and see what we could arrange.

Dylan flashed me a smile. "Sounds good to me."

"Where's …?" I searched for the name of Dylan's girlfriend but came up blank.

"Georgina?" Dylan said. "She's long gone."

"The three of us are free and single again." Ryan beamed at me. "We should celebrate. Get the shots in, Dylan!"

Dylan looked hesitant until Matt and Chrissie voiced their approval.

"I don't want a shot," I told him when he headed for the bar.

"If *I* have to, *you* have to," he told me with a grin.

"Why do you always make me do shots?" I asked the rest of the group, but only got shrugs and grins in reply.

"Can we get out of here?" Dylan asked after we'd

downed our tequila. "I'm sick of the place."

"We get free drinks, though," Ryan said.

"Only because I pay for them!" Dylan said. "Let's go somewhere else and you can buy me drinks for once."

"Go on then," Ryan agreed. "It's pretty dead in here, anyway."

I looked around the place, hesitating as the others stood. "I think I migh—"

"No, you're not going home," Dylan interrupted me. "Don't even try to wriggle away. You're not leaving me to deal with Ryan alone."

"I can hear you," Ryan said.

"You've got Matt and Chrissie," I told him.

"Love's young dream will be off snogging in a corner somewhere – they're disgusting!"

"That's true," Matt agreed. "Come on."

"I want to go somewhere we can dance," Chrissie announced.

"What a surprise," Dylan said, leading us out of the door.

Hannah Ellis

Chapter 30

The world was a horrible place when I woke, fully dressed, in Matt and Chrissie's spare room. My brain was having a boxing match with my skull, relentlessly pounding as though it wanted out. When I realised where I was, everything came flooding back to me. My life had fallen apart and I'd ended up here, passing out drunk in my friend's spare room. My life was terrible. Awful. Everything was bad.

I'd apparently lost my ability to think rationally somewhere in a bottle of tequila. Now all I was left with was a head full of negativity, and my hangover attacking me – not only with a headache that threatened to kill me, and limbs that ached before I even moved, but by removing any shred of positivity from my mind. My life was a disaster. I was a horrible person. I was never going to leave the bed. I'd just stay there until I withered away – the slow painful death I deserved.

My desire to go back to sleep and never wake up was hampered by my body, which was insisting that I go in search of water.

Matt and Chrissie were drinking coffee in the kitchen when I walked in. I filled a glass with water and gulped it down before refilling it. "I think I lost my phone."

"It's here," Matt held it out to me. "We had to confiscate it."

"Why?"

"You wanted to call Adam at 2am and we didn't think it was a great idea."

"Thank you," I said, taking the phone. "I do need to talk to him, though."

"No," Chrissie said.

"Not today," Matt agreed. "It'll end badly."

"How much worse can things get? I just want to talk to him. I need to check the girls are okay."

"Don't make me take your phone back," Matt said. "Wait. Call him tomorrow."

"Okay."

"Do you want something to eat?" Chrissie asked.

"I think I'm going to go back to bed." Thank goodness it was Saturday and I didn't have to be a functioning human being for another forty-eight hours.

"Good plan," Matt said. "Sleep it off. You'll feel better later. The shots probably weren't a good idea."

"I tell you that every time you make me drink with you." I went back upstairs, nausea sweeping through me at the mention of alcohol. I changed into jogging bottoms and a T-shirt and collapsed back onto the bed, pinned down by my hangover and the weight of the world. I drifted in and out of sleep for a few hours and then, when my willpower had run out, reached for my phone.

"It's me," I said, sounding pathetic and trying hard not to cry.

Adam didn't say anything.

I don't know what I had expected him to say, but I

was suddenly lost for words myself. "How are you?"

"Fine," he replied flatly.

"How are the girls?"

"Fine."

"That's good," I said, wishing I'd taken Matt's advice and waited until later to ring. "I'm staying at Matt and Chrissie's place."

"Okay."

"I was wondering if I could come and see the girls sometime. I thought maybe we could talk…"

"I don't think there's much to say." His voice was cold, full of anger and bitterness. "And I think it's better if you stay away for a while."

"Oh no, I need to see the girls," I told him, unable to hide the desperation in my voice.

"I don't want them to be confused. I think it's best that they don't see you for a while. They need to get used to you not being around."

"You can't ban me from seeing them."

"I can, actually. I'm their legal guardian. I decide what's best for them."

"That's not what's best for them." I sat bolt upright, ignoring the throbbing in my head. "You're just angry with me. Don't take it out on the girls."

"I have to go," he told me.

"Don't you at least want to talk things through?"

"Why? You left. What's there to talk about? You don't want to be here. I don't want to talk about that, and I don't want to see you."

"Adam…" My voice trembled and tears fell down my face. "I need to see the girls. We need to talk."

"Not now. Maybe in a few weeks when things are more settled."

"A few weeks? Adam, I can't not see them for a few weeks—"

But he'd already hung up. I felt as though I was being torn apart. I wanted to hate him, I was so angry with him. I'd left, but that didn't make everything my fault. I wanted him to take some responsibility too. Part of me had expected him to grovel – had wanted him to, I guess. My pride was hurt that he didn't want to fight for me. It was stupid, because I'd decided I'd had enough and I knew it was over when I walked out. It stung that he had reached the same conclusion so quickly.

Now he was going to punish me. I missed the girls so much, and he knew it. He knew he could use them against me. He'd keep them from me, and I couldn't do anything about it. I gazed at my screensaver, which was a photo of the girls, and hugged my phone to me while I curled up and cried.

Chapter 31

The weekend dragged. I lazed around Matt and Chrissie's house eating junk and watching TV. The girls filled my thoughts, but I tried to think clearly. I couldn't stay with Adam just because of Hailey and Emily.

I hadn't expected Adam to cut me off from the girls. I don't know why. I knew he'd be angry with me, but somehow I'd thought that when it came to the girls, things would be amicable. He just needed time, I kept telling myself; he was angry now but he'd calm down eventually.

I kept reminding myself of how bad things had been between us in the past few months. Okay, I missed the girls now, but eventually things would settle and I'd be able to spend time with them regularly. Breaking away from Adam was a positive thing, but it would be hard at first.

Hanging around the house feeling sorry for myself left me in a fog of self-pity, and it was a relief to go to work on Monday and get back into some sort of routine. I arrived early and stood looking out of the window which overlooked the playing fields. Kids were milling around, chatting and playing. My mind wandered to the girls again. I imagined them having their breakfast. I glanced at my watch and realised that Adam would have left for work by now. On a whim, I decided to ring the house phone, hoping that Emily would pick up.

However, it was Ruth who answered, and I hesitated, tempted to hang up and try again another time.

"It's Lucy," I finally said, holding my breath to see what reaction I got.

"Oh, how are you?"

"I've been better," I told her. "Thanks for not hanging up on me."

"I take it you want to talk to Emily? She's just finishing her breakfast."

"Yes, please." I heard her moving around the kitchen, and muffled voices.

"Lucy!"

It was so good to hear her voice. I hugged the phone to my ear.

"Hi, sweetheart. How are you?"

"Good. When are you coming home?"

"I'm not sure."

"Today?"

"No, hon, not today. How's school?"

"It's good. Mrs Tierney said I'm the best at spelling!"

"That's great."

"Can you come home tomorrow?" she asked.

"Not tomorrow, but I'll see you soon." Tears sprang to my eyes and I needed to get off the phone before I started blubbing. "Can you put Gran back on the phone for a minute? You'd better get ready for school."

"Okay."

"I love you, Emily. Don't forget, will you?"

"Okay."

"Thanks for letting me talk to her," I said to Ruth.

"No problem. I don't know what's going on between you and Adam, but you're part of the girls' lives. They need you."

"Adam doesn't see it that way," I said. "Can you talk to him? He won't speak to me."

"I've tried but he won't talk to me. He just got cross with me for interfering."

"Can you try again?" I asked, desperately.

"Not now. I'll just end up falling out with him and things will be even worse. Give him some time to cool off. I'm sure you two will sort things out after a bit of breathing space."

"Oh, Ruth." I hated having to explain it to her. "We're not going to sort things out. We just need to figure out a way for me to still be in the girls' lives."

"Don't be daft! You and Adam will be back together before you know it. Relationships have their ups and downs."

"It's more than that. Things have been bad for a while."

"Well, you've had a lot on your plates; it's bound to be tough."

"Ruth!" I yelled. "Surely you could see what was going on?"

There was a pause.

"I'm sorry. I didn't mean to snap at you. But I had to leave. I couldn't take it any more."

"I know it's been difficult for you," she said sadly, "and I know I haven't always helped matters."

"I'm sorry," I told her, remembering that I used to

get on well with Ruth, back when life was simple. "I'm so sorry." Tears pricked my eyes. I should have been there for Ruth more too. I'd stopped asking how she was a long time ago. We could all have supported each other better. We'd kept our heads down and got on with life as best we could – but it hadn't turned out to be a good strategy.

"Me too," she whispered. "Now I need to get Emily to school. Call again soon. It's good for the kids to talk to you."

I was sitting on one of the children's chairs, sobbing, when Sarah walked in and found me. "Sorry." I wiped at my eyes and took deep breaths.

"What's wrong?"

"Everything." I laughed at the mess I'd made of my life. "Adam won't let me see the girls. He won't talk to me."

She patted my arm affectionately. "I'd tell you to go home, but I don't think it would go down well with Mrs Stoke."

"I need to be here, for my sanity. What else am I going to do? Plus, I can't afford to lose my job."

"Well, I put a good word in for you last week, so hopefully that'll keep Mrs Stoke sweet for now."

"Thank you. At least I won't have to be rushing off for sick kids or any other crisis any time soon." I managed a sad smile as I went to get a tissue, wiping my face to make myself presentable before the kids came in.

"Did you give up on the idea of becoming a teacher?"

"No. I just never found a good time to talk to Mrs Stoke."

"I think it would be good for you," Sarah told me. "It would give you something to focus on. Something positive."

I turned my back to her, straightening out the book corner to try and distract myself.

"Did I say the wrong thing?" she asked.

"No. Yes! I'm sorry. I can't think about it now; my head is going crazy."

"You'll be okay," she said. Then the bell rang, the door burst open, and a horde of seven-year-olds swept in.

I stayed for the full school day, figuring it might help to make up for some of my absences – and it would help keep my mind off things too.

I'd just pulled up at Chrissie's house when my phone rang and I answered it. It was Hailey.

"Emily said she spoke to you, and I told Gran that's not fair so she said I could call you!"

"Hi, hon. It's great to hear from you. How was school?" I asked.

"Good. When can we see you?"

"I don't know. Soon, I hope."

"I hope so too. It's boring around here without you."

"I'm pretty bored without you as well," I told her.

"Uncle Adam's in a bad mood all the time."

"Be nice to him."

"I'm always nice!" She laughed, making me smile. "Gran's cooking shepherd's pie, and I'm supposed to go and help her."

"Go on, then. I'll talk to you again soon."

"I miss you!" she said.

"I love you. Don't forget, will you?" I heard her

giggle before she hung up. I felt better for hearing her voice. The girls were so strong, they amazed me. It made me realise that I had no choice but to get through each day and hope that eventually Adam would calm down enough to talk to me.

Chapter 32

Late on Wednesday evening, I finally plucked up the courage to call Adam. I'd psyched myself up and was determined to state my case calmly and rationally, leaving him no option but to agree to let me see the girls.

I said a quick hello before getting to the point. "I want to arrange a time to come and see the girls."

"I told you to leave it for a while," he said, his voice so full of anger that I didn't recognise it.

"I know, but I'm not going to leave it for a while because I miss them and they must miss me too."

"You chose to leave," he said.

My teeth ground together and I had to make a conscious effort to relax my jaw to speak. "Well, we need to come to some agreement," I told him, my plan to stay calm and rational slipping away from me. "Because one way or another I will see them and you'll have to take out a restraining order to stop me. You may as well just tell me when is convenient."

"Fine. Next Saturday morning. You can collect the rest of your things while you're here."

His words rang around my head long after he'd hung up. Collecting the rest of my things would make everything so final. And how were we going to come to any sort of arrangement when he was so angry with me? It crossed my mind that I should have tried harder with Adam; I should have fought to keep us together. We should never have ended up in this state.

I *had* tried, though; I'd battled every day for the past year and a half and all I'd succeeded in doing was exhausting myself. At some point you have to know when to move on, and that's what I'd done – or at least what I was trying to do. I lay on the bed in Matt and Chrissie's spare room and hated myself. How had my life come to this?

I woke to a message from Sarah saying she was ill and wouldn't make it into work. She wanted to give me the heads-up that I'd be with a supply teacher for the day. I fired a quick message back telling her to rest and get well soon.

I arrived at work early. Jean Stoke arrived in the classroom shortly after I'd stowed my handbag in the cupboard.

"Sarah won't be in today," she told me.

"Yeah, she messaged me to say she's ill."

"Unfortunately, she was the third member of staff to ring in sick! There's a bug going around, apparently. I can't find enough supply teachers to cover. I wonder if you could cover the class today?"

"Oh." I was stunned. I'd never taken the class myself before. "Yes. That's fine."

"Great. Thanks. I'll pop in, but I'm sure you'll be fine, judging by what Sarah tells me."

She left me to go and organise supply teachers for the other classrooms. I was slightly worried. I couldn't concentrate on anything for more than five minutes; my mind constantly wandered to Adam and the girls. Teaching the class felt like a mammoth task.

In the end it turned out to be a good thing: being so busy kept my mind occupied and the day flew by. I hardly thought about my problems at all, giving me a much-needed break.

Mrs Stoke spent some time hovering in my classroom. I felt as though she was assessing me, but I ignored her and took over the class to the best of my ability. In the end I was happy to have the chance to show off my skills in the classroom. I might not have been the most reliable employee, but I was good at my job, and I was a very capable teacher. Jean Stoke had also unwittingly done me a favour by breathing down my neck for the day: the kids were always on their best behaviour when she was around.

Sarah was absent on Friday too and Mrs Stoke left me in peace to teach the class for the day. Again, the day flew by and I was surprised by how much I enjoyed teaching. The kids responded well to the lessons, and at the end of the day I had a real sense of achievement. I would definitely find time to talk to Mrs Stoke about doing teacher training.

Hannah Ellis

Chapter 33

My heart raced as I drove through Havendon on Saturday morning. I parked in my usual spot on the driveway, beside Adam's car. I was apprehensive about seeing him, but was hopeful that talking to him face to face would be easier than over the phone. I was confident that he wouldn't make a scene in front of the girls, anyway.

I missed them more than I imagined I would. I missed Emily crawling into my bed at night, and her incessant chatter. I missed Hailey's laugh and her sense of humour, and how she could win an argument with just a look.

When I reached the door, I hesitated, unsure whether it was appropriate for me to let myself in. The thought of knocking was absurd, so I pushed the door gently and shouted hello, waiting to hear the girls' footsteps as they ran towards the door. Nothing happened. When I ventured into the hallway, I caught a flash of movement from the corner of my eye, and saw Adam standing at the top of the stairs.

"Hi," I said, trying desperately to sound calm.

"Hi."

"Where are the girls?"

"Mum's taken them shopping." His voice was void of emotion as he walked down the stairs. I should've known. With a great effort, I hid my disappointment, swallowed my anger and held my ground.

"Maybe it would be a good time for us to talk then." I hoped he hadn't noticed the tremor in my voice. I wasn't prepared for this. I'd expected the girls to jump all over me and lighten the atmosphere with their chatter and energy. I didn't even know what I would say to Adam.

"Okay." He moved into the kitchen and I followed him, surprised that he'd agreed to talk so easily.

"I'm sorry I left so abruptly," I said.

He leaned against the sideboard, his arms folded across his chest. "You can take whatever you want," he said. "Furniture, whatever. I think that's only fair."

I stared at him for a moment, trying to comprehend what he was saying. "Don't you want to talk?"

"Why? What do you want to talk about? You want to kiss and make up and pretend nothing happened – until the next time you have a bad day and decide to leave? How long are we going to do this for?"

"I didn't have a bad day, we had a bad year and a half!" My words were angry. I paced across the room, stopping to clutch the back of a chair. "And I don't want to make up! I didn't leave on a whim; I didn't just run out without thinking about it." I was amazed he could think that, and I suddenly felt sorry for him. He thought I'd wanted to fix things between us!

"You could have given me a clue how you were feeling," he said, glaring at me.

"Oh come on! You can't seriously have been surprised," I shot at him. "You have been living here too. Surely you've noticed how awful it's been?"

He laughed then, and the look in his eyes scared

me. "My sister died," he told me, enunciating every word. "My dad died. My nieces lost their parents. My mum lost her husband and daughter. I'm sorry it's not been a party around here. I just didn't expect you to leave me because of all that."

"I didn't leave you because of that!" I screamed at him, unable to control my emotions. "I stuck by you through all of that. But you wouldn't talk to me. So much has happened that you just brush under the carpet. You should be the one person in the world I can talk to, but you just want to bury your head in the sand and pretend everything is fine."

"I thought everything *was* fine!" he said, his voice rising. "At least, between us. I thought we were a family and we would stick together. And then you just walked out. If you were expecting me to apologise, you can forget it. You left us. Did you even think about how hard it would be for me to tell the girls that you'd left them?"

"I didn't leave *them*," I told him, tears springing to my eyes. "I left *you*. I couldn't live with *you* any more. It breaks my heart to not see the girls, but what was I supposed to do? Stay for them and forget about my own happiness? I couldn't live like this any more."

"So, take what you want and leave. Get your things and get out!" He turned away from me.

Tears streamed down my face. "It's not that simple, though, is it?" I said. "I want to talk about the girls. I want to make things as easy as possible for them, but I don't know ho—"

"I think it's too late for you to start worrying about that!"

"We could sit down together and talk things through with them," I offered, sniffing. "Surely after everything we've been through we can figure out a way to make this okay for the girls."

"I don't know how we can make things okay," he said, his voice calmer, under control. "I don't understand what you think will happen. Are you expecting us to be friends, or what?"

"I don't know," I cried. "I just don't want us to hate each other."

"Maybe you leaving wasn't the worst thing that could have happened," he said bitterly. "Maybe we do make each other miserable." He turned and looked at me. A flicker of something – Sympathy? Pain? Regret? – flashed across his face before his expression went blank and he walked past me. "I'll leave you to pack. We'll figure out a time for you to see the girls later, when things have settled down."

The front door closed behind him. I slumped into a chair, sobbing into my hands. I allowed myself a few minutes, then I picked myself up and looked around. I plucked a photo of the four of us off the fridge. Hailey had taken it with my phone; we'd been watching a movie on the couch and Hailey had been in a silly mood. She'd jumped across us to take a selfie, directing us to move in and smile.

I found a shopping bag by the back door and moved from room to room, adding anything I wanted. There was little of mine that I cared about. I ended up with a bag of random objects: a hair slide of Emily's, a bottle of Adam's aftershave, a photo of Adam and me taken when we were first dating, a cushion from Hailey's bed (I knew she'd notice it was gone, but she wouldn't mind I'd taken it. She had so many cushions).

When I walked out of the house I was furious with Adam. I pulled roughly at the car door and threw my bag of treasures onto the passenger seat.

I'd already begun to drive away when I glanced in the mirror and caught sight of the garage. On impulse I reversed to it and jumped out of the car. I went into the garage, picking out framed photos from the stacks. They were old now and Adam would say they weren't his best. I left the biggest pictures, collecting a mix of the smaller and medium-sized ones and making a pile in the middle of the room. Adam never came in here any more – and even if he did, I didn't think he'd notice some missing photos, there were so many. Besides, he had said I could take whatever I wanted.

By the time I'd loaded up the car, my anger had subsided and all I felt was sadness. I walked back into the house and went slowly up the stairs to our bedroom, where I took Adam's camera out of his wardrobe and placed it carefully in the middle of the bed.

Hannah Ellis

Chapter 34

There was a good chance I was losing my mind. I left Havendon and drove straight to The White Kitchen, my car full of Adam's framed photographs. I'd debated calling first but decided I had a better chance of making my case in person.

Adam had been all set to display his work in the restaurant, but then his sister died and he pulled out, taking six weeks off work before returning full-time to the television studios. Back then, The White Kitchen had been an up-and-coming restaurant. The owners, Jonathan and Ollie, shared a passion for great food and great art. Their vision was to combine the two, showcasing a mix of work by new and established artists on the walls of the restaurant.

I'd Googled the restaurant and learned that the place had really taken off: during busy periods, people queued along the street to get in. They had a Michelin-starred chef and it had become *the* place to be seen.

The stonework at the front of the restaurant was painted white and an understated slate sign hung over the door, announcing *The White Kitchen* in simple white letters. I peered through the window and saw movement at the back of the restaurant. Knocking gently on the door brought no reply, so I rapped loudly. A middle-aged woman finally opened the door a fraction.

"We're not open yet," she told me.

"I know, sorry. I'm here to talk to Jonathan and Ollie about artwork for the walls."

"You're early," she said, opening the door wide. "They're not expecting any artists until later."

"My mistake," I said. "Should I come back later?"

"They're in with the chef, discussing changes for the menu, but I'll see if they've got a few minutes for you."

I walked past her when she stood to one side.

"Wow!" My eyes feasted on the room. The concept was simple. Elegant décor, all in white: bright white tablecloths and napkins, plain white walls. Nothing about the restaurant was striking, but that meant the eye was immediately drawn to the artwork on the walls. It was an effective strategy. It was like a restaurant in an art gallery.

"Peter Vincent." The woman followed my gaze to the nearest painting. "Have you heard of him?"

"No," I told her.

"He's taking the art world by storm. I'd get one of these for myself if I could afford it. But I think that about most of the art that graces these walls. I'm surrounded by this all day and then go home to an Ikea rainforest print!"

I smiled at her. "How often does the artwork change?"

"There's a different artist every three months," she told me. "And they have artists queuing up to display their work here. What did you say your name was?"

"I'm Lucy Mitchell," I told her. "I'm here on behalf

of Adam Lewis. The photographer." At the mention of Adam's name her brow furrowed slightly. She looked as though she was about to say something, but then carried on through the door.

I wandered the room, looking at the artwork and losing hope. Now that the restaurant was so well established, I wasn't sure how much luck I would have in persuading the owners to display Adam's photos. Although that might not be a bad thing, since I'd technically be dealing in stolen goods.

"Hi." A voice broke into my thoughts. I turned to see two men who looked to be in their early thirties walking through the door.

"I'm really sorry to bother you," I said, walking towards them and offering my hand. "I'm Lucy Mitchell. I wanted to talk to you about artwork for the restaurant walls, but it seems like there's probably a long waiting list."

"There is. I'm Ollie."

I was drawn to his striking ginger hair, which was cut short and neat. He wore a crisp white shirt and smiled warmly at me.

"Jonathan," the second guy said when he shook my hand. He had a similar lean build to Ollie, but had dark hair peppered with grey. "We're not taking on any more artists for the restaurant at the moment."

"Okay," I said. "Thanks anyway." I smiled at them, feeling suddenly awkward under their scrutiny. "I'll let you get back to work, then."

"But Stephanie said you were here for Adam Lewis…" Ollie said as I made to leave.

"Yes, that's right." I turned back to them and caught them exchanging a look.

"Interesting," Jonathan said. "Do you have any of his work with you?"

"Yes, in the car."

"Let's go and have a look, then," he replied.

I opened the boot of the car and they looked through the pictures without saying a word.

Ollie finally straightened up and looked at me. Jonathan continued looking through the pictures. "We're interested," he said.

"Oh!" I frowned in surprise and at the same time realised the absurdity of what I was doing. I couldn't actually sell Adam's photos. "I thought you weren't looking for anything at the moment?"

"Not for the restaurant," he said.

"Come with us," Jonathan said, closing the car door. I followed obediently as they set off down the road. A few doors down from The White Kitchen was another white-fronted building adorned with a similar slate sign that read *White Ice*.

"We're sticking with the white theme," Ollie told me. "But this is our latest venture." He opened the door and led me into a bar. It was decorated in the same style as the restaurant but had different artwork hanging on the walls.

"It's amazing," I said, looking around and ignoring the panic that was rising steadily.

"We had so many people waiting for tables that we thought we'd open a cocktail bar and take more money off their hands while they waited." Jonathan smiled and motioned for me to take a seat at a table. "And then we realised it also helped us turn tables quicker if we could offer an alternative place to carry on drinking and chatting once people had finished eating."

"That's great," I said, panicking. Why couldn't the conversation have ended when they said they weren't looking for any artwork at the moment? I had the feeling I'd wandered into quicksand and was sinking fast.

"In the restaurant we display one artist's work for three months," Jonathan went on, "but in here we change artists every week."

"It's a logistical nightmare." Ollie laughed. "But it keeps us on our toes."

"I'll bet." I looked around, trying to keep my nerves under control.

"We should probably be honest." Jonathan glanced at Ollie. "We have a running joke about Adam."

I felt my eyebrows dart upwards.

"He's the one that got away," Ollie leaned in and told me quietly. They exchanged another look and shared a laugh. I smiled awkwardly.

"Sorry," Jonathan said. "We're making you uncomfortable, aren't we? You're his girlfriend, right? The one from the reality show?"

"Yes," I said, trying not to show any emotion. I didn't think it would go down well if I said that I was his ex who'd swiped a load of pictures when he kicked me out.

"Adam's the only artist who ever turned us down," Ollie said. "We never really got over it."

"He was also one of our favourites," Jonathan confided. "We liked him as a person and we loved his photographs."

"And then he ditched us!" Ollie chimed in. "Didn't even reply to our emails."

"So we discussed him a lot!" Jonathan said. "It became a joke with us: what we'd say if he ever came crawling back."

"I'm sorry," I said. "It must have seemed really unprofessional."

"We thought he must have got a better offer, but we're well connected in the art world and we never heard anything about him."

"It was a personal matter," I told them, feeling they were owed an explanation. "A tragedy in the family. He gave up photography for a while."

They nodded and looked at each other again.

"We have a standard contract for artists," Ollie told me. "But for you we'd have one more condition."

I nodded and he continued.

"We'd each like a picture."

"That's it?" I asked, disappointed that it wasn't the sort of thing that I could withdraw the deal over.

"When Adam cancelled on us, I was mostly annoyed that I'd missed out on the chance to get one of his photos," Jonathan said.

"I don't think that will be a problem," I told them.

"Great."

"When would you display them?" I asked, hoping the waiting list would be long enough for me to think of a good excuse and wriggle out of the crazy idea.

"Hard to say," Ollie said. "We've got quite a lot lined up but we try and keep things pretty flexible in the bar. It might be a couple of months."

"That's fine," I told him. That bought me a bit of time.

"We've got a garage out the back that we use for storage, if you want to leave them there. We've got plenty of space at the moment."

"That would be great," I said. I wasn't sure what I would do with them otherwise. In a couple of months, Adam might have calmed down and I could tell him about it. He might be happy about it. And if not, I'd just come and get them back and make up an excuse.

"I can get you a copy of the contract now," Ollie said. "We'll just need Adam's signature on it."

"Of course." My hands were suddenly clammy and I felt my sweat glands jump into action.

"We'd need to talk about the price. A lot of new artists either under- or over-value their work, so we like to have a say in the price. If our price points don't match up, then we tend to part ways with artists."

"I'm sure we could come to an agreement," I said, doubting we'd ever get that far.

"We display the photos for a week and then at the end of the week you can come and pick up any that didn't sell – and the money for those that did," Jonathan told me.

"That sounds good," I said, standing when Jonathan and Ollie did.

"We have to get back to the chef now, but we'll get Stephanie to help you unload the pictures and give you the contract. You can fax or email it back to us. Leave your details with Stephanie and we'll be in touch."

I thanked them and we walked back to the restaurant together. The dishonesty left me feeling uneasy. I told myself that, with everything that had gone on, I was bound to have a crazy moment here and there. But I knew that wasn't really an excuse for what I'd done.

Hannah Ellis

Chapter 35

"Is Hailey here?" Max asked when I walked into Dad's house on Sunday.

"No, she's at home," I told him. He sighed in disappointment and disappeared up the stairs.

"What a welcome," I said, hugging Kerry.

"It's just the age, I'm afraid. Big sisters aren't that cool any more!"

"Obviously. Where's Dad?"

"Hiding up in the study. Do you need him?"

"No." I followed her into the kitchen. "How are you guys?"

"Same as ever. Surviving! How are you doing?"

"Hovering somewhere between not very good and terrible…"

She gave me a sympathetic look and poured me a coffee from the pot.

"Did you manage to talk to Adam?"

"I was there yesterday, but he won't let me see the girls. We had an argument and he told me to get the rest of my stuff and get out. I don't know what to do. I understand that he's angry with me, but I can't believe he's keeping me from the girls."

Kerry took a seat at the kitchen table and pulled a chair out for me. I sank heavily into it.

"You probably won't remember," she told me

softly. "But when you were about five, you ended up in hospital with pneumonia. Your dad rang me to say they were taking you into intensive care and I left work and rushed over to the hospital. When I got there I made the mistake of telling the nurse that I was your dad's girlfriend. She told me that only parents were allowed in to see you…"

She paused and her eyes welled up with tears. "I wanted to punch her," she went on. "I'd been with your dad for almost two years and you spent most weekends and holidays with us. I'd been up at night with you and looked after you when you were sick, and suddenly this stupid woman made me feel like I was nobody."

I'd never heard this story, and I listened intently as Kerry recalled it.

"I waited for three hours in the hospital café until the nurses changed shift and then I told the next nurse that I was your stepmum and I'd just nipped out for a coffee. She let me straight in. At that point I think I really would have knocked out anyone who told me I couldn't see you." Kerry shook her head as though shaking away the memories.

"Thank you," I said, moving to hug her. "You were always such an amazing mum to me and I don't think I ever said thank you."

"Shut up!" she said, sniffing as she pulled away from me. "I'll be blubbing all day!"

I'd never really looked at things from Kerry's point of view. It wasn't that I hadn't appreciated her; I had. I was always grateful that she was in my life. Since I had been looking after the girls, I'd been able to see what the other side of the relationship was like, and I knew I wanted them to be sitting in my kitchen in twenty years telling me their problems. I couldn't let Adam keep me away from them now.

"I need to go," I told Kerry, only halfway through my coffee.

This time when I walked in the door and shouted "hello" the girls came running, nearly knocking me over when they flung themselves at me.

"I missed you so much," I cried, clinging to them and covering them with kisses.

"I knew you'd come back." Emily grinned at me. "Are you staying forever?"

"I've just come for a visit today," I said.

"I want you to stay forever," she said, sticking out her bottom lip.

"I'll stay for a while," I told her with a smile. Adam glared at me from the bottom of the stairs.

"Can I have a quick word with you outside?" he said calmly.

"Can you do some colouring with me?" Emily asked.

"In a minute," I promised. "I just need to talk to Uncle Adam for a minute." I shot Hailey a look and she directed Emily into the living room.

"What are you doing here?" Adam asked me on the doorstep.

"I came to see the girls."

"I told you I don't want you coming over."

"You can't just cut me out of their lives. It's not fair. I have a right to see them."

"You don't, though," he snapped. "You don't have any rights!"

"Please let me have an hour with them," I pleaded. "I'm not just going to walk away from them."

"It's confusing for them," he said.

"Their whole life is confusing! And that's not the reason you don't want me to see them. You're angry with me and you want to hurt me. But you're punishing the girls, and that's not fair." I took a breath and he stayed quiet, pacing in front of me. "Look me in the eyes and tell me that you honestly think it's better for the girls not to see me."

He stopped pacing. Our eyes locked. I watched his anger slip away until there was only pain in his eyes. For the briefest moment, I caught a glimpse of the Adam I'd fallen in love with. An image of him laughing shot through my mind, and I chased it away again. I wished things had worked out differently for us, but there was no point dwelling on it. I had to focus on the girls.

"You can have an hour with them," he agreed before turning and walking away down the drive. I stood and watched him leave, my heart feeling as though it was crumbling in my chest. The man I had loved could barely stand the sight of me.

Pulling myself together, I took a deep breath and slapped on a smile and went to see Emily and Hailey.

When I couldn't stand to be in the house any longer, I hustled the girls outside and down to the playground. I'd never felt as though I could make the house my own with Ruth constantly hovering over me, but somewhere along the way it had crept into my heart and had become mine anyway. Even with the girls' constant chatter, I was still assaulted by a million memories and tormented by the knowledge that I was just visiting. It wasn't my home any more; I'd have to leave soon and go back to living in a lonely room in someone else's house.

I messaged Adam to let him know where we were, worried that he would have me arrested for kidnapping. We had the playground to ourselves and we played around together as though we didn't have a care in the world.

Adam arrived an hour later and told the girls it was time to go. He didn't look at me. I hugged the girls, promising them that I'd see them soon. I waved until they were out of sight and then took a seat on the bench, trying desperately to be brave and focus on the positive – at least he'd let me see the girls.

Hannah Ellis

Chapter 36

The situation with Adam's photos played on my mind all week. Had I gone mad? They weren't my photos to sell and Adam didn't want to sell them. I couldn't figure out if I thought I was doing him a favour or if I secretly enjoyed making him angry. Because he would be furious, I knew that much. Deep down, I think I wanted to get back something of what we'd lost. I'd always wanted him to make a career from selling his photos and, after so long nagging him and getting nowhere, it suddenly felt like I had nothing to lose. Maybe if I'd done this earlier – pushed him into it instead of just making the odd comment – things would have turned out differently for us.

It took a lot of effort to push it from my mind. I decided I'd go back soon, tell them it had been a mistake, and get the photos back. Then I'd be able to forget about the whole thing.

I talked to Adam on Friday and had to bite my tongue to stop myself from blurting out what I'd done. He was curt and monosyllabic on the phone, and my heart broke a little more as we spoke.

He agreed that I could come over on Saturday to spend some time with the girls. He'd be at work, he told me, but he'd let Ruth know to expect me. The phone call left me feeling drained.

Before I set off for Havendon, I called Angela and asked if she and the kids had time to meet up. I wanted to avoid spending too much time in the house when I visited the girls; it felt weird to be there. I missed my chats with Angela too: it would be nice to catch up.

Ruth hugged me when I picked up the girls. I ushered them into my car and we set off on the short drive to Angela's place. The girls chatted incessantly from the moment I picked them up, filling me in on everything I'd missed.

"What will you do?" Angela asked me as we sat on a bench at the playground, watching Emily dangle from the climbing frame. The big kids were at the other side of the field, building a den in the woods. Poor Emily was left to play on her own; the older kids didn't want a baby around them.

"I don't know. I'd like to do my teacher training next year. It would be good to have something to focus on."

"Can you keep living at your friends' place?"

"No." I sighed. "Not really. They won't kick me out, but it's only supposed to be a temporary arrangement. I just can't bring myself to look for anywhere else. The thought of living on my own is so strange. I'll have to start looking for somewhere, but it's going to be hard, financially and emotionally."

"How're things with Adam now?"

"Awful. But at least he's letting me see the girls, so things are better than they were a week ago."

"Things will get easier. I think Adam was just so shocked when you left that he didn't know how to react. He misses you."

Tears filled my eyes and I silently cursed myself for not being able to keep my emotions under control. "At the moment it just seems like he hates me."

"Maybe a bit," she said lightly. "But he still loves you too."

"I'm not so sure about that," I told her, dabbing at my eyes. "Things have been over for a while. It's just hard to admit it. I'm not in love with him any more." I was surprised at how easily the words fell off my tongue. "I feel like I don't really know him any more."

"It's been such a hard time for you all," she said. "It's a shame you can't work things out."

"Have you spoken to him?" I asked.

"No. Not really. I've bumped into him a couple of times at the school gates but he doesn't say much."

"The girls are doing okay, aren't they?" I asked.

"It seems like it. They're both doing well at school and they're always lovely and chatty when I bump into them. They're such good kids."

"Ruth must have stepped in to look after the girls after school," I said, leaping to my feet when Emily fell off the climbing frame, and then sitting again when she brushed herself off and carried on. "I wonder if Adam's working any less. I don't know if he just went to work today to avoid me. He might not be at work at all. Just staying out of the way."

"Stop overthinking everything," she said, patting my knee. "You'll drive yourself mad."

"I think I probably will. That's if I'm not mad already!"

"Have you spoken to Mike since you left?"

"No," I told her. "I dropped a note through his door the day I left, apologising. Adam punched him and I felt terrible about it. I meant to call him, but I haven't got around to it."

"There was a bit of gossip flying around the place after their little punch-up…"

I looked at Angela and exploded with laughter. She joined me, and Emily grinned over at us as we cackled away.

"Poor Mike," I said, wiping my eyes. "I should go and talk to him. He was always a good friend. I didn't mean to drop him in it."

"He knows. He is a good friend. I wish he'd find himself a girlfriend, though."

I rolled my sleeves up and stretched my legs out in the sun, the bout of laughter lifting my spirits. "Did he tell you he's been trying internet dating?"

"Yeah. He was supposed to meet up with someone but he had to cancel due to his black eye."

"Just when I think I couldn't feel any worse!"

"Don't worry about it. I didn't mean to make you feel bad. It's Mike – you know what he's like, he can see the funny side. Adam apologised and everything is fine."

"How did I cause so much drama?" I asked.

"I think Adam can take some of the credit. Anyway, it gave people something to talk about for a few days."

"That's all right, then!" I smiled. "Sometimes my life just seems so surreal. If someone had told me two years ago where I'd be now, I'd have laughed at them. It's like a bad dream that I can't wake up from."

"Ah, but it's not been all bad. Look at the

relationship you have with the girls. It's incredible."

I nodded and my emotions betrayed me again. "I want my Adam back," I said sadly. "How we were before, when it was just the two of us. I miss him. It all seems so unfair."

"I wish I could help," she told me, rubbing my back.

"Thanks. This helps. It's nice to talk to someone properly."

"Any time."

"Can I go and climb trees with the others?" Emily asked then, running over to us. We turned to see Hailey, Imogen and Zac up a tree, waving back at us.

"Come on then," I told her, taking her hand.

I dropped the girls back with Ruth and left before Adam got home. I'd had a nice afternoon with the girls and I didn't want it ruined by running into Adam. We'd no doubt just end up arguing or he'd give me the cold shoulder, and I'd go home feeling even more depressed.

I slowed when I drove by the pub in the village, wondering whether I should pop in and talk to Mike. I was torn between wanting to talk to him and not wanting to give the gossips any more ammunition. The idea of Adam driving past and seeing my car outside the pub also didn't sit well with me. Who knows how he would react to that? I didn't want his macho pride causing Mike more problems.

There was a knock on the window, and I realised I'd stopped the car in my contemplation.

"Hi!" Mike's cheerful voice greeted me as I lowered the window.

"I was just wondering whether I dare come in and talk to you," I told him.

"Probably better not, to be honest."

"That's what I thought. I'm really sorry about everything. I can't believe Adam hit you."

"Don't worry about it," he said, leaning on the car. "I spoke to Adam and it's all sorted out."

"I didn't mean to involve you in our mess."

"I know – don't beat yourself up about it. Are you doing okay?"

"I guess so," I said. "It's all a big mess still."

"It'll all work out in the end."

"I hope so. How's the dating scene?"

"Surprisingly fun," he told me with a grin.

"So you managed to go on your date?"

"Yes, I rearranged it. I told her I was ill. Didn't like to say I had a black eye and had to hide from the world until it faded!"

"So how was it?" I asked. "When are you seeing her again?"

"She was pleasant enough, but I don't think I'll see her again. It was just good to have a night off and do something different. I need to get out more."

"That sounds positive," I told him. "Maybe I should give dating a go."

"I'd better get back to the pub." He smiled and straightened up. "It was nice to see you."

"You too."

On the drive home, I looked out for Adam's car. I don't know why. I thought I might pass him along the way, and I got a bit obsessed by the idea. It made the drive go quickly, but there was no sign of him and I wondered how late he would have to work. Again, the thought popped into my head that he mightn't be working at all, just keeping out of the way until I left.

Angela was right; I needed to stop overthinking things.

Hannah Ellis

Chapter 37

Slowly, my life got back into some sort of routine. I threw myself into work and spent time with the girls on Saturdays while Adam was either at work or staying out of the way, avoiding me. After a month, I still hadn't seen him. Our phone chats were limited to arranging when I could see the girls. I'd been overwhelmed by sadness for a while, mourning the loss of our relationship and all the promise it had once held, but I was gradually starting to look forward, wondering what else life might have in store for me.

Chrissie and Matt had insisted I stay with them. They claimed I was doing them a favour; they could use my rent money for their wedding. I'd gratefully agreed but had set a limit of six months. That would give me time to get back on my feet. I didn't like the idea of living alone at the moment.

"I've been thinking about dating," I told them one evening as we sat in front of the TV, eating Matt's chicken fried rice.

"Really?" Chrissie asked. "So soon?"

"I feel I need to do something proactive," I said with a shrug. "I wasted a lot of time in a stale relationship. It's time to move on. Anyway, I'm not talking about jumping into a serious relationship, just having a bit of fun. I hear internet dating is fun and easy: swipe left if you like them, and right if you don't?"

I watched in amusement as Matt shook his head, trying desperately to swallow his mouthful of food so he could impart whatever wisdom he had for me. "No need." He waved his fork at me. "I've got someone for you!"

"Oh God!" Chrissie sighed. "Who? Don't set her up with one of your weird friends!"

"Which of my friends is weird?" He shook his head. "Don't answer that! Lee who I go to the football with. I went to school with him. Nice guy, recently divorced."

"No!" Chrissie said firmly.

"I'm only twenty-nine," I reminded Matt. "Surely I can find someone who hasn't been married yet?"

"I don't know," he mused. "You're getting on a bit. It might be slim pickings!"

Chrissie gave him a quick slap on the arm and I carried on eating. "I'll just try the swiping thing," I told them.

"What about Damian?" Chrissie said, looking at Matt.

"From my uni crew?" he asked, screwing his nose up. "He's a bit boring, isn't he?"

"No, he's lovely," Chrissie said. "And he's nice-looking."

"I don't think I mind boring guys," I told them. "No drama would be good."

"I'll give him a call," Matt said.

"Just be subtle," Chrissie warned him. "Ring him for a chat and drop it into conversation that I've got a hot friend staying with us … But don't say why she's staying! Play it cool."

"Hey!" He laughed. "Matchmaking is a talent of mine. I don't need any help from you."

I laughed. This was probably a bad idea but it would be good to have something else to think about.

"I'm going to talk to the head tomorrow," I said, feeling suddenly confident. "I'm going to ask if I can do teacher training next year. I need to stop being scared of Jean Stoke and just tell her what I want!"

"Go for it!" Chrissie beamed at me.

When I walked into school the next morning, Jean Stoke was standing in the hallway, and all my courage and determination ran in the opposite direction.

"Morning, Miss Mitchell," she greeted me loudly.

"Morning!" I managed a quick smile and continued past her.

"Could you come to my office?" she asked. "I need a quick chat with you."

"Of course," I said. "Now?"

"Take off your coat and get settled," she said. "I'll see you in a few minutes."

I nodded and hurried off to the classroom, feeling like a naughty child. I should just ask about the teacher training anyway, I decided. Although that wouldn't be appropriate if she fires me …

"Come in," she told me when I knocked weakly at her door. "I want to talk to you about your contract for the next school year." She indicated the chair opposite her. "I wondered if you'd be interested in going back to full-time?"

I was surprised. I thought I'd have to beg for another contract. "Yes," I told her. "I think that would be good. I've been meaning to talk to you about it, actually."

"And what about your teacher training? When you started with us it was with a view to doing your teacher training here too. I know you've had a difficult time in your personal life, but I wonder what your plans are now."

"That's still my plan. There's just been so much going on at home…"

"I have to say, I was very impressed watching you teach when Sarah was away, and Sarah only ever has good things to say about you. With your training and experience, I can offer you a salaried teacher training programme to start in September. You'd be a qualified teacher in a year."

"Thank you," I said, surprised but happy at the offer. It's always nice when you don't have to beg for what you want.

"I presume you'll need some time to think it over, but I would appreciate an answer soon."

"Yes!" A smile spread over my face. Something in my life was finally going right. "I'd love to. I accept."

"You don't need time to think about it?"

"No. It's a wonderful offer and I'd love to take it. Thank you."

"Perfect." She smiled at me. "I know we had a conversation about your commitment to the job, but I presume that's all behind us now…"

"Definitely. I'm fully committed." Sadly, I had the feeling that work would become my main focus in life, but at least I had something to concentrate on while my personal life was in disarray.

Beneath these Stars

*****

Chrissie and Matt insisted on taking me out to celebrate. We ended up going from their kitchen to Dylan's pub after I told them the news. It was Friday night and I decided I'd earned a drink or two.

"Congratulations!" Dylan said when he sat down with us. "It's about time you had some good news. Any word on Adam?"

"He hates me and would happily never see me again, but he's letting me see the girls – which is as much as I can hope for at the moment."

When I left Mrs Stoke's office, I'd wanted to speak to Adam, to share my news with him. It was an annoying echo of our life together: he'd randomly pop into my head, making everything feel bittersweet. It had felt weird not to be able to call and give him my good news. I reminded myself that Adam hadn't wanted me to do my teacher training; it was part of the reason I'd left. Really, I should be angry with him, but I couldn't quite manage it. I just needed to keep looking forward.

"He'll calm down," Matt said. "He's just pissed off, but he'll come around."

"At least he's letting you see the girls," Dylan said.

"I know. It's so weird, though, just seeing them once a week. Let's not talk about this. Are we going to eat here? I'm hungry."

"I'm not really hungry yet," Matt said. "Let's wait a while."

"That might be the most shocking thing I've ever heard you say," I told him teasingly.

"We can't stay long," Chrissie said. "We've

promised to nip over to my mum's."

"Really? I thought you were going to help me celebrate. You'll stay out with me, won't you, Dylan?"

"Well, I'll be over there at the other side of the bar," he told me. "I'm only having a break before it gets busy."

"Don't look so upset," Matt said. "We'll stay for a bit." He stood up and waved to someone across the pub, then walked off.

Chrissie leaned over to me. "I'm so sorry," she said. "Don't hate me. It was Matt's idea…"

"What was?"

"I think I'd better get back to work," Dylan said, winking then slipping away.

"What's going on?" I asked, looking around to see Matt coming towards us, chatting away to the guy at his side. "Oh no." I looked back at Chrissie. "No, no, no!"

She winced, and mouthed another apology.

"This is Damian," Matt told me cheerfully when the two of them joined us at the table. "We went to uni together."

Chapter 38

I was soon left alone with Damian, and was torn between being angry at my friends for setting me up and thinking I should make the most of it and try and have a good night. Damian was reasonably attractive. There wasn't anything off-putting about his appearance, anyway: he had short dark hair and was dressed in jeans and a polo shirt. I'd been saying I wanted to move on, and this seemed to be my chance to take the first step. Maybe it was a positive thing. I should probably stop trying to catch Dylan's eye and focus on my date.

"Matt said you'd just got a promotion?" Damian said, taking a sip of his beer.

"Yes. Kind of. I'll be doing teacher training, which I've been wanting to do for ages."

He set his beer down and laughed. "What's the saying? 'Those who can, do; those who can't, teach'?"

Stunned, I put a hand to my mouth, sure that I was about to splutter wine all over him. Which maybe I should have done. Hurriedly, I swallowed my wine. Had he really just said that? I opened my mouth but had no idea what to say.

"Sorry! It's a joke I have with Matt. I like to wind him up."

"Right," I said, glancing at the bar and wondering whether to just stand up and shout to Dylan that he needed to save me. I took a breath and decided not to judge Damian on one stupid comment. Perhaps he was nervous. "What do you do?" I asked, trying to move past his comment.

"I work in online marketing," he told me.

At this rate, I'd be drunk in no time. I couldn't seem to stop putting my wine glass to my lips and it was almost empty already. "What does that involve, then?" I asked, trying to keep the conversation flowing without really caring what his job entailed.

"You know those creepy ads that pop up on the internet and somehow know what you want or like? I run those campaigns. I work for a fashion company so I figure out who to target and where to place our ads."

"That sounds interesting." I had nothing to say and I was losing interest in Damian quickly. Why did I think dating would be fun? This was not fun. I needed to find some common ground – and quickly. "What do you do in your spare time?" I asked, desperate for him to redeem himself.

"I'm really into online gaming," he told me happily. My mouth managed to smile while I cried inconsolably on the inside. Why on earth did Chrissie think we would be a good match? Next time I would try online dating and at least I'd only have myself to blame if I chose awful dates. That's if I ever dated again. Maybe there's only one love for everyone – and I'd had mine with Adam. I was probably destined to be alone forever now. My mind drifted to my early dates with Adam, and I felt my fixed smile start to fail me.

"Sorry," I said, standing and interrupting Damian, who was in the middle of telling me about his online gaming friends around the world. "I'm going to get another drink. Do you want one?"

"I'm okay at the moment," he said, holding up his half-full pint.

I marched to the bar and glared at Dylan when I got there. "Please help me," I said.

He winced. "Not going well?"

"No! I'm going to kill Matt."

"I told him it was a bad idea."

"I'm just so bored!" I complained. "I can't be bothered to meet new people. It's too much effort. And this guy's definitely not for me. How can I politely get out of this?"

Dylan handed me another glass of wine. "Has he been telling you all about himself?" he asked.

"Yeah. That's why I've been drinking so fast. It's all very boring."

Dylan leaned closer to me with a cheeky smile. "Maybe it's time you told him a bit about yourself…"

"What do you mean?"

"Tell him about your life … Be honest with him." He grinned. "I bet you can scare him off pretty quick if you want to!"

"Dylan!" I leaned over the bar to give him a shove. He walked away from me, laughing, and I took a sip of my wine before turning to look at Damian.

"It must be nice, knowing the owners of a bar," Damian commented when I re-joined him.

"It has its perks," I agreed. "I'm afraid I can't stay long tonight. I've got to be up early tomorrow."

"Got something fun planned?"

"A day out with my kids," I told him casually. "Well, not my kids – my ex-boyfriend's kids, but we have a sort of joint custody arrangement since we split up. It's a long story, and probably not something I should bore you with on a first date!" I smiled, finally enjoying myself. Damian squirmed in his seat. "What were you telling me about the guy in Australia ... the one you play the computer game with?"

He stuttered a little before regaling me further with tales of his online interactions. His heart wasn't in it, I could tell. Dylan was right, he scared easily. Far too easily for me.

It was still early when I walked into Matt and Chrissie's house.

"Hi!" Chrissie called from the living room.

"Home already?" Matt shouted. "What happened?"

"I'm not talking to you," I shouted back, kicking my shoes off and heading for the stairs. "Either of you. Ever again!"

"It was all Matt's idea," Chrissie called after me. I managed a smile when I heard Chrissie telling Matt off and him attempting to defend himself. I decided an early night was in order and curled up in bed. My re-entry into the world of dating had left me disappointed. It wasn't as much fun as I'd hoped.

Chapter 39

When I arrived in Havendon the next day, Adam was in the kitchen. He was busy cleaning up milk, which was all over the table and dripping onto the floor. Tension radiated from him and I could hear Emily crying upstairs. I would've rung the doorbell if I'd known Adam was home.

"Hailey!" he shouted, glancing up but not acknowledging me. "Help your sister get changed. Please!"

"Everything okay?" I asked.

"Fine," he said, squeezing out a sodden cloth into the sink.

"I thought you'd be at work."

"Nope," he said fiercely. "Sorry!"

"I'll go and help Emily," I told him calmly. I found her standing beside a pile of wet clothes, her knickers on back to front, attempting to put a T-shirt on inside out. "Here, I'll help you," I said and pulled off the T-shirt to start again.

"I spilt milk everywhere," she told me sadly. "And Uncle Adam's cross with me."

"Don't worry," I said. "He's just tired."

"Can you stay forever?" she asked, while I pulled a pair of jeans on her and searched for matching socks.

"I've just come to see you for a while," I said,

unable to look her in the eye. "What shall we do today?"

"Can we go swimming?" she asked.

I frowned. "I didn't bring my swimming things." Truthfully, they were probably still here, but I didn't feel like swimming. I liked to be at the pool when it opened on a Saturday, otherwise it would be heaving. "It's nice and sunny. We could play outside, or go to the playground?"

"Okay," she agreed and held my hand. We went to Hailey's room to see what she was doing.

"Morning," I said, pushing the door open.

"Hi!" Hailey grinned at me and pulled her earphones out. "I'm so glad you're here. Uncle Adam is being a nightmare!" She sounded like a teenager, and it made me smile.

"Do you want to come to the playground with us?"

"Yes! Anything to get away from him!" She jumped up and gave me a hug then we clattered downstairs.

The girls put their shoes on. I stuck my head into the kitchen, to find Adam filling up the washing machine. "I'm going to take the girls out for a walk, if that's okay?" I asked tentatively.

"Okay," he said without looking up. I thought I heard him mumble "thanks" as I turned back to the girls.

We stopped at the village shop and bought drinks and snacks, then we spent some time at the playground before going for a walk over the hills and through the woods. The girls were happy and energetic – and oblivious to my attempt to keep them out of the house for as long as possible. The house was tidy when we got back, but there was no sign of Adam. We ate sandwiches at the kitchen table and played card games for a while.

When the girls went out to play in the garden, I crept upstairs. Adam was fast asleep on the bed. I stood watching him. He looked so stressed – even while he slept. His jaw was covered in stubble. Once, I'd thought stubble made him look rugged and roguish, but now it just made him look worn. He didn't look like someone who'd decided not to shave, but someone who didn't have the time, the energy, the motivation. He looked like somebody who didn't care enough to look after himself.

Suddenly his eyes opened, as though he'd sensed me watching him. I stayed in the doorway, unable to move or pretend that I'd been doing anything other than watching him sleep.

He wiped at his mouth when he sat up and then glanced at his watch. "Sorry," he muttered. "Do you need to go?"

"No," I said. "Just wanted to check you were okay."

He swung his legs off the bed and rubbed his eyes. "Sorry about this morning. Mum's had flu all week so it's been a bit hectic."

"The girls told me she was ill. You should've called. I would've helped."

"It was fine." He shook his head, standing up. "Angela helped with the girls after school. It's just the housework that defeated me."

"I would've had the girls after school," I told him, angry that he'd not called me, and jealous that Angela had been looking after the girls.

"I didn't want to bother you," he said flatly. "I was

going to take the girls to the cinema today. We should probably get going. Have they had lunch?"

"I made them sandwiches."

"Thanks," he said, already halfway down the stairs.

I followed him down. "I guess I'll go then."

"Thanks for coming over," he said without looking at me. I slipped out of the back door and said goodbye to the girls before I left. The drive home was torturous: I was angry, certain that Adam was doing his best to keep me out of their lives just to spite me. Surely there was a better way for us to manage things. I wanted to help him. I wanted him to call me when they needed something. It wasn't enough for me to see them for a few hours on Saturdays.

*****

My bad mood lingered through the next week. I thought I'd been making positive steps in my life, but I suddenly felt that I was drowning again. I hadn't slept well on Wednesday night and pressed snooze on my alarm a few times too many on Thursday morning.

When I ran into school just before the bell, Jean Stoke happened to be walking down the corridor. I slammed on the brakes and tried to act casually, giving her a quick smile when I passed. People started work at different times; did she really remember when everyone should arrive? Probably. I was in before the kids were, I consoled myself, so it could have been worse. The fact that I should have been in to set up the classroom was no big deal, surely.

I slipped into the classroom just as the bell rang and the corridor filled with kids.

"I'm so sorry," I told Sarah, who was sitting at her desk. I pulled off my coat and shoved it into the cupboard in the corner with my handbag.

"Don't worry about it. I set everything up."

"Thanks," I said, catching my breath. "I bumped into Jean in the corridor. Just my luck!"

"It's not like you to be late. Everything okay?"

"Fine," I told her. "I'm just tired."

"I know that feeling!"

I spent the first half of the morning helping the children with group work on mini-beasts. It was a fun topic and the kids responded well. It was easy to get them excited and inquisitive when it came to creepy-crawlies. The morning went fast and it was break-time before I knew it. Once the kids had run out to play outside, Sarah and I got on with straightening out the classroom.

After ten minutes, it had started to drizzle. I glanced at my watch. The kids would be back any minute. I was about to return my phone to the cupboard when it buzzed. It was an unknown number. I frowned as I recognised the area code to be that of Havendon.

"Lucy, it's Mike," the voice told me as I accepted the call.

"Hi – how are you?"

"I didn't know if you knew..." He trailed off, his voice full of uncertainty.

"Knew what?"

"Hailey's missing."

My heart immediately started to pound as though it might crash through my chest. "No one's seen her since last night."

"I didn't know," I said, my voice sounding strange

in my head. "Thanks for calling. I'm coming now."

I pressed end and tried to get my brain to function faster.

"What's happened?" Sarah asked.

"Hailey's missing."

"Okay," she said calmly. "I'm sure she's fine. Go over there and find out what's happening." She retrieved my coat and handbag from the cupboard and passed them to me. "Remember to breathe, and drive safely."

"Thanks."

"Keep me updated."

"I will." I ran down the empty corridor and was almost at the main entrance, pulling my arms into my jacket, when Jean Stoke stepped out of a classroom and called my name. "I'm sorry, I have to go," I told her, unwilling to stop and explain.

"Miss Mitchell…"

"I can't talk, I have to go."

"Miss Mitchell, if you leave now…"

"I have to," I shouted back to her in a panic. "Stuff the job. I have to go." I ran through the rain to the car.

The drive seemed to take longer than it ever had before. Every traffic light was against me and the traffic was worse than I'd ever known it. My mind went into overdrive, imagining where Hailey could be. What could have happened to her? And why hadn't Adam called me? What if Mike hadn't called? When would I have been told?

As if on cue, my phone rang. It was Ruth.

"Has she turned up?" I asked.

"There's no sign of her. Half the village is out looking. I don't know what to do."

"I only just heard. I'm on my way. We'll find her. Everything will be fine."

"Adam kept saying she'd turn up, but there's no sign of her. He's just called the police!" Ruth sounded frantic, and the worry in her voice made me panic even more.

"I won't be long," I said, ending the call and pressing my foot harder on the accelerator.

Hannah Ellis

Chapter 40

The drizzle had changed to pouring rain by the time I pulled up at the house. A police car had taken my space so I couldn't park on the driveway. My stomach lurched. I ran towards the house, not sure what I would walk into.

A policeman sat at the kitchen table, Ruth beside him. Adam was pacing and stopped when he saw me.

"Where is she?" I cried.

"We don't know," Ruth said, getting up.

On impulse I ran upstairs, passing a policeman on the landing and running into Hailey's room. Somehow, I expected her to be on her bed with her earphones in, listening to music.

Ruth was waiting at the bottom of the stairs when I hurried back down. "The police just got here. I'm sure they'll find her soon."

"They will," I told her, as confidently as I could manage. I gave her a hug and she sobbed quietly into my shoulder.

We moved back into the kitchen and I glared at Adam. He looked worn and weary, worry etched over his face. "When did you last see her?" I asked tearfully. I sounded accusing, but I couldn't help it: I was so worried.

Finally, he met my gaze. "I looked in on her before

I went to bed. When I got up this morning, she was gone."

"Did you check the garage?" I asked frantically. "She likes to go in there sometimes."

"Of course I checked the bloody garage!" Adam snapped at me. "I've looked everywhere. She's not here. I've called her friends and no one's seen her. I didn't know what to do."

"You could have called *me*," I said scornfully. "Why didn't you?"

He turned away from me to look out of the window.

"You're here now," Ruth said, lowering herself into a chair. "That's all that matters." She looked suddenly frail and I went over to her, resting a reassuring hand on her shoulder.

"I have a few more questions," the policeman said calmly. I noticed the photos of Hailey laid out on the table beside his papers, and my heart raced. "It would be really helpful for us to know if any of Hailey's things are missing."

He escorted Adam and me up to Hailey's room. When Adam looked nervously around the room, I strode past him. "She wouldn't run away," I stated, sure that was what we were trying to establish.

Adam shuffled to the window. "Maybe she did," he muttered.

"No! She wouldn't." I was sure of it.

I yanked open her drawers and rifled through her familiar clothes. Nothing seemed to be missing. The wardrobe was its usual mess, and the desk was scattered with her things. I couldn't find any clues and I felt the policeman's eyes on me. The sight of the photo on Hailey's bedside table made me burst into tears. I picked it up. It was a family photo: Hailey and Emily with Becky and Will.

"She wouldn't leave without this," I cried, holding it out to show Adam. He crossed the room and wrapped his arms around me.

"We'll find her," he told me through his tears. Part of me felt like clinging to him, while another part wanted to punch him. He was supposed to look after them. It wasn't his fault, I told myself. He loved the girls and he'd always done his best for them.

"She didn't run away, though," I spluttered. "I know she didn't. Where is she, Adam? What's happened to her?"

Adam looked down at me, fear and worry in his eyes. "I don't know."

Satisfied that nothing was missing, the policeman led us back down to the kitchen where Ruth was making tea with shaky hands. "I just need something to do," she told us.

The policeman asked for the names of Hailey's friends and any places we thought she might go, explaining that once his colleague had finished searching the property, they would start looking further afield. He was scribbling on his notepad when something caught my eye.

"Did you move my cardigan?" I asked Adam. "The big green one that's always in the kitchen?" I used to leave it hanging on the back of the kitchen door for Emily's little trips to look at the stars. It was entirely possible that Ruth or Adam had moved it, but I wanted to check. They looked blankly at me. "There was a cardigan on the back of this door," I said. "Did you move it?"

They shook their heads.

"And you looked in the garage?" I asked Adam again.

He nodded.

I heard him call my name as I ran out of the back door into the rain, but I didn't look back. I had to find Hailey.

The garage was unlocked.

Inside, the air was cool and everything was still. I bit my lip when there was no sign of Hailey. I'd imagined her sitting on the table, swinging her legs and looking sheepish. Storage boxes were piled at one end of the airy room and Adam's photos stood propped against the walls. Everything was as it should be. I was about to walk out again when I noticed the broken picture.

Crossing the room, I saw it was a photo of me, taken when I'd first started dating Adam. He'd given it to me and we'd hung it in the living room at our old house when we moved in together. We'd never got around to putting it up when we moved here. It had been condemned to the garage, gathering dust. In the picture, I sat on a bench in the distance, oblivious to Adam snapping the photo as I basked in the warmth of the sun.

The glass was cracked and tiny shards glistened on the floor. I was shocked at the sight of Adam's camera lying broken among the glass – his old favourite Nikon, the one I'd left out on the bed when I'd come to pick up my things.

"Lucy."

I turned at the sound of his voice. He stood in the doorway, his hair damp.

"What happened to your camera?" I asked quietly.

"I-I was angry. I just missed you so mu—" He stopped at a sound – a shuffle of movement that drew our attention to the corner of the room. Quickly, Adam pushed boxes away from the long wooden table. I gasped when I saw Hailey sitting under the table, hugging her knees, my green cardigan wrapped around her. Relief washed through me in a torrent, and I found myself torn between wanting to shake her and wanting to hug her and never let go.

"Oh, thank God," I whispered. I was beside her in a shot and squeezed her tightly when she emerged from under the table. Her face was red and blotchy from crying.

"I'm sorry!" she cried, clinging to me. "I'm so sorry."

"What happened?" I asked, glancing at Adam. Relief flooded his face.

"I woke up early and came in here," Hailey explained tearfully. "I fell asleep, and when I woke up I could hear Adam and Gran shouting and I got scared, so I hid. I was going to come out, but then I saw the police car…" She buried her head in my chest as she sobbed. Adam came to hug us both.

"It's okay," he told her soothingly. "Just as long as you're okay."

Hailey tensed and wriggled out of my embrace, hitting out at Adam.

"It's not okay!" she screamed. "I hate you. I hate living here. I hate you!"

Adam stood stunned. I pulled Hailey away from him. "Calm down," I said firmly. She curled into me again and I stroked her hair, murmuring soothing words.

"It's horrible here," she told me when she caught her breath. "He's so sad all the time, and we never do anything fun."

I looked at Adam. His face was ashen and his haunted eyes were too much for me to bear.

A policeman stepped into the doorway.

"I take it you're Hailey?" he asked, his mouth breaking into a kind smile.

Chapter 41

When I led Hailey in through the back door, Ruth burst into tears and rushed across the kitchen to embrace her.

I was watching Adam. He looked as though he'd walked through hell.

Hailey cried some more, cocooned in Ruth's arms. When she looked up, her gaze landed on Adam. "I'm sorry," she said, looking concerned. Now that she was calm she must have realised how much her outburst had hurt him.

He stood up and drew her to him for a hug. "It's okay. Just don't ever disappear on me again." He took a step back, his hands on her shoulders, his voice trembling. "Promise me."

"I promise," she sobbed. "I'm sorry. I didn't mean to."

Adam hugged her again. The policeman spoke into a walkie-talkie, telling someone Hailey had turned up. Ruth fussed over Hailey, tearfully asking where she'd been and why.

While Adam spoke to the police, I took Hailey into the living room and cuddled up with her on the couch. Ruth left to collect Emily. Apparently Angela had taken her over to her place before the police arrived, not wanting to scare her more than necessary.

"I don't hate Uncle Adam," Hailey finally said to me.

Adam saw the policemen out, then came to join us on the couch once they'd left.

"I don't hate you," Hailey told him, getting tearful again. "I'm sorry I shouted at you."

"It's all right," he assured her. "I'm sorry too. I'll make sure things get better, okay?"

Hailey nodded and leaned into him.

"I love you so much," he whispered to her, his eyes welling up. "I'll fix things. I promise."

"I love you too," she replied.

I left them to get drinks and when Adam joined me in the kitchen moments later, I automatically hugged him. I needed the comfort after the emotional morning.

"Are you okay?" I asked when he moved away from me.

"No," he said miserably and buried his head in his hands at the kitchen table. It was hard to see him so defeated. He was always the one telling me that everything would be okay. It had always annoyed me before; it made my concerns feel trivial. Ironically, I now had the overwhelming desire to tell him everything would be okay.

"Why didn't you tell me she was missing?" I asked instead.

He shook his head. "I don't know. I should've done. I've messed everything up. Everything I do is wrong."

I couldn't quite bring myself to disagree. "You have to make things better for the girls."

"I know!" His head snapped up at me. "I know

that."

"I can help you. If you'll let me."

His eyes softened, pleading with me. "Come home."

I pulled my hand away when he reached for it. "I can't."

"Why not?" He spoke quickly. "Everything was better when you were here. We all miss you so much. Can't we try again?"

"You never even saw that there was a problem between us, so how could things be any better than before?"

"I can see it now," he told me. "After my dad died, and Becky, I just got so used to things being awful that it started to seem normal. But I see it now. I can make things better."

The kettle boiled. I got up to make drinks, trying to figure out what to say. "I've moved on," I said, sounding cooler than I'd intended. "At least, I'm starting to. I don't want to go back. Things are finally starting to feel normal for me: my job's going well and I'm getting on with my care—." Then I stopped abruptly and stared at Adam, stricken.

"What?"

I dumped tea bags out of the mugs and into the sink, remembering the look on Jean Stoke's face when I ran out of school that morning. "I probably lost my job today," I told Adam wearily. Would things ever go right for me?

He looked puzzled. "Because of Hailey? I'm sure, given the circumstances…"

"It doesn't matter," I said, placing a mug of tea in front of him. "It really doesn't. Let's just think about the girls. I want to see them more. And I want you to be able to call me when there's a problem, or for anything to do with the girls."

"It's not that simple," he told me seriously. "I wasn't trying to shut you out to hurt you. I just can't stand to be around you if we're not together. It kills me." His honesty took me by surprise.

"We'll have to figure something out," I said.

"Okay. I'll try."

I couldn't bring myself to look at him. Instead, I busied myself making hot chocolate for Hailey and then sat with her until Emily burst through the door a while later. She jumped into my arms and I hugged her tightly.

Ruth made us sandwiches and then left us alone. The four of us cuddled on the couch watching films all afternoon, then ordered pizzas for dinner. It was cosy and relaxed and I wished we could always be like that.

I enjoyed the routine of putting the girls to bed. It was something I missed, settling them down for the night with stories and cuddles.

"Adam?" He jumped when I walked into the kitchen to find him clearing up the dinner things. "What happened in the garage? With the picture and your camera?"

He looked thoughtful. "I was annoyed that you left it out on my bed. It was like you were still nagging me about it even after you'd left. I was just going to store it in the garage but…" He paused, looking sheepish. "I threw it across the room instead!"

"You win, then," I said, unable to do anything but make light of it. "You can't take photos without a camera!"

A smile flashed across his face and quickly disappeared. "There were too many memories." He looked at me earnestly. "That's why I didn't want to take photos any more. Every time I looked at the camera it brought back all these memories of my dad and Becky. And it felt wrong, somehow, for me to carry on playing around with my camera when they were dead."

"I'm sorry," I said, surprised by him. "I never understood why you gave it up." Thoughts of the photos I'd taken to The White Kitchen sprang to mind and I wanted to tell him what I'd done. I hesitated too long, not wanting to argue when we were getting on.

"It doesn't matter," he said, straightening up. He seemed embarrassed now by what he'd told me. If only he'd been able to open up to me sooner.

"I'd better go." I pushed my feet into my boots in the hallway. "The girls are fast asleep."

"Thanks for coming over."

I picked my coat up. "Next time there's a problem…"

"I know. I'll call you."

I went to hug him, and immediately wished I hadn't. Everything about him was so familiar. He held me tightly and I breathed in his scent until I felt the tears threatening to fall. It was hard to let go. "I'll come over at the weekend?" I said, my hand on the door.

"Good," he said. "See you then."

I finally managed to meet his eyes. Smiling weakly, I walked out and left him again.

Hannah Ellis

Chapter 42

"If you explain the situation, I'm sure she'd reconsider." Sarah looked at me sympathetically as I sat on a kid's chair, my head in my hands.

I was drained from my time in Jean Stoke's office. She'd called me in first thing and told me that she wouldn't be able to keep me on the following school year, either as a teaching assistant or in the teacher training programme. It was no surprise. I knew when I left the previous day I would lose my job. I barely had the energy to care.

"I just couldn't bring myself to argue," I told Sarah. "Besides, she's right – there's always something. It seemed like time to bow out gracefully. There was a limit to her patience and I definitely pushed her to it."

"I can't believe you won't be here next year," Sarah said sadly, taking a seat beside me.

"I know. I'll miss you."

"New kids *and* a new TA. That's depressing enough. Now you won't even be in the building."

"Jean said she'd give me a reference at least. Maybe it's a good thing. A change might be good for me. A fresh start."

"Will you still do teacher training?"

"I don't know," I said, stretching out my legs. "I was happy about doing it here, where I already knew everyone. It seemed so natural and easy."

"You should still do it."

"It just feels like my whole life is a mess. Maybe I should pack a bag and go travel the world."

Sarah smiled at me and I laughed. "Except I have no money, so I guess I wouldn't get far."

"You could try hitch-hiking?" she suggested.

"Hitch-hike my way around the world? Now that could be interesting!" I sighed. "I don't know what I'm going to do. I need to think of something, though."

"At least Hailey's okay," Sarah said. "Kids really know how to scare you, don't they?"

"I was petrified," I said. "My mind wandered to a hundred horrible scenarios. Thank God she's fine."

"Adam must have been out of his mind. Are things any better with you and him?"

"I think so. He still wants us to get back together, though, which makes things hard."

"It was never going to be easy to stay friends after breaking up, was it?"

"I know," I said, peering into the hall at the kids milling around. "I just don't know what to do."

"You'll figure it out," she said kindly. "Are the kids here already?"

"They are," I said, glancing at my watch. I opened the door and let the rabble in.

My mind definitely wasn't on my job. I smiled at the kids when they spoke to me, but hardly registered what they said. Try as I might, I just couldn't focus. I was glad it was Friday.

I decided I'd head into Manchester after work and walk around the shops. A bit of window shopping might be fun. It would be better than moping around Chrissie and Matt's place anyway; that was doing me no good at all.

My phone rang just as I parked the car in the multi-storey, and I was surprised to hear Mike's voice when I answered.

"Please tell me there're no more emergencies today?" I said.

"Only a very minor one," he said, chuckling. "It's a bit awkward. Don't tease me…"

"Don't make me promise that!"

"Okay, fine! I drove into Manchester for a date, but she's just rung and cancelled."

"Oh no," I said. "I'm sorry."

"Thanks for not laughing. I just thought, since I'm already in the city… if you're not doing anything, maybe we could meet up. Grab some dinner?"

"Oh!" I leaned back against the seat of the car.

"If you're busy or whatever, it's fine. I just thought you might take pity on me."

"I'm not busy," I told him slowly. "I'm actually in the city already. Dinner would be good."

"Great. Where are you? I'll come and meet you."

When I got off the phone it was with mixed feelings. I'd always enjoyed Mike's company, but guilt niggled at me. I almost felt like I was going behind Adam's back; like I was cheating on him. I got out of the car and shook off my guilt. It was a stupid thought for a number of reasons. First, Adam and I weren't together any more so how could I cheat on him? And second, it was just dinner with a friend; it wasn't a date. It was just Mike. My friend.

Hannah Ellis

Chapter 43

We met nearby. Mike greeted me with a hug.

"You look smart," I told him, taking in his khaki trousers and black shirt, sleeves rolled back to reveal his toned forearms – the result of working in a pub.

"Scrub up okay, don't I?" he said. "I think it's important to look good when you get stood up!"

"Definitely," I said with a smile. "I came from work, so…" I shrugged and looked down at my black trousers and plain V-necked top.

"Perfectly dressed to save me in my hour of need," he said with a cheeky grin.

We fell into step, heading to the city centre, and when Mike casually stuck out his elbow, I hooked my arm through his. The sky was clear and the sun beat down while a warm breeze whipped at my hair. It was beautiful weather for a stroll.

"What do you want to eat?" Mike asked.

I shrugged. "I don't mind."

"Good. My cousin's got a bistro – she's always on at me to visit."

"That sounds nice."

"Great. It does involve me taking you down a few back streets; it's a bit hidden away, over by the Northern Quarter."

I laughed. "I trust you."

"This way, then." He pointed, and we crossed the road.

"I think you know your way around Manchester better than I do," I said as we navigated a number of back streets, finally coming to a cobbled street lined with small independent shops.

"You must have been here before," he said.

"Not for years," I said, looking around. "My stepmum, Kerry, used to bring me shopping here when I was a kid. Actually…" I pulled him to the opposite side of the street to a small jewellers. I peered into the window and my mind flooded with memories. "I got my ears pierced here. My dad didn't want me to get them done. I was eight and he said I had to wait until I was ten! I was so angry with him. Kerry said she'd deal with my dad, and she let me get it done. She bought me little dolphin earrings." I smiled at the memory. "I'd forgotten about that."

I slipped my arm back into Mike's and we continued along the cobbled street, stopping occasionally to window shop.

"Here we are," Mike announced when we stopped in front of a little bistro sandwiched between a bookshop and a shop selling candles and incense sticks. The smell wafting out filled the warm air with a mixture of scents which put my nose into action. I sniffed the air like a dog, much to Mike's amusement.

There were people sitting at two of the four tables outside the bistro, and the sign above the door read *Melody's*. I followed when Mike ducked his head through the low doorway. The inside was brighter and more spacious than I was expecting. Soft piano music came from an old upright in the corner.

"There's a ghost that likes to play," Mike told me, following my gaze.

"That's amazing," I said, watching the keys move up and down by themselves. I ignored the black box of technology sitting on top of the piano, choosing instead to believe in the magic of a piano playing itself.

A tall, skinny woman walked out of a door at the back of a room. Her red hair was scraped messily into a knot on top of her head and her nose was bony and too big for her face, but her green eyes sparkled and her face lit up when she spotted Mike.

"Finally!" she said jovially. "It's been far too long." She glanced at me before returning her attention to Mike, enveloping him in a hug.

"This is my friend, Lucy," Mike said when she finally released him. "Lucy, this is Melody."

"Hi!" we said, and she gave me a warm smile.

"Elliot!" She turned to a guy in white who was peering through a hatch at the back of the room. "This is my long-lost cousin, Mike. That's my chef, Elliot." He gave us a toothy grin and a quick wave before he disappeared again.

"The place looks good," Mike said.

"Thanks. I can't believe you're here. How long have I been nagging you now?"

"It's not that long since I was last here," he said cheerfully. "Maybe a year or two."

"Or three!" She laughed and turned to me. "It's always me who has to venture out to the middle of nowhere to visit him in his back-of-beyond pub!"

"Okay!" Mike held up his hands. "I'm here now! Stop complaining and feed us, will you?"

"Go on, then." She slapped his arm good-naturedly. "Inside or out?"

He looked at me and raised his eyebrows. "Out?"

I nodded. "Sounds good."

We followed Melody to a little round table and she pulled a lighter out of her apron to light the candle in the middle of the white tablecloth, even though it was still bright outside.

We ordered red wine and Melody left us with the menu.

"Don't choose a salad," Mike said, scanning the menu.

I looked at him, my eyes wide. "You're going to tell me what I can eat?"

"No, just what you shouldn't eat! You're starting to look like someone who only eats salads." He lifted his eyes from the menu and I was surprised to find that his teasing look had been replaced by something else. Concern, maybe?

"I was looking at the steak, actually!" I said.

"Good." He snapped his menu shut. "Me too!"

It was fun to sit outside, watching the shoppers wandering in and out of the shops. The tinkling of the piano could be heard now and then, when quiet settled around us. The aroma from the candle shop wafted past.

"Who's looking after the pub?" I asked as we waited for our food.

"James," he told me. "He helps out now and again. You've seen him on quiz nights – he always helps me out then."

I nodded. I knew all the villagers by sight, but I wasn't very good at names. I hadn't had time to get to know people. I'd expected village life to be quiet. It was for others, I guess, but my time living in the village had been far from peaceful.

"Where did you grow up?" I asked Mike.

"Princess Road."

"Oh, so you really were a city kid! Right in the heart of things."

"Well, the other end of Princess Road, the quiet end. But yeah, the city was my playground."

"What did you do before you took over the pub?"

He squinted, scratching his forehead. "Where should I start?" he said with a smile. "I've done a lot of jobs."

He kept me amused until our food arrived, running through his colourful résumé and telling anecdotes about all his jobs. He'd worked as everything from a milkman to a baker, to jobs in call centres and pet shops.

"A real-life jack-of-all-trades," I teased him as Melody put our food in front of us.

"No one in the world has had as many jobs as our Mike," Melody told me. "He was good at them all, though; he always managed to leave with glowing references."

Mike smiled, a hint of bashfulness in his eyes as he put his napkin in his lap and reached for his cutlery. Melody patted my shoulder and left us to eat in a companionable silence.

Afterwards, Melody wouldn't let us pay, insisting she wanted to treat her cousin and didn't want to have to worry about all the freebies she got when she visited the pub. She laughed, promising to drink the place dry on her next visit. She kissed my cheek when we said goodbye. I wobbled slightly on the rough stones as we set off back down the road.

"That's the trouble with cobbled streets." I grinned at Mike. "Very uneven and difficult to walk on!"

"How are you getting home?" he asked.

"Don't worry, I'm not going to drive," I said. "I can leave my car in the car park and pick it up tomorrow." It would cost me a fortune, but never mind. The wine had gone down so easily that I'd forgotten all about the car until it was time to leave. I'd only had two glasses of wine, but I could feel it buzzing through my system. "I'll hop on the bus."

"I can drive you," he offered.

We walked on in silence, the setting sun leaving a chill in the air. Mike pushed his hands into his pockets and I rubbed my arms.

"You didn't ask about Adam," I commented as I settled into the passenger seat of Mike's car.

"Was I supposed to?" he asked, starting the engine.

"No. It's just that everyone does. Most of my conversations revolve around Adam and the girls."

"Did you want to talk about them?" he asked.

"No," I mused, clicking my seatbelt into place. "It was nice to talk about something else for a change."

"Good. Thanks for saving me from eating alone," he said.

"You're welcome. I enjoyed it. Sorry your date didn't work out."

"You win some, you lose some. You'll have to direct me," he said, looking at the road ahead.

"Turn right at the traffic lights and keep going for a while," I told him. Traffic was light and I gazed out of the window, watching the bustle of life that filled the city streets. "I don't really feel like going home yet," I told Mike. "Do you want to go for another drink?"

"I can't," he said, slowing at another set of traffic lights. "I've got to drive home."

Matt and Chrissie had gone away for the weekend. The thought of going back to their house to sit and watch TV alone didn't appeal to me at all, and I definitely didn't want to go to bed yet. The night was still young. Then the thought of going to Dylan's pub entered my mind, and I couldn't shake it.

When the lights turned green, I directed Mike to turn left. Which was not the way home.

Chapter 44

"You're such a gentleman," I said to Mike as we walked the short distance from the car to the pub. "You really don't have to chaperone me, though. I know my way around here."

I'd asked him to drop me off at Dylan's pub, but he said he'd come in for a Coke and make sure I was okay.

"I know. I just think you might be a bit tipsy, that's all."

"I only had two glasses of wine," I told him.

"Three! And you're wobbling."

"Am not," I said, bumping shoulders with him and laughing.

Mike pulled the door open and the noise and heat of the pub hit us. It was busy: all the tables were occupied and there were a lot of people standing around in groups, cradling their drinks and talking loudly. I drank in the atmosphere as I walked over to the bar. It was just what I needed: I wanted to be out having fun, not sitting at home.

"Hi!" I had to shout over the din.

Dylan looked over from where he was busy pulling pints and gave me a warm smile. He finished serving and met me at the end of the bar for a hug.

Mike reached out and shook Dylan's hand when I

introduced them.

"Mike has a pub too," I said.

"And you get a night off?" Dylan asked. "How do you manage that?"

"Happens about twice a year! My place never gets as busy as this, though."

"This is pretty hectic for us too," Dylan said. "I don't know where everyone's appeared from tonight." He moved back behind the bar, taking our drinks order as he went.

"This makes me appreciate village life," Mike said, looking around. "I couldn't cope with all this."

"Do you ever think you might be getting old?" I asked cheekily.

"Definitely!" he said. "Old and boring. And happy with it! I like the quiet life."

We slipped onto bar stools when a couple next to us left, and Dylan put a bottle of beer and a Coke on the bar in front of us.

"They're on the house," he said. "Just don't tell Ryan – he thinks all his drinks should be free!"

"Is he here?"

He nodded, looking behind me. "Over at the back there."

"I'll go and say hello in a bit."

"I wouldn't bother," Dylan said. "He's with his little gang, and they're drunk and obnoxious. Someone's twenty-first, I think."

I took a long swig of my beer and Dylan left us to serve more customers.

"I love it in here," I said, beaming at Mike. "It always brings back so many memories. I used to come in here all the time before I moved to Havendon."

"You seem to be settling back into city life well," he said.

"It's okay. But did I tell you I lost my job?" A laugh escaped me. Suddenly, everything seemed funny, and I picked up my beer, taking another long drink, then started to pick at the label.

"How did that happen?" Mike asked.

"The boss questioned my commitment to the job," I told him. "So she won't give me another contract for the next school year. To be fair, I had a lot going on in my personal life, and I didn't put work first. When Hailey went missing, I dropped everything and left the school, even though the head teacher, Mrs Stoke, told me to stop. That was the final straw."

The beer was going down far too easily, but it felt good to be out and having fun. I looked over at Mike, who set his Coke down in front of him and eyed me sympathetically.

"It doesn't matter," I said, refusing to let it ruin my good mood. "I'll get another job."

"I'm sure you will," he said. "Why don't we finish these and I'll drop you home."

"It might be a good idea," I agreed. My eyes roamed the pub for a moment before I turned back to Mike, changing the subject abruptly. "Have you seen Adam lately?"

"Only in passing," he said, sympathy flashing in his eyes.

"I just wondered," I said, shrugging. "Did I tell you I went on a date?"

"Really?"

"Yeah. My friends set me up on a blind date! It was a disaster."

"I guess blind dates usually are," he said with a smile. "Hmm, you're very thirsty tonight!"

I nodded, looking at my almost-empty beer bottle. I'd been drinking it as if it were pop. "I better go and say hi to Ryan before we leave."

"I'll wait here."

Dylan was right. Ryan was with a bunch of young guys, all sporting a similar boy band look: gelled hair and skinny jeans.

He waved when he saw me. "Lucy!"

"Ryan!" I shouted back at him and he put his arms around me, almost knocking me over when he hugged me.

"This is my Lucy!" he told his friends, who cheered wildly. "Have a shot with me," he said, reaching for a drink on the table in front of him. "We're celebrating Rich's birthday! He's twenty-one today."

"Happy birthday!" I said to Rich, who came over and slung an arm around Ryan's shoulders. I tipped the shot down my throat. I had no idea what it was, but it burned all the way down.

"I was just leaving," I told Ryan. "I only came to say hi and bye."

"Spoilsport!" Ryan complained. "Stay out with us. We're going to a club later; you can come with us."

"I'd better not," I said, placing the shot glass down and reaching to give him another hug before I headed to the toilets. It seemed hilarious when the tap sprayed water all over me, and I patted the front of my T-shirt down, before reaching for the door handle and missing. When I returned, Mike was still sitting at the bar, chatting to Jack, the landlord, now. No doubt they were swapping pub stories.

I turned and headed to the pub's back room. Nostalgia swept over me when I walked in. It looked the same as when we used to hang out there, with a bar on one side of the room and the pool table in the middle, although today it was only being used to prop people up while they drank and chatted.

We'd spent so many evenings there after we'd been on the TV show, and memories washed over me like waves. Adam was always there with us. Always happy and laughing. Sadness crept in and I walked back to find Mike.

I leaned over the bar to give Jack a kiss hello and asked for another beer when he offered.

"I thought we were going?" Mike said.

"I'm just going to have one more," I told him. "But you don't have to wait for me. I can get a taxi."

"I don't like leaving you," he said. "I'll wait."

"It's fine. Dylan's here. And Ryan asked me to go clubbing with him. I'll be well looked after."

Dylan was serving a group of girls next to us, and I was vaguely aware of him giving Mike a meaningful look. I decided to ignore it. If they wanted to be overprotective, that was up to them.

My good mood was slipping. It was no fun being out with people who would rather be at home.

"Fine," I said to Mike. "I'll finish this and you can take me home."

I lifted the bottle to my lips and drank until I felt someone taking it away from me.

"Behave!" Dylan grinned. "Go home and go to bed. You've had enough."

I reached over and squeezed his cheek. "You're so boring these days!"

Mike followed me when I walked towards the door, waving goodbye to Jack as I went.

"Nobody wants to have fun with me any more!" I told Mike, pouting. We stepped out into the fresh air, and the sudden quiet left a ringing in my ears.

"I already told you, I'm old and boring!"

"You didn't have to prove it!"

From the pub, it was only a five-minute drive to Matt and Chrissie's place, and we'd pulled up outside before I knew it.

"I'm so glad your date cancelled," I said, unclipping my seatbelt and shifting in my seat to face him. "I had a brilliant time."

"It certainly seems like it!"

"My blind date was rubbish," I blurted, feeling the words slurring. "I just want to go on dates and it be like this…" I reached over and touched his arm. "Just like friends going out together."

I leaned over to him, intending to give him a kiss on the cheek – I think. But my lips hit his when I moved at the last minute. It didn't occur to me to pull away. I liked the feel of his lips on mine. He didn't respond, though, and I felt his hand on my shoulder, gently pushing me back into my seat.

I opened my mouth to apologise, feeling stupid and embarrassed, but my stomach lurched and I just managed to turn round and open the car door in time to vomit into the gutter.

My eyes watered as I coughed and spluttered. "I'm so sorry," I said to Mike, mortified, searching for a tissue in my bag and wiping my mouth. He was hovering on the pavement and held out a hand to me as I got out of the car, avoiding the pool of sick by the door.

"Don't worry about it," he said. "I'm fairly experienced when it comes to drunk people."

"Honestly, I'm so sorry," I said again, tears filling my eyes as he walked me up the front steps to the door. "I don't know what's wrong with me sometimes."

"Come on, you're just drunk," he said. "Sleep it off and you'll be fine."

"I'm so embarrassed. I can't believe I kissed you." I fumbled in my bag for my key and shoved it into the lock.

"I'm always fighting off women who throw themselves at me," he said jokily. "Happens all the time!"

I appreciated his attempt to make me feel better but my humiliation was overwhelming and my stomach was still churning. I felt awful.

"Will you be okay?" Mike asked.

"Yes," I said, managing a smile. "Thanks for bringing me home and looking after me."

"No problem." He backed away down the steps. "Just sleep – you'll be fine."

I waved and walked inside. Once I'd had a glass of water, I headed upstairs and got changed for bed. I should've taken Mike's advice and gone to sleep then, but instead I took out my phone. It had been at the bottom of my bag all night, unchecked. I should have left it like that.

There were no missed calls or messages. I should have gone to sleep. Instead I searched for Adam's number and pressed dial. I lay back on the bed while it rang.

"Hello?" Adam sounded sleepy and confused.

"It's Lucy," I said.

"Is everything okay?" he asked. "What time is it?"

"Nothing is okay," I told him miserably, tears springing to my eyes and spilling down my face. "I lost my job. And I'm living in someone's spare room."

I heard movement and imagined him sitting up in bed, switching on the lamp to check the time, and rubbing his eyes as he tried to wake up. "You've really lost your job?" he asked, his words thick with confusion.

"Yeah, and I got really drunk," I blurted through a sob. "And I kissed Mike. And I went on a stupid, awful blind date – and it's all your fault!"

"You kissed Mike?"

"Yes. And then puked everywhere. Everything in my life is a mess."

There was a brief pause. "It probably seems worse now than it really is," he said, his soft voice throwing me. I thought he would've hung up by now. Or shouted at me.

"I thought we would get married," I said, unable to control my sobs. "And now I'm drunk and kissing people who don't want to be kissed, and throwing up in the street. I thought my life would be so different – our life." I trailed off, shaking while I cried.

Adam stayed quiet. By the time I'd managed to calm down, I wondered whether he was still there.

"I'm sorry," he said quietly.

"I should sleep," I said. "I'm sorry for waking you. I shouldn't have called."

I thought I heard him say it was fine, just before I

hung up. I kept the phone in my hand, too exhausted to move.

Hannah Ellis

Chapter 45

The next morning, I was woken by an odd noise. I had no idea what it was for a couple of confusing minutes. By the time I realised it was my phone, the dreadful ringing had stopped. I lifted my head, squinting into the sunlight that streamed spitefully through the window. Curtains are a great invention – when you remember to use them.

The memories came back to me in a vicious assault, one after the other – *bang, bang, bang*. I groaned and lay back, not sure which part of the night I felt worst about.

Then my phone started up again, its noise gnawing into my head. After some scrabbling, I found it right beside me. Adam's name flashed up on the screen.

"Hi," I said, trying to recall exactly what I'd said to him last night.

"Are you okay?" he asked.

"I'm fine," I said, staring wide-eyed at the ceiling. I was so embarrassed. *Why on earth did I call him? And I told him I kissed Mike! I'm such an idiot!* "I'm sorry for waking you last night."

"It's okay. Don't worry about it. I'm on my way to work. I just wanted to check if you'll still make it over to see the girls today."

I groaned again. I hadn't even thought about the

girls. Tears flooded my eyes and a wave of self-loathing stormed through my body. "I'm sorry," I said, sniffing. "I won't make it until later."

"That's fine," he said calmly. "I told Mum and the girls you wouldn't make it until lunchtime; I presumed you might be feeling delicate this morning. But if that's not okay, I'll let them know now. The girls will be getting excited."

"Lunchtime is fine," I said quickly. "I want to see them. I'll sleep a bit more and I'll be fine."

"Great. They always look forward to seeing you. It gives them a break from Mum and me. Hailey seems to think we're awful people most of the time!"

I managed a laugh, more of a snort really, surprised by the normality of the conversation. After my drunken rant, I'd thought he'd be even more distant.

"She's just a ten-year-old," I told him. "I wouldn't take it personally."

"I try not to. I should let you get back to sleep. How's the head?"

I moved to get comfy, pulling the duvet around me. "Terrible."

"I'll bet. Get some more sleep and drink plenty of water. That should help. Have fun with the girls later."

"I will," I said, hanging up, turning onto my side and closing my eyes.

I napped for an hour. The hangover calmed down after a shower and some toast, but returned with full force when I got the bus into town to retrieve my car. There were too many people in the confined space and the air was stale and stuffy. I got off a stop early and enjoyed the fresh air as I walked the final stretch to the car.

The weather was nice, so I took the girls for ice creams in the park and then we drove into Brinkwell for a walk around the shops. I bought Emily new hair slides with fairies on and a pair of sunglasses for Hailey. They were both pleased with their purchases when we got in the car and headed back home.

The house smelled delicious when we walked in. Adam was in the kitchen with an apron tied around his waist.

"You're cooking?" Hailey asked, surprised.

"Hey! I'm a good cook," he told her, looking at me. I nodded my agreement, though it had been a long time since I'd seen him do any cooking.

"I'll leave you to it," I said. "I should head home."

The girls groaned and their disapproval felt like hands tightening around my heart.

"You're welcome to stay for dinner," Adam said, turning his back to me to stir a pot on the stove.

"Thanks, but I should get going."

"Please stay," Emily said.

"I'll see you soon," I told her, giving her a big kiss on the cheek. "Bye, Hailey." She smiled her goodbye and Adam followed me to the front door.

"Thanks for today," he said.

I hovered awkwardly. "I had fun."

"Are you sure you won't stay for dinner?" he asked. "Maybe we could talk later."

Great! Now he wants to talk when I'm hungover and can't think straight! "Not today, Adam. I'm tired." I really didn't have the energy. I couldn't bring myself to look at his face: he'd look wounded or angry and I couldn't deal with either so I said goodbye and walked quickly away.

On the drive home, I struggled to make sense of my feelings. I'd been so sure that I wanted to move on from Adam, and yet I was wracked with guilt over kissing Mike – and my stupid blind date. It felt like a betrayal. How would I feel if I found that Adam had been out for dinner with another woman? What if he kissed someone else? It was bound to happen at some point. Eventually, he'd meet someone new. Someone to take my place in his heart – and in our home. Suddenly, I felt sick.

I arrived back at Matt and Chrissie's empty house. There were times when I'd lived with the girls when all I'd wanted was peace and quiet, but now I had that, it seemed louder than anything. I switched on the TV to fill the silence and stared blankly at a nature documentary for an hour. My mind wouldn't focus and my thoughts constantly wandered to Adam. A bridal magazine on the coffee table seemed to be taunting me, and eventually I stuffed it under a cushion out of sight.

The evening stretched out before me. I'd just pulled a packet of crisps from the cupboard, wondering if they would pass for a full meal, when the doorbell rang.

Adam stood on the front steps.

"I thought I'd take you out for dinner, since I couldn't tempt you with my cooking," he said, skipping pleasantries. "Unless you have other plans?"

"I had planned on having these," I told him, holding up the bag of crisps and trying to hide my surprise that he'd driven all the way over to ask me out to dinner.

"Well, that's hard to compete with," he said, looking vulnerable.

I smiled. My feelings were so jumbled that I didn't trust myself around him. This didn't feel like moving on. It felt like he was asking me on a date! But I could hardly turn him away without even talking to him.

"I'm sorry about last night," I said, beckoning him in and closing the door but not moving from the hallway. "I was really drunk."

"I know. It's fine."

"It doesn't change anything," I told him, leaning against the wall.

"Just come for dinner with me," he pleaded.

I shook my head in frustration. "Why? Because you're jealous that I kissed Mike? Or that I went on a date?"

"Yes. Partly. But mostly because I miss you and I want my best friend back. I want you back with us. Where you belong."

He held my gaze and I looked at the floor. I missed him too. But things had been awful between us. I had to keep reminding myself of that.

"I need to move on," I told him. "We both do. You said yourself that we make each other miserable."

"I only said that because I was angry at you. And at the world." He paused, his eyes boring into me. "I've been talking to Hailey's counsellor, Amelie Bright. I know how bad things were, and how much I messed up, but I want to make things right."

I looked up, surprised by the revelation. "I can't think straight now," I told him. "I'm hungover and confused. I think it's better if we talk another time."

I opened the door for him, avoiding his gaze. If I

looked him in the eye, I knew I'd cave.

He walked towards the door but stopped in front of me. "Just have dinner with me," he said quietly. I stared at my feet until I felt his hand on my chin, forcing me to face him. "Please."

"Adam—"

"You don't even like cheese and onion crisps," he said, smiling as he took the packet of crisps from me. "And I put a shirt on and drove all the way here."

My resolve crumbled. "I'll get changed," I said reluctantly, sure that going out with him would only complicate matters but unable to resist.

"Thank you," he said, closing the door. "You home alone?"

"Chrissie and Matt have gone away for the weekend."

Adam was perched on the couch when I returned, his elbows on his knees and his head resting against his clenched hands as though deep in prayer.

"Ta-da!" I said awkwardly and did a quick twirl to show off my new dress. It was an impulse buy from the day I'd spent shopping and having a mini-makeover.

I'd spent too long mulling over what to wear. I wasn't sure what was appropriate: I didn't want to look like I was making too much effort but I was keen for my new dress to have an outing.

He turned to look at me. "I was starting to think you'd left me down here to starve."

"I gave you snacks!"

"Long gone." He motioned to the empty crisp packet, then stood and looked at me, his gaze travelling over my body. "You look great."

"Thanks," I said, suddenly self-conscious. "Sorry I took so long – I decided I needed a shower."

"No problem. You're slightly overdressed for Burger King, though…"

"You'd better not take me to Burger King!"

"Okay, plan B then!" He escorted me out of the door and into his car.

"Where are we going?" I asked.

"There's an Italian place nearby. I drive past it on my way to work. It looks nice." He glanced at me. "Or do you want to go somewhere else? I guess we eat pizza and pasta a lot."

"It's fine. I don't care what we eat." I was only thankful that he hadn't suggested The White Kitchen. I'd had an email from Ollie a few days before, asking me to return the signed contract to them as they wanted to display Adam's photos. I'd ignored the email. I was intending to call them and confess what I'd done. I needed to get the photos back.

Adam was right; the Italian was a lovely little restaurant a five-minute drive away. It was surprisingly quiet for a Saturday night, and we found a table tucked away in a corner. The evening was relaxed: we managed to avoid talking about the girls and the mess we'd made of our lives. Adam told me light-hearted anecdotes about his job and I told him stories about the kids in my school. Neither of us mentioned me losing my job and I neglected to mention the teacher training course – which now wasn't going to happen.

Adam was quiet when he drove me back to Matt and Chrissie's place. I felt his awkwardness before we pulled up at the house. It just seemed so wrong, him dropping me off and then driving away. This is why I should have held my ground and not agreed to go out with him. What we needed was a clean break.

"Do you want a coffee before you head back?" I asked to fill the silence, registering how tired he looked.

"That would be good, actually."

"Is Ruth staying at your place?" I asked as we walked inside.

"No, I dropped the girls with her. They were excited about having a sleepover. Well, Emily was, at least."

I flicked on the kettle and Adam leaned against the kitchen counter. "Hailey's new counsellor seems to be working out well," he told me awkwardly.

"Yeah? That's great. And you've been talking to her too?"

"Yeah. When I first met her, she asked a lot of questions about how I was coping and how things were going with the rest of the family."

"That makes sense, I guess."

"I told her I was fine," he said, shifting his weight. "I said we were all fine! And she told me I was welcome to call her once I'd had enough of the denial."

I smiled at him as I made him a cup of instant coffee and a tea for myself.

"I met with her once after you left."

I nodded and motioned for him to follow me into the living room.

"I told her how pissed off I was with you and that I didn't know why you'd left now. A year or eighteen months ago, I wouldn't have blamed you ... but now? I just didn't get it."

I shook my head sadly. "You must have realised how bad things were between us."

He shrugged, silent for a moment. "Amelie seemed to think that you leaving was sensible. But I also think she's a bit crazy sometimes! Anyway, I went back to her last week to discuss Hailey and I ended up talking about you again. And I made a deal with her: I'll see her once a week and bare my soul, and in return she'll tell me how to get my girlfriend back."

A smile crept slowly over my face. "She agreed to that?"

His nose wrinkled. "No. She didn't seem keen on making deals!"

He'd taken me by surprise, and I wanted to tell him it wasn't that simple. We should be concentrating on moving forward, not back. I opened my mouth but Adam interrupted me before I could voice my concerns.

"Just give us some time," he said. "Maybe you could talk to Amelie too?"

"Me?" I looked at him mock-seriously. "But I'm fine!"

He laughed, and the sound rattled round the room. "Maybe I'll give you her number for when you've had enough of the denial..."

"Maybe." I smiled at him and he sank back into the couch, his legs stretched out in my direction.

His face was suddenly serious again. "I think I got so caught up in making sure the kids were okay that I forgot about us. I bottled everything up for the sake of the kids – but at our expense."

I sighed. I didn't know what to think. I'd been so sure we were better off apart, but Adam was finally opening up – which is what I had wanted for so long.

I didn't pull away when his hand slipped into mine, our fingers lacing together.

Chapter 46

Adam had ended up sleeping on the couch, but was gone when I got up. He started calling me everyday after that. It'd taken me by surprise at first but over the next week I got used to our daily chats, I even started to look forward to them. We'd talk about work and the girls, filling each other in on our days. It began to feel normal, and when Adam asked me to stay and have dinner with them after I'd taken the girls out on Saturday, I'd readily agreed.

The relaxed meal had been marred only by my thoughts about The White Kitchen. When I hadn't responded to Ollie's email, he'd followed up with a phone call. I didn't dare explain the situation over the phone and promised to call in on Sunday. My plan was still to take the photos back. It would be embarrassing, and Jonathan and Ollie would be unimpressed, but I had no choice. I couldn't bring myself to tell Adam what I'd done, and the photos couldn't be displayed without his signature on the contract.

I hadn't had time to think about what I was going to do with Adam's photos once I'd picked them up. After weighing up my options on the drive to The White Kitchen, I decided I'd take them to Dylan's. He had space in his apartment above the pub, and he was the one person I knew who wouldn't ask too many questions or pass judgement. He'd probably be amused by the predicament I'd got myself into, but I was sure he'd let me store them there for a while. It wouldn't be for long; it'd be easy to sneak the photos back with the rest of Adam's collection over the school holidays when Adam was at work.

With that clear in my head, I knocked on the door of The White Kitchen. After a moment, I knocked more loudly, but still got no reply. I walked slowly in the direction of White Ice, already feeling relieved at the thought of being able to drive away and deal with the situation another day.

When I looked through the window into the wine bar, I felt as though I'd just taken a steep drop on a big rollercoaster. *How did I get myself into this mess?* I was tempted to turn and run, but Ollie looked out and saw me, so I had no choice but to face up to the mess I'd caused. It was going to be much worse than I'd anticipated; they were going to be so angry with me.

"What do *you* think?" Jonathan asked, turning to me when I pushed the door open. "Left a bit, right a bit?" He was standing on a chair holding up one of Adam's photos. Adam's work was propped up all around the room, and a man with a tool belt hovered next to Ollie, helping to direct Jonathan.

"A bit higher?" I suggested and then felt faint. *A bit higher?* Surely what I really meant was a bit further out the door, a bit down the road … a bit more in my car! Not a bit higher!

"She's right," Ollie said. "Stop there – it's perfect." He looked at me and I nodded my approval without taking my eyes off the picture. It was a photograph of local woodland, dense with trees whose leaves shone in autumnal tones. Adam had captured the moment the wind had blown leaves from the trees, and the beautiful golden shapes blew across the path in the foreground. I wanted to jump into the photo and run away down the path.

"We were joking that Adam was going to leave us high and dry again," Jonathan said as he took out a pencil and marked where the picture should hang before climbing down from the chair.

"We are all set, aren't we?" My head snapped towards Ollie as he spoke. "You've got the contract for us?"

I nodded and wondered if my smile did anything to hide my panic. When I saw Ollie looking at my hands, I let out a laugh, shaking my head as though I couldn't believe what a scatterbrain I was. "I left it in the car! I'll be right back." I was surprised at how confident I sounded when I waltzed back out of the door.

Opening the passenger door, I took a seat and went over my options: I could go back in, explain everything, apologise profusely, take the photos and leave; or I could call Adam, confess what I'd done and try and convince him to sign the contract; or I could go with the most appealing option, which was to drive away, abandon the photos, change my phone number and email address, and possibly move to a different country!

Taking a deep breath and making a conscious effort not to repeat my 'vomiting in the street' incident, I opened the glove compartment and took out the contract, which had been hiding there since I got it.

Then I rooted around in the door pocket for a pen … and switched my brain off.

Chapter 47

On Tuesday afternoon, I left work and headed straight to Havendon. I parked the car on the road by the church and walked across the churchyard, enjoying the warm wind on my face. Fresh flowers lay on Tom's grave and Adam sat in my spot next to the headstone, his back to me as he looked out across the valley.

"Hi," I said.

He jumped. "I wondered if you'd come today."

I nodded as I fought off tears. "Thought I'd come and wish him a happy birthday," I said, running my hand across the top of the headstone. "I miss him," I told Adam, feeling pathetic and fraudulent. He wasn't my dad and I'd only known him for eighteen months. I'd always felt close to him, though: he saw me for exactly who I was and I always felt loved by him. He was warm and kind and a pleasure to be around.

I looked at Adam but he'd turned away from me. Guilt hit me. I seemed to carry it with me constantly. "I'm sorry I wasn't with him when he died," I said, quietly. Adam looked back at me, the confusion on his face prompting me to continue. "I always felt bad. You told me to look after him and then he died all alone." I wanted to sit with Adam but instead I hovered awkwardly. Maybe he wanted to be alone.

"I'm sorry," I said again, moving away. "Tell the girls I said hi."

"What do you mean, I told you to look after him?" he asked.

"The night before he died, we spoke on the phone and you told me to look after him. I promised you I would. I should've stayed at the house with him."

My conversation with Adam had haunted me ever since. Adam had been so upset about Becky when I spoke to him that night – I wanted to fly back out to France to comfort him. I'd asked him what I could do and he said I should just look after his dad.

"You couldn't have known what was going to happen. And you staying at the house wouldn't have made any difference," he said gently. "You couldn't have done anything. He had a massive heart attack."

"But I promised you I'd look after him – and then he died."

"I don't even remember having that conversation," he said, looking me in the eyes. "I don't remember speaking to you on the phone. Those days are all a blur."

"I remember everything," I told him. "That last day with your dad – he was talking about how you'd be the girls' guardian. That they'd come and live with you. He said Becky had talked to you about it when the girls were tiny and you'd laughed about it."

"We joked about how much I could screw up her kids," he said with a sad smile. "It's not quite as funny now."

"Your dad said you'd be great with the girls, and I said I'd be around to help too. He said no one would blame me if I walked away, and I said I wasn't going anywhere. I promised him I'd stay."

I looked out over the hills and felt relieved. The wind lifted my hair from my shoulders and I closed my eyes and enjoyed the warmth of the sun on my face.

"You're not great at keeping promises, are you?" I could sense the smirk on Adam's face before I looked at him.

"It's definitely something I could work on." I gave him my hand as he reached out to me. Our fingers entwined and his thumb stroked mine. "I should get back," I said.

He stood and walked with me back towards the road. "Can you come home with me for dinner?"

When I walked into the kitchen, Ruth embraced me, and I hugged her back tightly. She rubbed my back and I struggled to keep my emotions under control. She seemed to be fighting the same battle.

"It's good of you to come over today," she said.

"I was up at the grave. The flowers are nice."

"He wouldn't like them," she told me. "He'd say it's a waste of money."

I shrugged. "He's not here to complain, is he?"

She smiled at me. It was also the sort of thing Tom would've said.

"How are you?" I asked.

She shrugged and her bottom lip quivered. I felt bad for not asking her more often. She'd been so stoical that it was easy to forget how horrendous everything had been for her. She'd lost so much, and all at once. I hugged her again as tears streamed down her face, and we stayed that way until we heard the girls bounding down the stairs. We pulled apart and managed to laugh as we both quickly wiped away our tears.

The girls ran to me. I hugged them to me and tried to listen when they both spoke at once. "Calm down," I said. "I can't hear you. Let's go and sit in the living room and we can chat in comfort." They cuddled up to me and took it in turns to fill me in on what had been happening at school and with their friends.

The five of us ate together. Ruth insisted we sit in the dining room. I was worried that a cloud of dust would envelop us as soon as we opened the door, since the room was never used, but perhaps Ruth came in and cleaned it from time to time. I certainly never had.

Ruth perked up, and the atmosphere was relaxed and happy as we tucked into her roast chicken. Only Adam was quiet, his smile never reaching his eyes.

I stayed to put the girls to bed, saying goodbye to Ruth before I took them up to read stories. Once the girls were settled, having promised them that I'd see them soon, I went to look for Adam. I found him lying on our bed, staring up at the ceiling.

"All quiet?" he asked.

"Yeah, they were tired."

"I know the feeling."

"You okay?" I asked.

He met my gaze. "I have no idea."

I leaned against the doorframe. He shifted his gaze back to the ceiling.

"Do you need anything?" I asked.

He shook his head and smiled briefly at me. "Thanks for coming over today."

"You're welcome." I headed for the front door,

stopping halfway down the stairs and taking a deep breath. Maybe I should go back and comfort him. He was obviously upset. Leaving him alone seemed so wrong. I turned to go back up to him and then thought better of it. *I should just go home. We're over. Cuddling up in bed with him is hardly going to emphasise that point! Oh God, it would be nice, though. And he's been making such an effort. Would it really be so bad? Maybe we could work things out.* I hesitated again, torn. He'd be fine, I told myself. I'd call him tomorrow and see how he was. I needed to be strong and move on with my life.

I leaned my head against the steering wheel when I finally made it to the car, then I pulled out my phone and called Angela.

Hannah Ellis

Chapter 48

In the pub, I hopped onto a stool at the bar and smiled at Mike, who greeted me warmly.

"I'm meeting Angela for a quick drink," I told him.

"Wine?" he asked.

"Lemonade. I'm driving!"

He turned to pour my drink.

"Mike?" I hesitated and he glanced over at me. "I'm sorry about the other night."

"Don't worry about it," he said, his back to me.

"I'm really embarrassed." I lowered my voice. "I'm such an idiot."

He put my drink in front of me. "Maybe I shouldn't have invited you out for dinner. I hope I didn't give you the wrong idea. Adam's a friend. I only asked you as a friend."

"I know!" I said quickly. "I didn't think anything else. I just drank too much, and my head is a mess at the moment."

He shook his head slightly before looking at me with a boyish smile. "Shall we just pretend you didn't kiss me? Let's continue being friends."

"Yes." I gave a sigh of relief. "Could we forget about the vomiting too?"

He laughed at me. "Sorry, that's etched on my memory forever!"

"Great!" I took a sip of lemonade and buried my embarrassment.

"Have you been up at the house?" Mike asked.

"Yeah. It's Tom's birthday today. I think Adam's struggling. That's why I called Angela to meet me. I need her advice."

"Good idea," he said. "Angela gives good advice. She's very wise."

The door opened. We turned to see Angela walk in, a big grin on her face. "I'm so glad you called," she said. "It's nice to get out of the house!"

"Thanks so much for coming," I said, standing to hug her.

She said a quick hello to Mike who poured her a wine, and we headed over to sit by the window with our drinks.

"So what's going on?" she asked. "Tell me everything."

I gave her a quick rundown of everything that had happened, ending with me leaving Adam this evening when I absolutely didn't want to.

"I want to go back and check he's okay," I told her, "but I don't know if it's a good idea. What do you think?"

Angela bit her lip and frowned. "I don't know if I can give you impartial advice," she confessed. "I don't feel very objective."

I shook my head in confusion. "What? I was relying on you to tell me what to do! You're supposed to be the voice of reason."

"I would say go back to him." She winced slightly. "But that's because I want you and Adam to get back together and live happily ever after!"

I screwed my face up. "Angela! Really?"

"I know! But I've known you since you first got together and I've seen what an amazing couple you are."

"Were," I corrected her. "And that's the problem: I want things to be how they used to be when we were ridiculously happy."

"But you also want to be there for him today when he's upset, so what does that tell you? You must still care about him – and he obviously loves you. He's seeing this therapist, so he's obviously making an effort."

"I know. But I'm worried I'll get hurt all over again. Plus there's the whole issue of his photos," I added as an afterthought. I realised what I'd said when I saw the puzzled look on Angela's face. With a sigh, I covered my face with my hands. "I took some of his photos and gave them to a restaurant to display." I winced. "I forged his signature on a contract."

I'd been feeling so bad about it. Adam was making so much effort to repair our relationship – and I had gone behind his back with his photos. I should tell him, but I knew he'd be angry and I was just getting used to him being calm again. If I told him, he'd slip back to being grumpy and distant, and I hated the thought of that. Why couldn't life just be simple?

"Oh God," Angela said, her eyes wide with surprise and amusement. "You really like drama, don't you?"

"I don't know what to do," I told her.

"My advice," she said slowly, "is to go home."

"Home to Adam?" I asked.

She gave me a sly smile. "If that's where home

is…"

*****

When I pulled up outside the house again a while later, the sky was perfectly clear. I lingered on the driveway, craning my neck to look at the stars. The three stars on Orion's belt twinkled above me. I felt silly, but I couldn't resist waving up at them before I went inside. Adam was in exactly the same position on the bed when I knocked gently on the doorframe.

"I thought you'd gone," he said.

"I came back," I told him. "I was worried about you."

"I'm okay," he said. "Just thinking about Dad."

I walked over and lay beside him. We stared at the ceiling together.

"The first time I met your dad, he told me what a geek you were when you were a teenager!"

Adam laughed. "I remember. I was so embarrassed!"

"He was always telling me stories about you and Becky when you were kids." He used to take me out to the pub for lunch and regale me with stories.

"I bet most of them were embarrassing," he said. "He could always spin a good yarn."

"I miss his stories," I said.

"Me too." Silence settled, and memories of Tom whirled round my head until Adam spoke again. "When I was a kid he used to do magic tricks. For a while he actually had me believing that he was a member of the Magic Circle!"

I turned my head in Adam's direction and a laugh

escaped me. "He told me you believed that until you were twenty!"

"No way!" Adam flushed and I was overcome with laughter. "Not twenty! Maybe until I was twelve or something. I definitely wasn't twenty. God, my dad's so embarrassing."

Tears of laughter ran down my face. "You should talk about him more," I said.

"I should. It's hard. Sometimes I still can't believe he's gone. That they're both gone."

"I know."

"Thanks," he said. "I'm glad you're here."

His arms encircled me when I laid my head to his chest and curled into him.

When the sun streamed into the room the next morning, I was tangled up with Adam. He slept peacefully and I had a sudden urge to kiss him. I took a moment to breathe in his scent and enjoy his warmth before dragging myself away. Thankfully, I hadn't completely cleared out my clothes, so I was able to find a clean outfit for work. I tiptoed to the shower, hoping the girls wouldn't wake.

"Can I help with the kids in the school holidays?" I asked Adam when I walked back to the bedroom to find him sitting on the edge of the bed. It was the last week of the summer term, and I intended to spend as much time as possible with the girls in the holidays.

"Yes, please. I'll only work four-day weeks but I was still worried that spending so much time with my mum might push Hailey to run away for real."

"Your mum's not so bad," I said, perching beside him.

"Yeah, she's great when you don't have to see her every day. You looking forward to your summer break?"

"Kind of," I said. "I need to do some job hunting, and that's never fun."

"I'm sorry about your job," he said.

"It'll be okay," I told him. "I'm going to do my teacher training. Somehow!"

I hadn't really decided until that moment, but I didn't want to give up on it just because I couldn't do it at St Jude's. I'd have to apply to different schools – which wouldn't be as easy, especially since it was so late in the school year – but the idea was firmly planted in my head and I realised I really wanted to get on with my career.

"I need to go," I told Adam. "I want to be gone before the kids wake up. I don't want them to be confused or think I live here again."

"Okay." He laid his hand on mine, stopping me as I tried to get up. Butterflies fluttered round my stomach when he put a hand on my face and leaned in to kiss me. I kissed him back. A smile spread over my face as I pulled away.

"What's so funny?" he asked.

"I don't know," I said. "Us. Everything."

I turned when I reached the door. "Will you take me out on another date?"

"Yes. Definitely. Now get out before the kids wake up!"

Chapter 49

I'd had an email from Ollie on Sunday evening to tell me that the photos were up and looked great. When I'd handed over the contract to them, I'd spent some time blagging my way through a conversation about prices and then made my excuses and hurried away, leaving them to get on with hanging the pictures. In the email, Ollie invited me to view the photos, and asked if Adam would come too. He suggested we go down one evening for complimentary drinks.

Ollie's email distressed me for many reasons. I knew I shouldn't have handed over Adam's photographs – even though my intentions had been good – and when Adam finally found out, he would be furious with me – and rightly so. I hoped that the photos wouldn't sell, so I could return them to the garage at the end of the week and pretend none of it had ever happened.

Ollie's email also made me imagine a different life: one in which Adam was excited by all this, and we would spend an evening dressed up and drinking fancy cocktails while people around us admired his photographs. It'd be just like it used to be, when we couldn't get enough of each other and when other people envied us. After spending the night cuddled up with him, I had a glimmer of hope that we might be able to get back to that. But I knew it would all crumble when he found out what I'd done.

"I'm just nipping out for a while," I told Chrissie on Wednesday evening. She looked surprised.

"Meeting someone?"

"No, I just feel like a drink. I won't be long."

"Want company?" she asked.

I hesitated, feeling bad for shutting her out when she'd been so kind to me. Part of me wanted to tell her everything and take her with me to sit in the fancy cocktail bar to admire Adam's photos, but I knew it wasn't fair to ask her to keep my secret. Chrissie and Matt were friends with Adam too, and it would put them in an awkward position.

"I just feel like being on my own," I told her. "Thanks, though. Maybe we can go out at the weekend."

"Okay." She smiled and left it at that.

I found a parking spot near White Ice and decided I'd indulge myself with a cocktail and come back for the car the next day. Matt drove this way to work; he could drop me off on his way.

The place was busy. I slid onto a stool at the bar and ordered a mojito. I was overcome with emotion when I looked around at Adam's photos. They were amazing. I always knew they were special, but seeing them properly displayed made me realise how spectacular they were. It occurred to me that my idea of them not selling was ridiculous.

"We wondered if you'd ever show up."

I glanced over. Ollie was taking a seat on the stool next to me. Quickly I looked away, embarrassed, as I felt a tear roll down my cheek and fall into my lap. I could feel his gaze on me while I tried to discreetly wipe my eyes with a napkin. "They look great, don't they?"

"They're incredible," I said, managing a smile and finally meeting his gaze. He was wearing a dark suit which contrasted sharply with his red hair and highlighted the golden freckles across his cheeks.

"I especially like the red dots," he said. I looked at him quizzically. "The red stickers mean they're sold."

"Oh." I looked at the picture nearest to us and noticed a red dot next to the price. I scanned the other pictures, but most were too far away to see.

"All of them," Ollie said with a boyish smile.

"They all sold? Already?"

"The day they went up," he told me proudly.

"Really?" I struggled to speak through the lump in my throat. He nodded. I reached for a fresh napkin and openly dabbed at my eyes.

"Maybe you want to call Adam and tell him the good news?"

More tears welled and he smiled kindly at me. "He doesn't know you brought them in, does he?"

I shook my head, feeling pathetic. "Should I be worried you've put us in a difficult position?"

I shook my head again. "Not as far as the photos are concerned. Adam always intended to sell them. Life just got in the way. And I think he was always scared that they wouldn't sell." I took a deep breath. "He's going to be so mad at me, though." I was such an idiot. Just when we might finally be getting back on track, I was going to ruin it all.

Ollie nodded at the barman, who got me another

cocktail and handed Ollie a bottle of beer.

"I hate to complicate your life further," Ollie said. "But Jonathan and I didn't reserve our pictures before we hung these in here, so you still owe us two."

I caught his sly smile and laughed. "You'll get them." I finished off my cocktail then started on the next.

"See this one?" Ollie pointed to a photo hanging on the back wall. "The guy who bought this told me that he used to play there as a kid and whenever he'd been back as an adult it was never quite as he remembered, even though nothing had really changed. He said the photo was like someone had taken a picture of his childhood memories. It's the angle of the sunlight: it makes everything sparkle and glow."

I remembered something Adam had said once. "Adam told me he finds a spot he likes and then goes back at different times over weeks or months, waiting until the light is exactly right and everything is perfect."

"I wish I had that kind of talent," Ollie said.

"Looks like you've done all right for yourself," I said, glancing around the busy bar.

"True. I can't complain. And this is nothing; you've not even tasted the food yet. Come on, let's go and say hi to Jonathan and annoy the chef a bit while we're at it!"

After a quick tour of the kitchen, I sat at the back of the stunning restaurant with Ollie and Jonathan, enjoying yet another cocktail and their easy company. Ollie had filled Jonathan in on the situation with Adam. Jonathan hadn't seemed entirely surprised.

"I forged his signature," I told them, the alcohol

buzzing through my system. "On the contract."

They exchanged a glance and Ollie raised his eyebrows. "Did she just say something?" he asked Jonathan, mirth in his voice.

Jonathan shook his head. "I didn't hear anything. Are you hearing voices again?"

"I'm serious," I said. "I feel bad. I can't believe I forged his signature." I went unheard as Ollie and Jonathan stuck their fingers in their ears and drowned me out with some awful singing. "Okay, okay! I'll shut up."

"So when are you going to tell him?" Ollie asked.

"I don't know."

"The sooner the better, I should think," Jonathan said. "You don't want him to find out from someone else."

"I hadn't even thought of that," I said, lowering my head to the table. When I looked up, they were smiling at me.

"It'll all be okay," Jonathan reassured me, lifting his glass to mine.

"I'll drink to that."

Hannah Ellis

Chapter 50

On Friday, Sarah hugged me goodbye and I walked out of St Jude's Primary School for the last time. It was the last day of the summer term, and I was carrying enough wine and chocolates to last me through the summer holidays. I had hand-made cards from the kids, and flowers and bath sets too – I had to make two trips to the car.

For a moment, I looked back at the school, and then, with a heavy heart, climbed into the car and started the engine. After a second, I turned it off again and leaned my head against the headrest. *Why was I crying?* I was only vaguely aware of a car pulling into the parking space beside mine, and jumped when there was a knock on my window.

"What are you doing here?" I asked Adam, my hands shaking as I opened the car door and stepped out.

"I finished work early. Thought I'd stop on the way home and see if I could catch you."

"Thanks," I said, avoiding his gaze so he wouldn't see my tears.

When he wrapped his arms around me, I rested my head on his chest. "Everything will be okay," he told me gently.

"I know."

"You'll find another job," he said.

"I know." I was glad he'd turned up and I was impressed he was making so much effort. "But I liked it here."

"You'll like it somewhere else too."

I wiped at my eyes and took a step away from him. "Thanks for coming."

"Are you doing something to celebrate the end of term?"

"I'm going out with Chrissie and Matt," I told him. "At least, I'm supposed to be. I don't really feel like going out."

"I don't think you'll have much choice if Chrissie is involved. You'll be off to Dylan's pub, I guess?"

"I imagine so."

"It'll be fun."

"Yeah." I wanted to ask him to come along but hesitated too long, unsure whether I should.

"Are you coming over this weekend?" he asked.

"Yeah."

"Good," he said. "Have fun tonight and give me a call, okay?"

"Okay." I hated watching him leave.

I drove straight to Dylan's. Matt was propping up the bar. He gave me one of his bear hugs.

"You're going to have to cheer up, Little Miss Sunshine! We've got six weeks off and that's something to smile about. You look like the world's about to end."

"Sorry. Just get me a shot of something and I'll cheer up."

"Uh-oh!" He laughed. "I'm going to get you a beer to start with. We'll talk about shots later. I don't want to carry you home."

"Are you okay?" I asked him with mock concern. "Don't tell me you're finally growing up!"

"Fine!" He grinned at me. "You've talked me into it – we'll have a shot."

Dylan came over with a tray of empty glasses. He slid it onto the bar and gave me a hug.

"So you're unemployed again," he said. "I think we should drink to that!"

"Shots!" Matt told him.

"I'll join you for drinks later," Dylan said, moving around the bar to pour shots for us. "There's more staff coming in an hour and then I can take off."

"So what are you doing for the summer?" I asked Matt.

"Whatever Chrissie tells me to, I would imagine! Plus I'll be spending a fair amount of time sitting here." He raised his glass and we downed our shots before ordering beers. "My plan to spend the summer sitting naked on my couch has been foiled by an unexpected house guest."

"I'm very sorry!"

"No, you're not."

"Well, I haven't forgotten it's a temporary arrangement."

"Oh, shut up," he said, taking a swig of beer. "I was only messing with you. You can stay as long as you want."

"Thank you."

"Well, not too long…" He smirked and I gave him a shove. "I take it things are getting better with Adam, anyway?"

"Yeah, it seems like it."

He nodded. "I spoke to him the other day."

"What did he say?"

"Not much. He pretended to call for a catch-up and threw in a few questions about you. I felt used."

"Sorry." I smiled at his attempt to look wounded.

We ate sitting at the bar. By the time we'd finished, Ryan had arrived and Dylan had come to join us. I was tipsy and joking around with the boys by the time Chrissie joined us.

"You're cheerful for someone with no job," she said, jokily.

"It's taken a fair few drinks to get her to relax," Matt told her. "Don't come in here and ruin all my hard work!"

"I'll get another job," I said. "Don't worry about it!"

"Oh, I'm not worried," she told me and then ordered a drink, insisting we move to a table instead of sitting at the bar.

"Let's just do what the boss says!" Matt said, hopping off his stool and putting an arm around Chrissie's shoulders. "Everyone move along now. You're sitting in the wrong place."

Chrissie rolled her eyes at him as we got up and moved to a round table nearby. The place was filling up, and it was one of the only tables left.

"Why don't you just work in here?" Ryan asked me. "That's what I'd do if I lost my job."

"Please don't ever lose your job, Ryan," Dylan commented. "I see enough of you as it is."

"I'll keep it in mind for a backup plan," I told Ryan. "But I'm going to try and get a teaching job first."

"It's nice that you're around again anyway," Ryan

said. "You should've ditched Adam ages ago."

"Oh my God," Dylan said while Chrissie slapped Ryan's arm. "What is wrong with you?"

"What?" Ryan asked. "I'm just saying, it's nice to have Lucy back. What's wrong with that?"

I shook my head at him. "Thanks, Ryan."

Then my phone rang. Adam's number flashed on the screen. I couldn't hear anything over the noise of the pub, so I made my way through the throng and out onto the street.

"Is everything okay?" I asked.

"Sorry, I didn't know if you'd still be out," Adam said.

I glanced at my watch. It wasn't *that* late.

"Would you mind saying goodnight to Emily? She had a bad dream and was asking for you."

"Yeah, put her on," I said. I waited until I heard Emily's voice. I paced the pavement in front of the pub while I chatted to her for a few minutes.

"Sorry," Adam said when he came back on the phone. "I didn't mean to interrupt your evening."

"It's fine. I'm leaving soon anyway. I'll come over tomorrow."

"Good. I'm not working, so I'll see you then."

My little gang were surprisingly quiet when I rejoined them. "What's going on?" I asked.

Matt grinned up at me. "We've got a bet on whether talking to Adam will make you want to drink more or go home!"

"Thanks for the support! Everything's fine. I'll have another drink and then I'm going. I need some sleep."

Hannah Ellis

Chapter 51

It was mid-morning when I arrived in Havendon. Cautiously, I pushed the front door open and heard raised voices.

"You're not going anywhere until you sort out that mess," Adam shouted.

"I said, I'll do it later!" Hailey screamed.

I stood at the bottom of the stairs, looking up to where the noise was coming from.

"Do it later, then," Adam replied gruffly. "But you're not leaving your room until it's tidy."

I glanced into the living room and wondered at the irony of Adam telling Hailey to tidy her room when the coffee table was littered with pizza boxes and beer bottles.

"I'm not surprised Lucy left!" Hailey's voice was filled with rage. "You're so annoying!"

A door slammed.

Adam appeared at the top of the stairs, looking beaten.

"Hi." He frowned as he walked down the stairs. "I don't know what to do with her. We were getting on great and now she can't stand me again. I only asked her to tidy up a bit."

"She'll get over it," I told him, following him into the living room and watching him tidy up his own mess.

"She's driving me mad," he said, picking up the empty bottles. "I think she just enjoys arguing with me."

In the kitchen I switched on the kettle. "Where's Emily?"

"Mum took her to the playground. I think she'll be back soon. How was your night out?"

"Good," I told him. "A standard night at Dylan's. It feels like the place where time stands still."

"It's good that some things don't change."

"Definitely," I said, making a coffee and handing it to him. He kissed my cheek as he took it, and butterflies took flight around my stomach. When he lingered I leaned in and kissed his lips.

I flushed when I moved away from him. Somehow it felt like we were doing something we shouldn't.

"Will you move back in?" Adam blurted.

I caught the vulnerability in his eyes. "Don't rush me," I said gently, worried we'd fall into an argument.

"Sorry," he said quickly. "I don't want to pressure you. I just miss you!"

"I miss you too," I replied. "But I can't move back in until we're absolutely sure it's the right thing. After everything we've been through, I don't want us to rush things and end up back where we were before."

"You're right," he said. "I'm just being impatient."

"It's so quiet," I said, taking my coffee to the table. "I don't remember it ever being so quiet in here."

"It's nice, isn't it?"

"It's weird."

"Don't worry. I'm sure it won't last long!"

It was about a minute before we heard the front

door opening.

"Told you!" Adam said.

"Hi!" I stood up when Emily and Ruth came in. Emily was pale, and barely managed to return my smile. "What's wrong?"

"She says she has a stomach ache," Ruth said. "I think she needs a quiet day."

"Okay." I put a hand to Emily's cheek. Heat was radiating off her.

"Sorry, Lucy." Ruth kissed my cheek. "I didn't even say hello. I'm in a rush. I've got to get up to the church for a fundraising meeting."

"It's fine," I said. "You get off. I'll talk to you later."

Ruth hurried away and I bent down to talk to Emily. Without warning, she vomited all over me. Oh no! I winced and fought with my gag reflex as the yellow mess dripped down me.

"Sorry," Emily said and began to cry.

"It's okay," I told her and glanced at Adam, who had frozen, his coffee cup halfway to his mouth. It took me a few seconds to figure out how to deal with the vomit, which was all over Emily and me. "Let's get undressed," I told Emily, peeling her clothes off her and then stripping down to my underwear. "You're going to have to deal with the mess," I told Adam, picking Emily up. We were halfway upstairs when the next wave of vomit hit.

"Adam!" I shouted.

"I'm on it!"

After showering Emily, I wrapped her in a towel and sat her beside the bath while I showered. Afterwards, I put pyjamas on Emily and tucked her into bed, a bucket beside her. She looked pale and doll-like and was asleep within minutes.

My hair was still wet when I went downstairs, to find Adam putting away the cleaning supplies.

"She's asleep," I told him.

"I bet you're glad you came over today," Adam said.

"These things happen," I said with a shrug.

"If you'd rather go, we'll be fine…"

"I'll stay a while," I said, taking a seat at the kitchen table and propping my head up on my hand. "I've not even seen Hailey yet."

"Go in her room – if you dare!" He smiled, his gaze staying on me for too long.

"What is it? Do I still have puke on me or something?"

"No." He finally shifted his attention from me. "It stinks in here, though."

When Adam went into the back garden for fresh air, I ventured back upstairs, avoiding the three damp steps. I checked on Emily before knocking gently on Hailey's door.

She pulled her earphones out and turned her nose up. "What is that smell?"

"Emily threw up," I said. "Everywhere."

"Gross. Where's Uncle Adam? I can't come out of my room unless he goes out."

"You could just tidy up," I suggested.

"But it's *my* room," she complained as I sat beside her on the bed. "This is how I like it."

"It's disgusting," I told her.

"I know," she said, her mouth twitching into a smile. "But it'll take ages to clean, and if I wait until

Gran's here next, she'll do it for me. You know how she loves to clean! I think I'd actually be doing her a favour."

I stood and made my way through the clothes scattered on the floor. "You sound a bit like your Uncle Adam when I first met him."

"So I can just let Gran do it?"

I shook my head and smiled at her. "No – you made the mess. I'll see you later, when your room's all tidy!"

"Do you want to help me?" she called after me.

I laughed and pulled the door shut.

Adam was on the couch when I went back downstairs, two steaming cups of tea on the table in front of him.

"Emily's sleeping," I said, sitting beside him and picking up my tea. "And Hailey will be out of her room in a few days – when she's managed to tidy up!"

"Can you hang around for a while?" Adam asked. "We could watch a movie ... It doesn't even have to be Disney or mermaids!"

"That sounds nice," I said. "What do you want to watch?"

"Don't pretend you care what I want to watch. We can just skip to the bit where you pick a romantic comedy and tell me I'll like it!"

"Hey!" I laughed with him. "You can choose if you want."

"No, no, you can," he said, passing me the remote.

"How about you choose the movie…" I moved to the opposite end of the couch and rested my feet in his lap, "and I get a foot massage."

"Deal!"

I wriggled to get comfy while Adam looked for a movie. I really didn't care what we watched. I was just happy to spend two hours cuddled up with him on the couch. I ignored the doubts that niggled at the back of my mind ... and refused to think about the stunt I'd pulled at The White Kitchen.

Chapter 52

When I spoke to Adam about the school holidays, it turned out that Hailey was at a drama school with Imogen for the first week of the holidays and Emily's week was crammed with two birthday parties, an afternoon art workshop at the community centre, and a trip to Chester Zoo with the family of one of her school friends. That kid had a better social life than me!

Adam wasn't working on Friday, so I planned to go over then, but I felt pretty deflated at the time I had to kill until then. I felt as though I was in limbo. Until Adam and I had made some decisions, I wasn't sure what to do about finding a job. Should I assume I would be living out in Havendon again and look for something around there? Part of me worried that I might jinx things by making that assumption. Surely we could work things out, though. There were just a few things to straighten out. One was me confessing what I'd done with his photos. Every time I spoke to Adam, it felt more and more right that I should move back in, which meant that I absolutely had to tell him about the photos – and soon!

I'd thought I would spend the first day of the holiday in Havendon with the girls, but instead I found myself at Dylan's pub with Matt, feeling pretty glum.

"Your misery could actually work out well for me," Matt told me as we sat at the bar. "Obviously, I'm really concerned and sympathetic and all that, but Chrissie telling me to take you out to cheer you up is quite nice for me."

I managed a half-hearted smile.

"No!" Matt said. "Don't get all smiley and happy … we need to spend the next six weeks cheering you up. Let's not accomplish too much today."

"Sorry. I'll try and keep the smiling to a minimum."

"That's good of you. Now, what are you eating?"

"I was just planning on drinking," I told him.

"That would get me into trouble with Chrissie. You're going to have to eat, I'm afraid."

"I can't afford to eat," I said miserably. "I'm unemployed and I've spent all my money." To add to my list of recent bad decisions, I'd decided to celebrate Adam's successful sales by going on a shopping trip.

"How have you spent all your money?" Matt asked. "You have a sad, boring life, so when have you spent it all? And what's bothering you? I thought things were getting better with Adam."

"It's a long story."

"Well, we have no other plans for the day, do we? Come on – spill!"

"I did something stupid," I said. Then I told him all about Adam's photos and watched his eyes widen in disbelief.

"So you basically stole his photos?" he said when I'd finished. "And he still doesn't know? How long have you been keeping this to yourself? Since you came to stay with us?"

I nodded and winced.

"But that's, like, two months, isn't it?"

"Yes. Since I took them. But they've only just sold."

He rolled his eyes. "That's okay, then!"

"I know, it's terrible. I'm so worried about how Adam's going to react."

"You know how he's going to react! That's why you're avoiding telling him."

"I don't know what to do," I said pathetically.

"Tell him! Get it over with."

"Next time I see him," I promised and reached for my beer.

"What about the money? You were saying you've spent it all?"

"That's another story for another day," I told him. "One problem at a time."

"Okay," Matt said, clinking his glass against mine. "Here's to Adam. I can't believe all the photos sold. And immediately. That's brilliant."

"It is, isn't it?" I just needed to get Adam to focus on that part of the story.

Telling Matt was probably a good thing. Of course, he wasn't the most sympathetic of people, and he teased me about it, but it made me determined to tell Adam. I had to tell him now that Matt knew. It felt like another betrayal that Matt knew before Adam did.

My day with Matt passed pleasantly, and on Tuesday he woke me by banging on my bedroom door. Chrissie had given him the task of painting the living room while he was off work, and he'd decided to get it out of the way at the start of the summer break. He roped me in to help, so we spent the morning at B&Q buying paint before covering the living room with dust covers. We hadn't been painting long but my arms were already starting to ache.

"So you spoke to Adam last night?" Matt said. "But you still haven't told him about the photos?"

I swept the paint roller up and down the wall. "No. I need to talk to him face to face."

"Doesn't it feel weird every time you talk to him? Surely every time you speak to him without mentioning it, it's more of a betrayal?"

"You're not helping! I'm seeing him on Friday. I'll tell him then."

"Why not sooner? The longer you leave it, the worse it will be."

"Shut up!" I snapped, but smiled as I turned to flick paint at him.

He grinned and got back to work. He was right; I should get it over and done with. I wiped my hands on my paint-flecked jeans as I walked out of the living room in search of my phone. I arrived back a few minutes later.

"I rang him," I said, frowning. "He's going to come over on his way home from work. Are you happy now?"

"Very!"

Chapter 53

Chrissie was happy about the paint job, and rewarded Matt by taking him out for a meal. I guess she also didn't want to eat surrounded by paint fumes. The thought of finally telling Adam everything was making me increasingly nervous, and I sat tapping my fingers on the kitchen table while I waited for him. The doorbell startled me and I took a deep breath before answering it.

Adam looked relaxed and happy. Did I really need to spoil his mood? Maybe we could just have a nice evening together... No! I would tell him. I had to tell him.

"I'm glad you called," he said, kissing me on the cheek. "I thought you sounded a bit down last night. We should talk things through. Try and make some plans."

"Yeah, that would be good," I said, leading him to the kitchen. "Sorry about the smell. Matt and I painted the living room today."

"Ah! Chrissie's got you hard at work, has she?"

"Yeah. They've gone out for dinner." I distracted myself making coffee and braced myself for the conversation to come. Soon it would all be out in the open, and that would surely be a relief.

"Have you started job hunting?" Adam asked.

"No. To be honest, I'm not sure where I should be looking."

"I thought that was bothering you." He moved and rested his hands on my hips. "Look for something out near Havendon."

I moved away from him, my heart racing. I just needed to tell him.

"I know you don't want to rush into anything, and we've still got things to work through," he said, taking my silence the wrong way. "But I promise to support you with your career. I think it's great that you want to do teacher training."

I tried to jump in but he was determined to carry on. "And I'm going to talk to Mum. It's not fair on you having her around so much. I know how hard that was for you."

"Don't upset your mum," I said, side-tracked. "It is hard, but she's had such a terrible time. She needs to be around the girls. I'm sure that's the only thing that keeps her going."

"I know, but she's been talking about wanting to get more involved with her church committees and things again. I think she's doing better. She'll understand that things need to change. We could even redecorate! Make the house more our own?"

"Adam, slow down." My chest tightened and tears pricked my eyes.

"And I'm going to help more with the housework too."

"Stop!" I yelled at him. His cheerfulness disappeared when he saw the look on my face.

"What's wrong? You do want this, don't you? You want us to be a family again?"

"I need to tell you something first," I blurted, dropping into a chair.

"Okay," he said nervously.

I paused, searching for the right words.

"Is this about Mike?" he asked.

"Oh my God." I massaged my temples. "No! What? Why would you think that?"

"Sorry. I don't know. But you're worrying me. And you never really did tell me what happened with Mike. You told me you kissed him. I wasn't really sure what to think."

"I told you I kissed him in a moment of insanity when I was very drunk!"

"Okay," he said calmly.

"There's nothing for you to worry about with me and Mike," I said, looking him in the eye. "I promise."

"I'm sorry. I shouldn't have mentioned Mike."

"Yes, you should. We need to talk about these things. And if you don't believe that nothing happened with Mi—"

"I do," he interrupted. "I believe you. I wasn't worried about Mike, not really. I just panicked. You said you needed to tell me something, and it sounded bad. What is it?"

"I took some of your photos when I left," I told him.

He squinted, confused. "That's not so bad, is it?"

"Quite a lot of photos. From the garage. Twenty-five of them."

"What did you do with them?" he asked slowly.

"I took them to Ollie and Jonathan at The White Kitchen," I confessed, biting my lip. "I forged your signature on a contract and they displayed them in their bar, down the road from the restaurant."

Nervously, I waited while he processed the information.

His brow creased. "You did what?"

"I just thought … Well, I wasn't really thinking."

"You stole my photos?" he said, angrily.

"I didn't really steal them! You said I could take anything."

"I didn't mean my photos!" he shouted, pacing the room. "You knew I didn't mean that!"

"I know. It was wrong. I'm sorry. Bu—"

"But nothing! How could you do that? Why? Why did you do it?"

"I'm not sure," I cried. "I always hated that they were hidden away. You're so talented."

"But we'd talked about this. You knew I didn't want to pursue photography. You can't just do whatever you want all the time!"

"I'm sorry," I muttered.

"And why didn't you tell me before? I've been trying to make sure we communicate better. And the whole time, you've had this huge secret?"

"I know." I had no defence. I was an idiot. The silence unnerved me until he finally spoke again.

"Which ones did you take?" he asked, calmer now.

"I just grabbed any." I tried to remember exactly. "That one with the kites. One of the woodland with the leaves blowing around. The sunset over the lake…"

"I can't believe you did that," he said, bewildered. "Do they still have them on display?"

I shook my head. "They sold them."

"Which ones?"

I smiled nervously. "All of them."

He'd always been filled with self-doubt when it came to his photos, and the look of disbelief on his face now was further evidence of that. It really shouldn't have been a surprise that they had sold so easily.

"All of them?" He looked to me for confirmation.

"Almost as soon as they went up. And you shouldn't be so surprised!"

"I don't know what to think," he said, walking to the door. "I'm going to go."

"Adam. Please don't just run away. We need to talk about this."

"I know." He turned back to me. "But I'm not sure what to say now. Let me get my head around it."

Relief washed through me when he kissed me on the cheek before leaving. It could have gone worse, I supposed.

Later, Adam surprised me with his usual bedtime phone call. I had expected him to skip it. He was calm, though still sounded perplexed by my actions. At least he was interested in hearing more about it all; he'd been looking through the garage to try and figure out which pictures were missing. I had a list of all the photos from Jonathan and Ollie so I went through it with him. I told him how much the photos had sold for, and how amazing they looked in White Ice. It would've been nice if we had been talking about it under different circumstances: if it had been something we'd done together. At least I'd finally told him, though. I felt lighter when I climbed into bed that night. Now that everything was out in the open, we could work on moving forward.

Chapter 54

I apologised to Adam every evening when we spoke on the phone, and he seemed to be softening about the whole White Kitchen incident. It was early when I arrived in Havendon on Friday. I slipped into bed beside Adam.

"I'm sorry," I whispered. He groaned as he woke and pulled me to him. When he kissed me, my body tingled with desire.

"You're forgiven," he said when his eyes finally flickered open.

"Really?"

"Yes. I'm just worried that you'll be more determined for me to set up a photography business now. But I smashed up my camera because I couldn't stand the sight of it."

"I know. I only wanted you to set up your own business because I thought that's what you wanted, deep down. Do you really not want to? After how well it went at White Ice?"

He looked conflicted. "I don't know."

We were interrupted by Emily.

"Lucy!" she squealed and took a running jump at me. I pulled her on top of me for a big hug.

"What are we going to do today?" I asked her.

"Can we have a picnic? And fly kites? And eat ice

cream? And go to the toy shop?"

"That's a lot of things," Adam said.

"Yes, it is. And can we go to the pet shop to look at the animals? I'd like to get a puppy."

"We can't get a puppy," Adam said. "But I think we can manage the rest. Why don't you go and get dressed?"

Emily bounded away.

"What were you saying about the photography?" I asked Adam

"I'm thinking about it," he replied. "But I honestly don't know if it's something I want any more."

"Okay. It's good that you're thinking about it properly." I lay in his arms enjoying the peace. "You should get up," I said after a moment.

"Yeah. I need to wake Hailey. She's got her drama class."

"How's your mum, by the way? I haven't seen her for a while. I thought I might call in on her later."

"She's going to the garden centre with Anne from church today, and then she's got choir practice after that, so you might not catch her."

"Oh wow!" I said, surprised.

"I told you, she's getting more involved with things again."

I untangled myself from Adam and moved to get up. "That's great. I'm pleased for her. You really do need to get up…"

He pulled me back down on the bed. "In a minute," he said nuzzling my neck and tickling me. "I love you."

I squirmed under his weight, giggling.

"I'm ready!" Emily interrupted us. Adam propped

himself up on an arm. She stood in the doorway.

"Are the fairy wings and tutu just for breakfast, or will you wear them outside too?" he asked her.

"Outside too," she said.

"And the pirate hat?"

"I'm a fairy pirate!"

"Of course you are," he said. "And the swimming goggles?"

"Just in case," she said before walking away.

"Just in case?" Adam whispered with raised eyebrows. "What kind of a day is she expecting?"

"It's good to be prepared," I told him.

"Hi," Hailey said, walking past the door. "What's so funny?"

"Your sister," Adam told her. "Just don't laugh when you see her."

"Is she dressed like a weirdo again? She's so strange!"

*****

In the pet shop later that day, Emily was disappointed by the lack of puppies. She set her sights on a rabbit instead and watched them hop around the cages.

"We can't get one today," Adam told her. "But we'll think about it. Maybe we could get a rabbit?" He looked at me. I nodded.

"Oh. I don't want a rabbit," Emily said, moving away from them.

Adam rolled his eyes.

"I want this!" She pointed up at the notice board, where there was a flyer advertising Labrador puppies for sale. "That little one," Emily said, looking at the picture of the adorable little pups.

"They're all little," Adam told her.

"You have to ring that number if you want one," Emily said.

Adam glanced at me as Emily swung on his arm, pleading for the puppy. I turned away to survey the selection of fish food – and avoid getting involved. I'd find it very hard to say no to a fairy pirate.

"You can't just buy a dog," he told her slowly. "You have to think about it for a long time first. Dogs take a lot of looking after. Who's going to feed it, and train it, and walk it, and clean up after it?"

"But I want it," Emily whined.

Adam bent down to her. "We can't get a puppy," he said calmly. "But we could go and get some lunch and then you can have ice cream, okay?"

"Chocolate ice cream?" She pouted.

"Whatever ice cream you want."

"And can we have McDonald's for lunch?" she asked.

"Yes. I guess we can," he told her.

Emily ran to the door and we followed her out onto the street and in the direction of McDonald's.

"The puppies looked so cute," I whispered to Adam as we walked hand in hand a few paces behind Emily.

"I know," he agreed. "Maybe it would be nice for the girls to have a dog."

"And I thought you'd done really well not giving in to Emily!"

He smiled at me. We watched Emily skip ahead, getting faster the closer we got to the restaurant.

"Can I have a Happy Meal?" she shouted back to

us.

Adam nodded and she beamed at him.

"Are you still seeing the therapist?" I asked suddenly.

"Yes," he said. "Why?"

"You just seem so much more relaxed," I said. "It's good."

"You should come with me some time," he said. "You'd like Amelie."

"No, thanks," I said quickly.

"Go on," he said. "Come next week. Please."

He wrapped an arm around my shoulder and I relented. "Maybe."

I wasn't sure I liked the idea of talking to a therapist. The thought of discussing my personal life with a stranger made me uncomfortable. But I suppose anything that could help us get back on track – and stay there – was a good thing.

Hannah Ellis

Chapter 55

Adam was right; I liked Amelie Bright immediately. She had an energy about her that suited her name. The three of us sat together in her office in Manchester the following Friday afternoon. It wasn't very office-like; two armchairs and a worn couch formed a ring around an arty wooden coffee table.

Amelie made tea for us and put me at ease by asking me questions about the girls, and chatting as though we were old friends. She got us to talk without me noticing she was doing anything, and peppered my talk of the girls with her own easy questions.

After all the stilted conversations I'd had with Hailey's old counsellor, Mrs Miller, Amelie Bright was like a breath of fresh air. I was surprised when she said she'd love it if I came back with Adam again. Surprised, because I realised that was her subtle way of asking us to leave, and because I found myself not wanting to move from the comfort of her homely office.

"Is it always like that?" I asked Adam when we walked out into the balmy summer evening.

"Like you just popped in for a chat with a friend?" he said. "She went pretty easy on you, but yes, it's pretty much like that."

"She's amazing. If only we'd found her sooner."

"I know," Adam told me, taking my hand as we walked towards his car. "I'm sorry, about everything. I just didn't know how to deal with things."

"None of us did," I said. "But we're doing okay now, aren't we?"

"Yes. We are," he said, turning to kiss me. "Can I take you out for dinner?"

I beamed back at him. "Yes, please."

Adam called Ruth to let her know he'd be late, and we wandered until we found a funky-looking Mexican restaurant. The décor was brightly coloured and fun, and the staff were equally energetic. It was hip and cool, with a young clientele, and it made me smile just being there.

I sipped a brightly coloured cocktail while we ate tacos. I felt as though we were only just getting to know each other. Adam stroked my leg under the table and I leaned over to kiss him, like one of those sickening couples who I would usually complain about.

We were laughing when we finally left the restaurant, but my mood quickly dive-bombed at the thought of going back to Chrissie and Matt's place.

"How do you feel about me moving back in?" I asked Adam as we reached the car.

He snaked his arms around my waist and looked at me intently. "I think you know the answer to that. You've been gone for far too long."

"Things will be different, won't they? I can't go back to how we were before."

"I promise you, things will be very different. Just tell me if anything is worrying you, okay?"

"Okay. So maybe I'll pack up my stuff and come

back tomorrow?"

He kissed me. "That sounds great."

We drove in silence. Adam dropped me at Chrissie and Matt's house, and I kissed him goodnight, happy that it would be the last night I spent away from my family.

Hannah Ellis

Chapter 56

The next morning I woke early and quietly packed my bags, checking around the house for any odds and ends I had left lying around. Then I walked to the local shop to buy some food for breakfast.

Predictably, the smell of bacon drew Matt from his bed. He and Chrissie padded into the kitchen together, still in their pyjamas.

"That smells amazing," Matt groaned, looking over my shoulder at the bacon and eggs spitting in the pan. "You know I love a fry-up."

"We're supposed to be watching what we eat," Chrissie said. "The wedding will be here before we know it, and I don't want to have to hide the wedding photos away forever because we look like a pair of hippos."

"I don't think there's any chance of that," I said, smiling at her. "But I just wanted to do something nice to say thank you for having me."

"You're welcome," she said, rubbing my arm affectionately.

"I'm all packed," I told her. "I'll be out of your hair after breakfast."

"Oh." She frowned. "That's great. I guess. I'm going to miss you, though."

"Yeah, right – I'm sure you'll be glad to have your

privacy back."

"Definitely." Matt grinned. "We can reinstate naked Sundays!"

"In which case I might go with Lucy," Chrissie said, sitting at the kitchen table. I placed the cholesterol-loaded breakfasts in front of them and sat down to tuck into my own.

"Just make sure you keep in touch, won't you?" Chrissie said through a mouthful of bacon and eggs.

"Yeah – we don't want to have to go back to slagging you off for being the world's worst friend." Matt grinned at me. Chrissie slapped his arm.

"I will, I promise. I don't know what I'd have done without you guys. I guess I would've had to go and stay with one of my parents – and that would've been really depressing."

"We liked having you," Chrissie said. "And it was nice to know you were around to keep Matt out of trouble while he's been off."

"I don't know what I'll do without you!" Matt grinned. "Although I'll be back to school before I know it. Why do the holidays go so quickly?"

"Please don't complain to me about how fast your six-week holiday goes." Chrissie glared at him. "How long is it until your *next* holiday?"

"Too long," Matt laughed. "And the reason we have so many holidays is because we work so hard in term time, shaping the minds of future generations!"

"Let's not talk about work," I said. "You'll make me lose my appetite." I'd been searching for jobs, and had applied for a few. It was pretty late in the day, really, as school would be starting again in a few weeks. Thankfully, out of town, there was a bit less competition for jobs, so I hoped I would manage to find something.

*****

Adam's car wasn't on the drive when I arrived, and the house was quiet. As I walked inside, I realised the place felt strange; different, somehow.

I found Ruth in the living room, which looked very bare.

"I'm finally moving out properly," she told me, smiling sadly as she paused in packing a box of ornaments. "Adam said you were thinking of redecorating so I decided it was about time I cleared the last of my things out."

"You don't have to do that."

"I do," she said, taking a seat on the couch and patting the cushion next to her. "I should have done it ages ago. I just didn't want to leave this place."

I sat down beside her. "If it's any consolation, I didn't want to be here."

"I still can't believe I lost them both like that," she said.

"I'm so sorry," I said. "I can't imagine how you felt. It was all so awful. Sometimes I still expect Tom to walk in and make us all laugh with one of his jokes."

"I'd never imagined my life without Tom. I know he'd had some health problems, but he was always so full of life." She paused, fishing up her sleeve for a hanky. "I just take it a day at a time. But there were definitely moments when I didn't think I'd survive it." She wiped her eyes. "I'm glad you're back, anyway.

You had me worried for a while."

"I know. I'm sorry."

She waved off my apology and headed for the kitchen. "Let's get a cup of tea and you can help me with the rest of my stuff. I don't know where I'm going to fit it all. It might be time to get rid of some things. Adam's always telling me off for hoarding."

I unloaded my things from the car and then loaded Ruth's belongings and drove them round to her house. "If there's anything left that you don't want, just get rid of it," she said. "I'm busy with the church committee next week so I won't be around much, but shout if you need me."

"Thanks."

I drove back up to the house and waited there, in the silence, until I heard the crunch of tyres on the drive. I was so emotional – I was in tears even before the girls were in my arms. When Adam kissed me I knew I was exactly where I should be. The girls stayed near me the whole day, Emily asking me frequently if I was really staying forever.

The sun shone brightly and when it turned breezy in the afternoon we took the kites to the playground. It was a relaxed day. When Adam cooked dinner in the evening, the girls and I set up the patio furniture to eat outside. We draped a tablecloth over the weathered table and Emily picked flowers from the garden, arranging them in a glass. The girls stayed up late and when I came downstairs after tucking them into bed, I found the kitchen spotless and Adam sitting outside in the twilight.

"I poured you a wine," he called to me.

"I've got you a present," I said as I went to join

him. I placed the box on the table in front of him. It was a Nikon to replace his old one. I'd bought it on a whim a while back but hadn't found a good time to give it him. It had cost me a small fortune.

"Wow! This is the best one on the market," he remarked, sitting up to examine it.

"I know. I did my research." I'd spent a long time chatting to the nice salesman in the shop, who'd assured me this was what the pros used. "But if it's not right or you don't want it, I can return it."

"It's great," he said, but with little enthusiasm. I eyed him suspiciously. "You've caught me by surprise, that's all. Thank you."

"You're welcome."

"I'd been thinking of getting a new one," he said. "I don't want to give up my job just yet, but it might be nice to take some photos again – as a hobby. Maybe I could even do those family photos for Angela. She's really helped me out a lot in the past couple of months."

"She'd love that."

"By the way, do you have the paperwork from the sale of the photos?"

"No. I need to call in at The White Kitchen one day and collect it. Which reminds me…"

"What?" Adam asked, sensing my uncertainty.

"We owe Ollie and Jonathan a picture each! I promised them when they agreed to display the photos."

"I'll pull something out for them," he told me, leaning back in his chair. "I can drop them off and pick up the paperwork. I wouldn't mind saying hello to them."

"Great. They'll probably tease you a bit," I warned. "They haven't forgotten about you cancelling the original arrangement."

We talked for hours, Adam topping up my wine a couple of times throughout the evening. When I finally looked around, I saw the sky had filled with stars.

"Do you know any other constellations, or just Orion?" Adam asked when I leaned back and gazed overhead.

"Just Orion," I said, grinning.

I felt his eyes on me and remembered how disapproving he'd been when I'd comforted Emily out here, beneath these stars. "It's not such a bad notion, is it?" I said. "That they're watching over us somehow."

"No," he agreed. "It's not."

My eyes stayed on the three twinkling stars of Orion's belt. "Is it me, or are they shining brighter tonight?"

Adam chuckled. "I think you'd better pass me your wine – you've obviously had enough."

"I think they're happy I'm home," I said, ignoring him.

"I'm sure they are," he said gently. I reached over and kissed him.

Chapter 57

The following weeks passed in a blur. It was a happy time. Adam spent much of his free time with his new camera in his hand, snapping away happily, just as he used to. Hailey had taken an interest in the camera too, and I'd often find them hunched over it together, Adam showing her how to use it.

I was feeling very proud of myself: I'd found a job! It was at a primary school in Brinkwell. When I walked in to the interview, I'd been sure I wouldn't get the job. The head teacher, Mr Hatfield, was stern and overbearing – an older man with grey hair and unruly eyebrows. I explained to him immediately that, while I had applied for a TA position, I would really love to find a school-based teacher training programme. He'd told me gruffly that wouldn't be possible; school policy was to only train TAs who had already worked in the school. It was what I'd expected, but I was still disappointed.

Then Mr Hatfield asked where I lived. His features softened when I mentioned Havendon, and his eyes glazed over as though he was remembering something fondly. "A long time ago, we had a caretaker from Havendon," he told me. "A lovely man named Tom Lewis."

Proudly, I explained my connection to Tom. I'd

forgotten he had been a school caretaker before he retired. We chatted about him for a few minutes. It seemed Tom had left a positive impression everywhere he went.

The interview was a dream after that. Mr Hatfield's whole demeanour changed, and the atmosphere was suddenly more relaxed. At the end of the interview, he told me he would need to check my references but, if they were all right, he would be delighted if I joined the school as a teaching assistant. Happily, I accepted. It wasn't quite what I'd hoped for, but the school was conveniently located and I was confident I'd be happy there.

I couldn't believe my luck when Mr Hatfield called me a few days later, saying he'd spoken to Mrs Stoke, who'd assured him I was a great teaching assistant and believed I would make an excellent teacher one day. He'd decided he could bend the rules for once, and arrange for me to train as a teacher!

Adam had found me in tears following the phone call. He had been concerned – until he realised they were tears of joy. Everything seemed to be falling into place for us, and I treasured the time I got to spend with the girls in the rest of the school holidays.

When I bumped into Mike in the village one afternoon, he'd cheerfully told me about a date he'd been on. It turned out the woman who'd previously stood him up had had a genuine excuse, and they'd rearranged their dinner together. He'd had a great time and had a second date lined up. It was lovely to see him so excited, and I hoped it would work out for him. He deserved someone special in his life.

Suddenly it was the last weekend of the summer

holidays. Adam had arranged a treat for us. We were all going into Manchester to visit my dad and Kerry and spend the night with them.

"I've booked a table for dinner," Adam said as I threw a few things in an overnight bag and he sat on the edge of our bed watching me. "At a fancy place."

"Really? I thought we could just stay in and have a drink with Dad and Kerry."

"Kerry said they'd babysit. That was the whole point of us staying over."

"I know," I said, pausing. "But I'm tired and I'm not that bothered about fancy places."

"Can't you just let me be a bit romantic for once?"

"I'll have to get dressed up."

"Is that really so bad?"

"I guess not," I said, relenting. "Where are we going?"

"It's a surprise."

"Okay, now I'm intrigued."

In the early afternoon, we drove to my dad's house. The kids spent the afternoon playing in the garden. Hailey enjoyed the twins' company, and Emily followed Kerry around like a shadow.

Kerry cooked dinner for the kids and settled them in front of the TV once they'd eaten. I got Emily into her pyjamas before Kerry told me to stop fussing and go and have a nice night.

We'd booked a taxi. Adam jumped in first and whispered to the driver where we were going, so that I wouldn't hear. I kept quiet when we neared Matt and Chrissie's place, wondering what Adam had planned for the evening. It would be nice if he'd arranged for us to meet up with Chrissie and Matt.

I was very surprised – to say the least – when we pulled up in front of The White Kitchen.

"Don't get too excited," Adam said as we got out of the taxi. "But I've been thinking some more about my job and the photography business…"

"Oh my God!" I squealed. "You're going to do it, aren't you?"

He stopped and looked at me, his expression swinging between worry and excitement. "My contract with the studios ends in two weeks – and I don't want to sign another one."

"That's amazing." I circled my arms around his neck, grinning like an idiot.

"Hold on." He looked at me seriously. "I don't know how it's going to work out financially. It could be great, but it could also be a disaster. It's a risk."

"I know," I agreed. "But I want you to try."

He kissed me lightly on the lips. "Thank you."

I was giddy with excitement when I turned towards The White Kitchen. "We should get champagne to celebrate," I said. "And we should talk to Ollie and Jonathan about selling more of your photos."

"Yes to both."

I spotted Ollie straight away, and waved as he made his way over to us.

"It's great to see you," he said, giving me a big hug. "What do you think?"

He gestured to the walls. I glanced around, but I was too distracted to have a proper look. Instead, I was longing to talk to him about displaying more of Adam's photos.

"It looks amazing, as always," I told him as he shook hands with Adam.

"Well, we're very happy with it," he said. "And in case you're interested in the artist, here's his card…" He handed me a business card, a huge smile on his face. When I read the name on the card, I did a double take. I looked at the pictures on the walls again, and then at Adam, who had a delighted smile on his face.

Adam Lewis Photography, I read. I looked around the room but my eyes had filled with tears until everything had blurred. "It's amazing. I can't believe you didn't tell me!"

"Thought I'd surprise you." He squeezed my hand. "Let's get on with the champagne, shall we?"

I nodded, looking around the room in amazement as we followed Ollie to our table. Champagne was waiting in an ice bucket, and I laughed when Ollie popped the cork and poured us both a glass.

"Enjoy," he said with a wink before leaving us alone. Adam and I clinked our glasses together. I couldn't stop looking around at his photos. "That one's got a red dot." I pointed to one behind Adam. "That means it's sold!"

He leaned forward. "They've been up a week – and they've all sold."

"That's brilliant."

"They keep them up for two weeks and then I need to give them a new batch. I'm going to be busy."

"This is incredible. How did you manage this? I thought there was a huge waiting list."

"I'm not really sure," he told me quietly. "When I called in to give Ollie and Jonathan their pictures, we got chatting and I asked if they'd put me on the waiting list. But they'd been having some sort of dispute with an artist they had lined up, and offered me his spot. It was all a bit last-minute."

"I'm so happy for you," I told him. "How did you do all this without me noticing?"

"I had to do a bit of sneaking around," he said with a sly smile.

Adam's phone rang while we were waiting for our food to arrive. He told me it was Hailey before answering it. I briefly wondered if something was wrong, but there was no sign of panic on Adam's face as he chatted to her.

"Yep, she loves it. Yes … no … not yet. You should be in bed. No! Leave me alone!" He hung up after a couple of minutes.

"So Hailey knew about all this before me?" I asked.

"My partner in crime!"

"Are they okay with Kerry?"

"Sounds like they're having a great time. Emily's asleep, and Hailey's been watching movies with the boys."

"That's good," I said. I was happy that Hailey got on so well with the boys. She even managed to overlook the fact that they were two years younger than her.

"We don't need to rush back, then?"

"No."

"I was thinking I might message Chrissie and see what she and Matt are up to. They're not far from here, and they might come and have a drink with us later in White Ice." I didn't wait for his reply, but dug around in my purse for my phone. "You don't mind, do you?"

"No, it's fine."

I tapped out a message and hit send.

I savoured every mouthful of the amazing food. Excitedly, I chatted to Adam and tried to listen in when I thought anyone around us was commenting on Adam's photos.

"You're quiet," I said, finally realising that I was yammering away alone. "Everything okay?"

"Fine," he said. "I'm just taking it all in."

"Everyone loves your photos," Jonathan said when he came over to greet us and took a seat beside me. "How's the champagne going down? Need another bottle?"

"We're still working on this one," I told him. "Can you join us for a drink? Where's Ollie?"

"Go on, then. I'll grab a beer and leave you to the champagne."

He and Ollie sat and chatted to us for a while. When they excused themselves to get back to work, I suggested we move down the road to wait for Chrissie and Matt in the bar.

"Are you sure you're okay?" I asked Adam as we walked. He seemed distant and it worried me. I held on to him for balance when I wobbled slightly.

"Yeah," he said. "I just wanted to ask you about something…"

"Okay."

His phone rang and he pulled it out of his pocket.

"Hailey again?" I said, tugging on his arm to look at the screen. He hesitated, and I had to prompt him to answer his phone.

"What do you want now?" he asked. "No … why aren't you in bed? Does Kerry know you're still up? Go to bed. I'll talk to you tomorrow!"

"What's wrong?" I asked when he hung up.

"Nothing – she just has a million questions about the restaurant."

"She should be asleep by now. Should we just go home?"

"No, she's fine."

"Lucy!" I turned to see Chrissie waving frantically to us as she tottered along in high heels. She was wearing a little black dress and looked great.

"Hi!" I greeted her with a hug. "You look amazing!"

"She should do," Matt said. "It took her long enough to get ready!"

"It would have taken way longer if I'd had some warning," she said.

"Sorry – I didn't know we were coming. Adam surprised me with a night out. His photos are on display in the restaurant!"

"Seriously? That's amazing!" She gave Adam a congratulatory hug, then linked her arm in mine. "I want to see!"

"I'll show you," I told her excitedly.

"We'll get the drinks in," Matt shouted as he and Adam carried on to the bar.

"I've been wanting to go to White Ice for so long," Chrissie said. "I'm always nagging Matt but he says it's too fancy. We always seem to end up at Dylan's pub."

I introduced her to Ollie and Jonathan and we had a good look at Adam's photos before we headed back to find the boys in the bar. They had cocktails waiting for us and Matt was quizzing Adam about his new career path. It was so nice to hear him talk about his plans. After so long, I'd been ready to give up on ever seeing him follow his dream, and I was so excited that he was finally going to be doing what he'd always wanted to.

"Did you enjoy your summer break?" Adam asked Matt.

"It was great. It's gone too fast, though. I've got some private tutoring set up this term to make extra money for the wedding. I'll be glad when that's all over with!"

"Hey!" Chrissie shot him a look.

"It's a nightmare," he told Adam. "So far, I feel like proposing was a huge mistake – and we're not even married yet." He grinned widely at Chrissie – always the joker. "Don't do it!" he mouthed at Adam.

"Don't say that." Chrissie moved round to slap Matt on the arm. "You two will get married, won't you?"

I saw the look of panic that flashed across Adam's face, and decided to help him out. "Not any time soon," I said. "We've got enough on our plates. And we're happy as we are. Aren't we, Adam?"

"Definitely," he said putting an arm around my shoulder. "Very happy."

"Sensible," Matt said, earning another slap from Chrissie.

"I love this place!" Chrissie said, looking around. "Why don't you ever bring me to nice places?" she asked Matt.

"Because you want a bloody expensive wedding! You can't have everything."

I laughed, enjoying the easy banter between them. We moved from the bar to sit at a cosy table at the back of the room.

*****

"I love you so much!" Chrissie told me as we flagged down a taxi after a fun evening. Adam had seemed to relax, and was even a bit drunk by the end of the night. We shared a taxi, dropping Chrissie and Matt off at their place, ignoring Matt's suggestion that we go to a nightclub.

"That was fun," I said as we pulled away from Matt and Chrissie's place.

"They're a funny couple."

"They're so lovely," I said. "I'm happy they're getting married."

"I thought you told Matt you didn't agree with marriage?"

"Matt doesn't actually think that," I said. "And I was only saying that *we* wouldn't get married any time soon. I think it's great that they are, though."

"I never know what you're thinking," Adam told me. "So you don't want to get married? You're not going to be suddenly mad at me next week because Matt and Chrissie are getting married and we're not?"

"No." I smiled at him. "Their life is completely different to ours. I'm happy as we are. You don't want to get married, do you?"

"I'd like to – one day…"

"Yeah, of course," I said, suddenly feeling tipsy. "One day." I slipped my hand into Adam's and concentrated on keeping my eyes open for the drive back to Dad and Kerry's. It was quiet when we crept into the house and tiptoed upstairs. I refrained from checking on the kids, and collapsed onto the bed, where I immediately fell into a deep sleep.

Chapter 58

Adam was sitting in the living room, chatting quietly with Hailey, when I finally emerged the next morning. I said a quick good morning and carried on to the kitchen in search of coffee.

The twins were eating cereal at the kitchen table and Emily was chatting to Kerry. Hailey and Adam followed me in, Hailey sidling up to me as Adam leaned against the counter, sipping his coffee.

"What do you want for breakfast, girls?" Kerry asked.

They looked at me so I asked for them. "What have you got?"

"The boys are having coco pops," she said. The room fell into an uncomfortable silence.

"They're full of sugar," Emily stated.

"Have you got muesli or toast or something?" Hailey asked.

"Wow, you've got them well trained," Kerry said to me. "You'll have to tell me your trick."

My face burned at the memory of my crazy outburst over cereal, and I caught the sparkle in Hailey's eyes as she turned to Kerry. "We try not to even mention coco pops, never mind eat them." A smile crept onto her lips and she glanced at Adam, who grinned into his coffee.

"Did I miss a joke?" Kerry asked, placing a variety of cereals on the counter.

"Yes," I said. "You did. But we won't retell it, since it's at my expense." I went over to Adam and snaked my arms around his waist. He hugged me and kissed my cheek.

The girls sat at the table with the boys and helped themselves to breakfast. Hailey caught my eye and I nestled my head against Adam's chest as I returned her smile.

I went out into the back garden with my coffee, leaving the hum of noise that came from having four kids in the house. Tears filled my eyes when I took a seat on the bench beside the back door.

"You okay?" Adam asked, stepping out into the sunshine.

"Yeah. A bit embarrassed, but I like that we have a private joke." It was actually pretty amazing to me that my humiliating loss of control would be something that bound us together: the one moment I would have loved to delete was something that we could laugh about.

He sat beside me on the bench. "We're doing okay, aren't we?"

"Yeah."

Hailey appeared at the back door, her smile full of mischief. "Everything okay out here?"

"Fine," Adam said, glaring at her.

"Good, just checking!" She disappeared and then reappeared again, beaming at me. "Uncle Adam wants to ask you to marry him – but he keeps chickening out!"

I looked at Adam, stunned.

"Just ignore her," he said. "It doesn't matter."

"You were going to ask me to marry you?"

"I was thinking about it – but you're probably right. We've got enough going on."

I bit my lip. "I only said that because I didn't think you wanted to get married. I thought I was making things easier for you…"

"Easy?" He laughed. "Nothing in my life is easy. I bought you a ring and took you out for a romantic meal. It would have been *easier* if you hadn't asked Ollie and Jonathan to sit with us – and then invited Matt and Chrissie out and told them you didn't want to marry me!"

"Oh my God. I'm so sorry!" I squeezed his hand. "I'm such an idiot. Is that why Hailey kept calling you?"

"Yes. I should never have told her about it."

Hailey appeared at the door again. "What did she say?"

"I haven't asked her," Adam told her impatiently.

"Yes," I said when Hailey looked at me. I turned back at Adam. "Yes!"

"You could at least let me ask! If you want to wait, we can wait…"

"I don't want to wait. I want to marry you."

"I wanted to ask you properly," he said. "I had everything planned."

"Haven't you learned yet that nothing ever goes to plan with us?!"

He pulled a velvet ring box out of his pocket. "I love it," I told him, as he slipped the beautifully simple ring on my finger.

"Really?"

"Yes – it's amazing." I gazed at the small, sparkling diamond on a slim platinum band, then reached up to kiss Adam. "Have you seen this?" I asked Hailey.

"I helped choose it," she said, coming to sit on my lap and wrapping her arms around my neck.

Then Emily joined us, climbing on Adam's lap as she asked what we were doing.

"Adam and Lucy are going to get married," Hailey told her.

"Okay," Emily said.

"We'll be bridesmaids and wear pretty dresses," Hailey told her, grinning at me. I looked at Adam, who shrugged.

"And then we'll get a baby," Emily announced.

"Will we?" Adam asked.

"Yes." Emily turned to him with a frown, as though she couldn't quite believe he didn't know. "That's what happens."

I laughed with Hailey and then turned to look at Adam. "That's what happens," I told him with a shrug.

A smile spread over his face. "Couldn't we just get that puppy instead?"

Emily's eyes looked like they might pop out of her head. "We can get the puppy?"

Adam raised his eyebrows and shot me a questioning look.

"Oh, why not?"

"We're getting a puppy?" Emily squealed, wriggling off Adam's lap and jumping up and down, shaking with excitement. "A puppy, a puppy!" She ran inside. "Kerry! We're getting a puppy!"

Hailey got up to follow Emily.

"Well, you effectively moved the conversation away from babies," I told Adam. "And I don't think Emily will come back to it any time soon."

He put an arm around me and pulled me closer. "Babies, puppies – bring it on!"

"I'm not sure I like the plural…"

"One of each, then?" he asked.

"Isn't our house crazy enough already?"

"Nope," he said, planting a kiss on the top of my head. "Not yet!"

THE END

Printed in Great Britain
by Amazon